A Comprehensive Index to
Black Mask, 1920-1951

A Comprehensive Index to *Black Mask,* 1920-1951

With Brief Annotations, Preface, and Editorial Apparatus

E.R. Hagemann
Compiler and Editor

Bowling Green State University Popular Press
Bowling Green, Ohio 43403

DEDICATION:

Chin Hsiu Ch'iung

PREFACE

A Preface is unsuitable for a history, however brief, of BLACK MASK, the greatest detective fiction pulp magazine ever published; but a Preface is suitable for a brief history of this *Index*.

Some twenty-five years ago, when smog was smog and not air pollution, the late Philip C. Durham and I, both assistant professors in the Department of English, UCLA, both existing on inadequate salaries, were shopping through decrepit bookstores in West Hollywood when we came upon, to our delight, a "file" of MASKS and other pulps. The prices ranged from 25¢ to 50¢ an issue. I forget the dollar-amount quoted by the owner (who was primarily interested in used paperbacks), but it was more than we had in-pocket. We at once telephoned Wilbur J. Smith, Head, Special Collections, UCLA, now retired but still active, and asked if he would purchase the lot. He agreed.

This was the beginning of the MASK file at UCLA. Durham and I, avid readers of the hard-boiled fiction when such was frowned upon, especially in a "publish-or-perish" department, began to "index" the issues on hand on 4x6 cards. Soon enough, Smith acquired the Joseph T. Shaw estate which included most issues when he was editor of MASK and some issues by way of Raymond Chandler. We worked through these as time permitted.

In 1959, I departed the academic world, not to return to it until 1964 at the University of Louisville. However, I maintained an active interest in the Index and in the acquisition of hard-boiled, tough-guy writers by Special Collections. Durham and I published a checklist of James M. Cain, *Bulletin of Bibliography*, 23 (September-December 1960), the first ever done on him. With assistance from me and others, Durham produced the exhibit, "The Boys in the *Black Mask*," UCLA, 6 January-10 February 1961, and wrote the text for the handsome 17-page catalogue. This was a pioneering effort and the mauve-covered catalogue, designed by Marian Engelke, is a collector's item and scarce.

Smith continued to acquire pulps in the 1960s and Durham hired-out graduate students to help with indexing, the names of whom are unfortunately lost, one of whom did some fine work. It is not inaccurate to state that the Index was shunted aside thereafter. Many, many of the 340 issues were simply unavailable. Moreover, Durham had become busy with his book on Chandler, *Down These Mean Streets a Man Must Go*, and his Negro cowboy project. My own work, while in the business world and then back in the academic world, led me far afield from rough-paper magazines.

Philip Calvin Durham died on 27 March 1977 in Los Angeles, some six weeks after his sixty-fifth birthday—a real loss to the field of Popular Culture. His office remained as it was on the third floor, Humanities Building (Rolfe Hall), Westwood Campus.

In the Summer of 1978 I was once again "into" hard-boiled fiction and laboring away in Special Collections on my Paul Cain research when I had a need to examine the Index. I obtained proper permissions, entered Phil's office, and found it in two beat-up 4x6 card boxes. Obviously it had not been touched in years and was in disrepair if not, in fact, disarray.

Brooke Whiting, Special Collections, agreed to bring the boxes over to the University Research Library for safekeeping. When I examined the Index, I was struck by the many omissions, lost items, incomplete entries, and inconsistencies of style. There was only one possibility: Start over again. It was then that I decided to make the Index my Number One Priority during the Summer research trips to the city I love best of all in the United States.

In Summer 1979 I reconstructed and reorganized. Approximately fifty issues had never been examined; approximately fifty more issues were wanting (at the very least). During June and July I indexed and commenced retracing work done years before. Some of the gaps, e.g., Carroll John DALY, Erle Stanley GARDNER, Raymond CHANDLER, *et al.*, were due to cannibalization for Durham's several projects. On the other hand, many missing cards could not be accounted for.

In Summer 1980 I completed work at UCLA, having perused, page by page, each issue, having personally seen to it that all 4x6 cards were xeroxed on legal cap, three cards to the page. In Louisville I began the often frustrating search for the missing issues for the rest of 1980 and well into 1981. Finally, on 5 September 1981, I could honestly say (to myself): "The Comprehensive Index to BLACK MASK is now complete—thanks to the help of friends, acquaintances, and colleagues."

While I was thus engaged, I heard rumors (and I use the word deliberately) of the MASK Index completed by the late William J. Clark (1918-1976). I have *never* seen it and every effort to track it down, *sans* trench coat and snap brim, failed. Yet such eminent people in the field as William F. Nolan and Cliff McCarty swear to its existence, swear to having seen it, having handled it. I do not doubt. But my last effort, led by Ralph Hanna III, University of California, Riverside, which took me into the depths of Upland, California, July 1981, convinced me that *I* would never find it.

That Clark was an assiduous indexer there can be no dispute. His work on ADVENTURE (2 vols.), BLUE BOOK (1 vol.), and WESTERN STORY (1 vol.) is in UCLA for all to see and examine.

Then there was the "Index" put together by E.H. Mundell, in actuality separately printed (but not always accurate) table of contents pages with initial page number only and no annotations. Not until late in my work did I ever see samples.

Other rumors about yet other "indexes" I ignored.

No index is perfect, flawless. As the title says, this *Index* is comprehensive, not complete, the latter requiring everything, as it were, i.e., letters to the editors, letters and editorials from the editors, and sundries not pertinent. However, when letters to the editors are noteworthy, as were those from Dashiell HAMMETT, they are entered.

Every effort has been made to include *all* fiction and most non-fiction deemed of interest (see Charles SOMERVILLE and The Manhunters series). So-called departments and columns have been noted but once or not at all. Contests, etc., are treated similarly. I am quite aware that such decisions may prompt protests but hasten to remind the user that this *Index* is comprehensive.

The bibliographic technique used in the *Index* has been this: author's name (last name first), title of story or article, volume number, issue number, abbreviated date in parentheses, inclusive pagination, followed by selected, brief annotations, i.e., series figures, geographical locations, and/or genre. When appropriate, cross references and letters from authors are given. Each entry has been assigned a number for easy reference.

Towards the end of its existence, BLACK MASK rather often reprinted stories but only occasionally from the magazine itself. No effort, except when available in published checklists, was made to hunt down the original source. Since the demise of MASK, thirty-five stories from it have been reprinted in four anthologies devoted to hard-boiled fiction. These are noted in entries. For publishing data, see the selected bibliography.

When known (and this proved to be a constant, nagging problem), pseudonyms are provided. I can only suggest that some authors "hid" under divers names, and, as I have maintained elsewhere, there is an excellent chance that some of the early numbers, especially during the editorship of F.M. Osborne, were written by a handful of contributors. This idea is best illustrated by Harold WARD and Ward STERLING who were one and the same.

The editorial apparatus which follows this Preface, is a capsule history of the 340 issues of BLACK MASK. This *Index* considers the July 1951 issue as the last one and does not concern itself with MASK after it was assumed by Ellery Queen.

Holdings and collections utilized for *Index* are listed in The Register. The chief source, of course, was Special Collections, University of California, Los Angeles. The Patterson Room (Rare Books), University of Louisville (Kentucky), holds a decent-sized file of MASKS, chiefly duplicates from UCLA. Strange as it may seem, The British Library (London) has a fine collection, and this was of inestimable value during compilation. Finally, private collectors provided necessary data. Although The Library of Congress holds a superior file, I made use of it only once, but that was a signal moment: the October 1921 issue completed *Index*.

Acknowledgements are many and are herewith specified.

My thanks, as usual and always, go to the staff of Special Collections, University Research Library, UCLA, who have endured me over the years with unbelievable patience and have provided absolutely impeccable service: Hilda Bohem, Lilace Hatayama, Kayla Landesman, and Pearl Rosenfeld. Brooke Whiting and Wilbur J. Smith have been my associates for years and they know how much I appreciate their professionalism.

George McWhorter, Curator, Rare Books, University of Louisville Library, always gave me immediate access to and use of the MASKS in The Patterson Room for which I am grateful.

Peter VanWingen, Head, Reference and Reader Services, The Library of Congress, was very gracious and thoughtful when he sent me data on the October 1921 issue.

I cite the Research Committee, College of Arts and Sciences, University of Louisville, for money to travel, and Dean X. J. Musacchia, Graduate School, University of Louisville, for a grant. Their faith in my work was a boost to my morale.

To Professor (of Mathematics) Jack D. Irwin, Trenton State College (New Jersey), I owe especial thanks. He drew from his files so as to provide me, cheerfully and professionally, essential data and information when it was not possible for me to examine personally certain issues. His advice and counsel were always sound.

Much of the same holds true for Robert S. Powell, doctoral candidate, University of Manchester (England), who sent annotations and xerox copies of table of contents pages from needed issues held in The British Library.

Neil J. Petersen, Poolville, New York, and Robert Sampson, Huntsville, Alabama, both Popular Culture enthusiasts, were of great help in specific instances.

Will Murray, North Quincy, Massachusetts, an authority on Lester Dent and Doc Savage, *inter alia*, was a constant source of encouragement from the very beginning and never "lost the faith." His tips on the world of small publishers were unfailingly true.

William F. Nolan, Los Angeles, detective fictioneer, collector, and Hammett expert, cheerfully supported the *Index* and gave needed information. I remember fondly the long and good afternoon we spent together in Brentwood, July 1981, and I look forward to his next book on Dash.

Dave Lewis, Portland, Oregon, filled in some blanks when

I was working on Frederick L. NEBEL. Until then Grimes HILL was but another name in the *Index*.

I thank my publishers, Pat and Ray B. Browne, Popular Press, who took on the book and believed in it.

And now a special citation: the profuse help, encouragement, and generosity of my friend, David A. Orr, Louisville, Kentucky. More than once he gave freely of his collections, more than once he bore with me the many problems, more than once he advised and consented. "Nothing can be compared to a faithful friend."

With such a talented "staff" on call at all times, is it any wonder that I regard myself to have been a very fortunate Compiler and General Editor? As we used to say in the Marine Corps, "Well Done!"

E.R. Hagemann
Louisville, Kentucky
June, 1982

Register of *Black Mask*

(With Holdings)

Vol. 1, No.	1	Apr 1920	C		11	[1] Feb 1923	C
	2	May 1920	C		12	15 Feb 1923	P
	3	Jun 1920	P		13	1 Mar 1923	C
	4	Jly 1920	C		14	15 Mar 1923	C
	5	Aug 1920	C	Vol. 6, No.	1	1 Apr 1923	P
	6	Sep 1920	B		2	15 Apr 1923	C
Vol. 2, No.	1	Oct 1920	C		3	1 May 1923	P
	2	Nov 1920	P		4	15 May 1923	C,L
	3	Dec 1920	C		5	1 Jun 1923	C
	4	Jan 1921	C		6	15 Jun 1923	B
	5	Feb 1921	P		7	1 Jly 1923	C
	6	Mar 1921	C		8	15 Jly 1923	C
Vol. 3, No.	1	Apr 1921	C		9	1 Aug 1923	B
	2	May 1921	P		10	15 Aug 1923	C
	3	Jun 1921	C		11	1 Sep 1923	C
	4	Jly 1921	C		12	15 Sep 1923	B
	5	Aug 1921	P		13	1 Oct 1923	B
	6	Sep 1921	P		14	15 Oct 1923	C
Vol. 4, No.	1	Oct 1921	LC		15	1 Nov 1923	C
	2	Nov 1921	C		16	15 Nov 1923	C
	3	Dec 1921	C		17	1 Dec 1923	C
	4	Jan 1922	C		18	15 Dec 1923	B
	5	Feb 1922	C		19	1 Jan 1924	C,L
	6	Mar 1922	B		20	15 Jan 1924	C
Vol. 5, No.	1	Apr 1922	B		21	1 Feb 1924	C
	2	May 1922	C		22	15 Feb 1924	B
	3	Jun 1922	C		23	1 Mar 1924	C
	4	Jly 1922	B		24	15 Mar 1924	P
	5	Aug 1922	B	Vol. 7, No.	1	1 Apr 1924	C
	6	Sep 1922	C		2	15 Apr 1924	C
	7	Oct 1922	C		3	May 1924	B
	8	Nov 1922	C		4	Jun 1924	B
	9	Dec 1922	C		5	Jly 1924	C
	10	Jan 1923	C		6	Aug 1924	C

	No.	Date	Code		No.	Date	Code
	7	Sep 1924	C	Vol. 11, No.	1	Mar 1928	C
	8	Oct 1924	C		2	Apr 1928	C
	9	Nov 1924	C		3	May 1928	C, L
	10	Dec 1924	B		4	Jun 1928	C
	11	Jan 1925	B		5	Jly 1928	C, L
	12	Feb 1925	C		6	Aug 1928	C, L
Vol. 8, No.	1	Mar 1925	B		7	Sep 1928	C, L
	2	Apr 1925	B		8	Oct 1928	C, L
	3	May 1925	B		9	Nov 1928	C, L
	4	Jun 1925	B		10	Dec 1928	C, L
	5	Jly 1925	B		11	Jan 1929	C, L
	6	Aug 1925	C		12	Feb 1929	C
	7	Sep 1925	B	Vol. 12, No.	1	Mar 1929	C, L
	8	Oct 1925	C		2	Apr 1929	C
	9	Nov 1925	B		3	May 1929	C
	10	Dec 1925	B		4	Jun 1929	C, L
	11	Jan 1926	B		5	Jly 1929	C
	12	Feb 1926	B		6	Aug 1929	C
Vol. 9, No.	1	Mar 1926	C		7	Sep 1929	C
	2	Apr 1926	C		8	Oct 1929	C
	3	May 1926	C		9	Nov 1929	C
	4	Jun 1926	B		10	Dec 1929	C
	5	Jly 1926	B		11	Jan 1930	C
	6	Aug 1926	C		12	Feb 1930	C, L
	7	Sep 1926	C	Vol. 13, No.	1	Mar 1930	C
	8	Oct 1926	B		2	Apr 1930	C, L
	9	Nov 1926	C		3	May 1930	C
	10	Dec 1926	C, L		4	Jun 1930	C, L
	11	Jan 1927	C		5	Jly 1930	C, L
	12	Feb 1927	C		6	Aug 1930	C
Vol. 10, No.	1	Mar 1927	C		7	Sep 1930	C
	2	Apr 1927	C, L		8	Oct 1930	C
	3	May 1927	C		9	Nov 1930	C
	4	Jun 1927	C		10	Dec 1930	C, L
	5	Jly 1927	C		11	Jan 1931	C
	6	Aug 1927	C		12	Feb 1931	C
	7	Sep 1927	C	Vol. 14, No.	1	Mar 1931	C
	8	Oct 1927	C, L		2	Apr 1931	C
	9	Nov 1927	C		3	May 1931	P
	10	Dec 1927	C		4	Jun 1931	C, L
	11	Jan 1928	C, L		5	Jly 1931	C
	12	Feb 1928	C		6	Aug 1931	C

	7	Sep 1931	C, L	Vol. 18, No.	1	Mar 1935	C, L
	8	Oct 1931	C*		2	Apr 1935	C, L
	9	Nov 1931	C, L		3	May 1935	C, L
	10	Dec 1931	C, L		4	Jun 1935	C, L
	11	Jan 1932	C, L		5	Jly 1935	C, L
	12	Feb 1932	C		6	Aug 1935	C
Vol. 15, No.	1	Mar 1932	C, L		7	Sep 1935	C, L
	2	Apr 1932	C, L		8	Oct 1935	C, L
	3	May 1932	C		9	Nov 1935	C, L
	4	Jun 1932	C, L**		10	Dec 1935	C, L
	5	Jly 1932	C		11	Jan 1936	C
	6	Aug 1932	C		12	Feb 1936	C
	7	Sep 1932	C	Vol. 19, No.	1	Mar 1936	C
	8	Oct 1932	C		2	Apr 1936	C
	9	Nov 1932	C, L		3	May 1936	C
	10	Dec 1932	C, L		4	Jun 1936	C
	11	Jan 1933	C		5	Jly 1936	C
	12	Feb 1933	C, L		6	Aug 1936	C
Vol. 16, No.	1	Mar 1933	C, L		7	Sep 1936	C
	2	Apr 1933	C		8	Oct 1936	C
	3	May 1933	C, L		9	Nov 1936	C
	4	Jun 1933	C		10	Dec 1936	C
	5	Jly 1933	C		11	Jan 1937	C
	6	Aug 1933	C		12	Feb 1937	C
	7	Sep 1933	C	Vol. 20, No.	1	Mar 1937	C
	8	Oct 1933	C		2	Apr 1937	C
	9	Nov 1933	C		3	May 1937	C
	10	Dec 1933	C		4	Jun 1937	C
	11	Jan 1934	C, L		5	Jly 1937	C
	12	Feb 1934	C, L		6	Aug 1937	C
Vol. 17, No.	1	Mar 1934	C, L		7	Sep 1937	C
	2	Apr 1934	C		8	Oct 1937	C
	3	May 1934	C		9	Nov 1937	C
	4	Jun 1934	C, L		10	Dec 1937	C
	5	Jly 1934	C		11	Jan 1938	C
	6	Aug 1934	C, L		12	Feb 1938	C
	7	Sep 1934	C, L	Vol. 21, No.	1	Mar 1938	C
	8	Oct 1934	C, L		2	Apr 1938	C
	9	Nov 1934	C, L		3	May 1938	C
	10	Dec 1934	C		4	Jun 1938	C
	11	Jan 1935	C			[Jly 1938; no issue]	
	12	Feb 1935	C, L		5	Aug 1938	C
					6	Sep 1938	C

	7	Oct 1938	C		12	Apr 1942	C
	8	Nov 1938	C	Vol. 25, No.	1	May 1942	C
	9	Dec 1938	C		2	Jun 1942	C
	10	Jan 1939	C		3	Jly 1942	C
	11	Feb 1939	C		4	Aug 1942	C
	12	Mar 1939	C		5	Sep 1942	C
Vol. 22, No.	1	Apr 1939	C		6	Oct 1942	C
	2	May 1939	C		7	Nov 1942	C
	3	Jun 1939	C		8	Dec 1942	C
	4	Jly 1939	C		9	Jan 1943	C
	5	Aug 1939	C		10	Feb 1943	C
	6	Sep 1939	C		11	Mar 1943	C
	7	Oct 1939	C		12	May 1943	C
	8	Nov 1939	C	Vol. 26, No.	1	Jly 1943	C
	9	Dec 1939	C		2	Sep 1943	C
	10	Jan 1940	C		3	Nov 1943	C
	11	Feb 1940	C		4	Jan 1944	C
	12	Mar 1940	C		5	Mar 1944	C
Vol. 23, No.	1	Apr 1940	C		6	May 1944	C
		[May 1940; no issue]			7	Jly 1944	C
	2	Jun 1940	C		8	Sep 1944	C
	3	Jly 1940	C		9	Nov 1944	C
	4	Aug 1940	C		10	Jan 1945	C
	5	Sep 1940	C		11	Mar 1945	C
	6	Oct 1940	C		12	May 1945	C
	7	Nov 1940	C	Vol. 27, No.	1	Jly 1945	C
	8	Dec 1940	C		2	Sep 1945	C
	9	Jan 1941	C		3	Nov 1945	C
	10	Feb 1941	C		4	Jan 1946	C
	11	Mar 1941	C	Vol. 28, No.	1	Feb 1946	C
	12	Apr 1941	C		2	Mar 1946	C
Vol. 24, No.	1	May 1941	C		3	May 1946	C
	2	Jun 1941	C		4	Jly 1946	C
	3	Jly 1941	C	Vol. 29, No.	1	Sep 1946	C
	4	Aug 1941	C		2	Nov 1946	C
	5	Sep 1941	C		3	Jan 1947	C
	6	Oct 1941	C		4	Mar 1947	C
	7	Nov 1941	C	Vol. 30, No.	1	May 1947	C
	8	Dec 1941	C		2	Jly 1947	C
	9	Jan 1942	C		3	Sep 1947	C
	10	Feb 1942	C		4	Nov 1947	C
	11	Mar 1942	C	Vol. 31, No.	1	Jan 1948	C

	2	Mar 1948	C	Vol. 34, No.	1	Jan 1950	C
	3	May 1948	C		2	Mar 1950	P
	4	Jly 1948	C		3	May 1950	C
Vol. 32, No.	1	Sep 1948	C		4	Jly 1950	C
	2	Nov 1948	C	Vol. 35, No.	1	Sep 1950	P***
	3	Jan 1949	C		2	Nov 1950	C
	6	Mar 1949	C		3	Jan 1951	C
Vol. 33, No.	1	May 1949	C		4	Mar 1951	C
	2	Jly 1949	C	Vol. 36, No.	1	May 1951	C
	3	Sep 1949	C		2	Jly 1951	C
	4	Nov 1949	C			[Last issue]	

* TofC p. has No. 7
** TofC p. has Vol. 10, No. 9
*** TofC p. has No. 5

B = British Library
C = UCLA-SC
L = University of Louisville
LC = Library of Congress
P = Private

ISSUANCE:

Apr 1920 - Jan 1923:	Monthly
[1] Feb 1923 - 15 Apr 1924:	Bi-Weekly
May 1924 - Mar 1943:	Monthly
May 1943 - Jan 1946:	Bi-Monthly
Feb 1946 - Mar 1946:	Monthly
May 1946 - Jly 1951:	Bi-Monthly

EDITORSHIP:

Apr 1920 - Sep 1922:	F.M. OSBORNE
Oct 1922 - 15 Mar 1924:	**George W. SUTTON, Jr.**
1 Apr 1924 - Oct 1926	Philip C. CODY
Nov 1926 - Nov 1936:	Joseph T. SHAW
Dec 1936 - Apr 1940:	Fanny ELLSWORTH
Jun 1940 - Nov 1948 (?)	Kenneth S. WHITE
Jan 1949 - Jly 1951:	No editor listed [Henry STEEGER, President and Secretary]

TITLE: In this Index it is always *Black Mask*; however, it was originally called *The Black Mask*. Early in 1927, *The* was dropped. In 1950, the pulp became *Black Mask Detective*. The final issue carried *Black Mask Detective Magazine*.

PRICE; Originally, 20¢ per copy; $2.00, yearly subscription. In the early 1930s, it dropped to 15¢, then up to 20¢ again in Jan 1940, down to 15¢ in Jun 1940, then up to 25¢, May 1947, at which price it remained until demise.

Editors, Writers (Arranged by Debut), Frequency of Appearance, and Series Figures (If Any)

F. M. OSBORNE: Apr 1920-Sep 1922

J. Frederic THORNE: Apr 1920-Mar 1922 (7)

Harry C. HERVEY, Jr.: Apr 1920-Jly 1922 (8)

Harold WARD: Apr 1920-15 Apr 1923 (29)
    [see also Ward STERLING]

Julian KILMAN: Apr 1920-Dec 1927 (6)

Hamilton CRAIGIE: May 1920-Apr 1921 (9)
    [including collaboration]

Clinton HARCOURT: May 1920-May 1921 (6)

Merlin Moore TAYLOR: May 1920-Jun 1928 (6)

C.S. MONTANYE: May 1920-Oct 1939 (29)
    Captain Valentine

J.C. KOFOED: Jly 1920-Jly 1921 (9)

J. B. HAWLEY: Jly 1920-Apr 1922 (12)

Ward STERLING: Jly 1920-Oct 1922 (16)
    [see also Harold WARD]

Hubert ROUSSEL: Dec 1920-Oct 1921 (7)

John BAER: Jan 1921-1 Aug 1923 (24)

Walter DEFFENBAUGH: Feb 1921-Jun 1922 (14)

J. J. STAGG: Feb 1921-Sep 1922 (11)

Lloyd LONERGAN: May 1921-Aug 1922 (8)

Murray LEINSTER: Mar 1922-Oct 1927 (7)

J. S. FLETCHER: Apr 1922-Jun 1925 (2)

Jack J. GOTTLIEB: May 1922-1 Mar 1923 (8)

Howard P. ROCKEY: Jun-Oct 1922 (5)

Herman PETERSEN: Sep 1922-Jly 1926 (18)

Frederick C. DAVIS: Sep 1922-Sep 1950 (16)

GEORGE W. SUTTON, Jr.: Oct 1922-15 Mar 1924

Henry W. FISHER: Oct 1922-15 Jan 1924 (3)
    Executioners

Francis JAMES: Oct 1922-Oct 1927 (13)
    Prentice

Carroll John DALY: Oct 1922-Jly 1944 (60)
    Race Williams
    Satan Hall
    Clay Holt
    Pete Hines

Eustace Hale BALL: Nov 1922-15 Feb 1924 (9)
    [including collaboration]
    The Scarlet Fox

Joe TAYLOR: Nov 1922-Jun 1924 (14)
    [including collaboration]
    My Underworld

Peter COLLINSON: Dec 1922-15 Oct 1923 (4)
    [see also Dashiell HAMMETT]
    The Op

Ray CUMMINGS: Dec 1922-Sep 1926 (16)
[including collaboration]
   T. McGuirk

Dashiell HAMMETT: Dec 1922-Nov 1930 (45)
[see also Peter COLLINSON]
   The Op
   Sam Spade

Drayton DUNSTER: Jan 1923-15 Jan 1924 (9)

Charles SOMERVILLE: [1] Feb 1923-May 1926 (47)
   The Manhunters

Harford POWEL, Jr.: 15 Feb 1923-1 Mar 1924 (6)

John AYOTTE: 1 Mar 1923-Oct 1925 (10)

Willett STOCKARD: 15 Mar 1923-1 Dec 1923 (5)

William ROLLINS, Jr.: 1 Apr 1923-May 1934 (21)
   Jack Darrow
   Percy Warren
   Kenneth Osborne

Robert Lee HEISER: 1 Jun 1923-Dec 1924 (7)

. Paul SUTER: 15 Sep 1923-Mar 1929 (18)
   Reverend McGregor Daunt

Edward Parish WARE: 15 Oct 1923-Apr 1929 (9)

PHILIP C. CODY: 1 Apr 1924-Oct 1926

Erle Stanley GARDNER: Sep 1924-Sep 1943 (103)
   Ed Jenkins
   Bob Larkin
   Black Barr
   Ken Corning
   Pete Wennick

Donald MacGREGOR: Oct 1924-Oct 1926 (10)

L. King TICHENOR: May 1925-Jly 1927 (5)

Nels Leroy JORGENSEN: Aug 1925-Sep 1938 (40)
    Black Burton
    Rio Kennedy

Tom CURRY: Oct 1925-Dec 1933 (38)
    Macnamara
    DeVrite

Katherine BROCKLEBANK: Mar 1926-Jly 1929 (7)
    Tex

Raoul F. WHITFIELD: Mar 1926-Feb 1934 (66)
    [see also Ramon DECOLTA]
    Chuck Reddington
    Mac
    Gary Greer
    Ben Jardinn
    Mal Ourney
    Alan Van Cleve
    Don Free
    Scotty

Frederick L. NEBEL: Mar 1926-Aug 1936 (67)
    MacBride & Kennedy
    Donahue

JOSEPH T. SHAW: Nov 1926-Nov 1936

Cutcliffe HYNE: Nov 1926-Jun 1927 (8)
    Captain Kettle

Joseph T. SHAW: Dec 1926-Nov 1932 (3)

Carl L. MARTIN: Jly 1927-Mar 1929 (6)
    Lon Havens

Henry Wallace PHILLIPS: Jun 1927-Jun 1932 (12)
    Red Saunders

William Donald BRAY: Jun 1927-Nov 1935 (12)
    Hardsley

W.H.B. KENT: Oct 1927-Jly 1930 (6)
    Killer Blake

Everett H. TIPTON: Nov 1927-Oct 1928 (7)

Horace McCOY: Dec 1927-Oct 1934 (17)
    Jerry Frost

Carl W. & Marion SCOTT: Jun 1928-Feb 1932 (17)
    Craleigh
    Kirby

Eric TAYLOR: Jun 1928-Jly 1936 (7)

Eugene CUNNINGHAM: Dec 1928-Nov 1936 (14)
    Cleve Corby

Ramon DECOLTA: Feb 1930-Jly 1933 (24)
    [see also Raoul F. WHITFIELD]
    Jo Gar

James P. OLSEN: Oct 1930-Jun 1931 (6)

Stewart STIRLING: Apr 1931-May 1933 (8)
    Hi Gear

Ed LYBECK: Dec 1931-Feb 1934 (4)
    Harrigan

Paul CAIN: Mar 1932-Dec 1936 (17)
    Kells & Granquist
    Black

Norbert DAVIS: Jun 1932-May 1943 (13)

Theodore A. TINSLEY: Oct 1932-Apr 1940 (26)
    Tracy

Roger TORREY: Jan 1933-Apr 1942 (50)

Dal Prentice
Killeen
O'Dell
McCarthy & Marge
Connell
Bryant

Norvell PAGE: Feb 1933-Apr 1933 (3)
Jules Tremaine

H. H. STINSON: Apr 1933-Sep 1948 (27)
Ken O'Hara

John LAWRENCE: Jun 1933-Oct 1942 (14)

Thomas WALSH: Jly 1933-Mar 1936 (6)

W. T. BALLARD: Sep 1933-May 1945 (43)
Bill Lennox
Drake

Raymond CHANDLER: Dec 1933-Jan 1937 (11)
Carmady
Mallory

Dwight V. BABCOCK: Jan 1934-Dec 1939 (21)
Beeker (Beek)
Thompson

James DUNCAN: Feb 1934-Jan 1939 (10)
Ivor Small
The Parson

George Harmon COXE: Mar 1934-Mar 1943 (27)
Casey
Paul Baron

Hugh B. CAVE: May 1934-April 1941 (9)

John K. BUTLER: Nov 1935-Sep 1942 (11)
Rod Case

Edward S. WILLIAMS: Mar 1936-Jly 1940 (8)

ester DENT: Oct 1936-Dec 1936 (2)
    Sail

ANNY ELLSWORTH: Dec 1936-Apr 1940

ornell WOOLRICH: Jan 1937-Jly 1944 (24)

onald WANDREI: Feb 1937-Dec 1938 (6)

aynard H. KENDRICK: Feb 1937-Mar 1940 (14)
    Miles Standish Rice

yatt BLASSINGAME: May 1937-Mar 1942 (8)
    The Bishop

ale CLARK: May 1937-Mar 1947 (32)
    O'Hanna

rank GRUBER: Jun 1937-Mar 1940 (14)
    Oliver Quade

teve FISHER: Aug 1937-Apr 1939 (9)

awrence TREAT: Sep 1937-Apr 1942 (5)

tewart STERLING: May 1939-Jly 1943 (12)
    Vince Mallie
    Special Squad

eter PAIGE: Sep 1939-Sep 1942 (12)

ENNETH S. WHITE: Jun 1940-Nov 1948 (?)

leve F. ADAMS: Jly 1940-Mar 1942 (6)
    Canavan

im KJELGAARD: Jly 1940-Jly 1942 (6)

. L. CHAMPION: Jly 1940-Jan 1950 (30)
    Rex Sackler

.T. FLEMING-ROBERTS: Aug 1940-Jly 1951 (8)

Robert REEVES: Sep 1940-Sep 1945 (10)
    Cellini Smith

C. P. DONNEL, Jr.: Jan 1941-Jan 1948 (20)
    Doc Rennie

C. G. TAHNEY: May 1941-Jan 1946 (5)
    Nickie

William ROUGH: Jun 1942-Jan 1947 (5)
    Slabbe

Merle CONSTINER: Jly 1942-Jan 1948 (12)
    Luther McGavock

Henry NORTON: Dec 1942-Jly 1947 (6)

Julius LONG: May 1943-Nov 1949 (23)
    Corbett

Fergus TRUSLOW: Jly 1945-May 1949 (6)

Robert MARTIN: May 1946-Mar 1951 (8)
    Clint Colby

William Campbell GAULT: Sep 1946-Nov 1950 (9)
    Mortimer Jones

Robert C. DENNIS: Nov 1946-Jly 1951 (10)
    Carmody

John D. MacDONALD: Sep 1947-Jly 1950 (6)

Selected Bibliography

Bruccoli, Matthew J. *Raymond Chandler: A Checklist.* Kent, Ohio: The Kent State University Press, 1968.

Easton, Robert. *Max Brand: The Big "Westerner."* Norman: University of Oklahoma Press, 1970. [See especially, pp. 273-301, "A Faust Bibliography."]

Goulart, Ron, ed. *The Hardboiled Dicks.* New York: Pocket Books, 1967. [Contains four stories reprinted from *BM.*]

Hagemann, E. R. "Introducing Paul Cain and His *Fast One:* A Forgotten Hard-Boiled Writer—A Forgotten Gangster Novel." *The Armchair Detective,* 12 (Winter 1979), 72-76. [Contains a checklist.]

_____. "Raoul F. Whitfield, A Star with the *Mask.*" *The Armchair Detective,* 13 (Summer 1980), 179-184. [Contains an annotated checklist.]

_____. "Ramon Decolta, a.k.a. Raoul Whitfield, and His Diminutive Brown Man: Jo Gar, The Island Detective." *The Armchair Detective,* 14 (Winter 1981), 3-8. [Contains an annotated checklist.]

Hughes, Dorothy B. *Erle Stanley Gardner: The Case of the Real Perry Mason.* New York: William Morrow and Co., 1978. [See Ruth Moore, compiler, "Bibliography of Erle Stanley Gardner," pp. 311-341.]

Kittredge, William and Steven M. Krauser, ed. *The Great American Detective.* New York: New American Library, 1978. [Contains two stories reprinted from *BM.*]

Layman, Richard. *Dashiell Hammett: A Descriptive Bibliography.* Pittsburgh: University of Pittsburgh Press, 1979. [See especially, "First Appearances in Periodicals," pp. 121-135.

Nevins, Francis M., Jr., ed. *Nightwebs: A Collection of Stories by Cornell*

Woolrich. New York: Harper & Row, 1971. [See particularly, "Short Fiction," pp. 487-502, for checklist.]

Nolan, William F. *Dashiell Hammett: A Casebook.* Santa Barbara: McNally & Loftin, 1969. [See "A Dashiell Hammett Checklist," pp. 129-178.]

Reilly, John M., ed. *Twentieth-Century Crime and Mystery Writers.* New York: St. Martin's Press, 1980. [Contains myriad checklists.]

Ruhm, Herbert, ed. *The Hard-Boiled Detective: Stories from "Black Mask" Magazine (1920-1951).* New York: Vintage Books, 1977. [Contains fourteen stories reprinted from *BM.*]

Shaw, Joseph T., ed. *The Hard-Boiled Omnibus: Early Stories from "Black Mask."* New York: Simon and Schuster, 1946. [Contains fifteen stories reprinted from *BM.*]

BLACK MASK is unique among fiction magazines, appealing to a wide group of readers ranging from those who like action fiction for action alone, where it is real and convincing, to the most discriminating readers in the professional classes—clergymen, bankers, lawyers, doctors, the heads of large businesses, and the like.

While it is commonly classed as a detective fiction magazine, it has, with the help of its writers, created a new type of detective story which is now being recognized and acclaimed by book critics as inaugurating a new era in fiction dealing with crime and crime combatting.

Joseph T. Shaw
Editor

April 1932

A

ADAMS, Cleve F[ranklin]

1. "The Aunt of Sigmi Chi." 23, No. 9 (Jan 1941), 33-50.
   Lt. Canavan & Lt. Kleinschmidt; L. A. setting.

2. "Herrings Are Red." 24, No. 11 (Mar 1942), 34-58. Canavan
   & Kleinschmidt in L.A.

3. "The Key." 23, No. 3 (Jly 1940), 28-48. Canavan &
   Kleinschmidt.

4. "Murder Parade." 24, No. 1 (May 1941), 104-127. Canavan.

5. "Nobody Loves Cops." 24, No. 3 (Jly 1941), 60-77. Engelhardt &
   Dewey, Car 97; L. A.

6. "That Certain Feeling." 23, No. 5 (Sep 1940), 45-55. Engelhardt
   & Dewey.

ADDISON, H. G.

7. "The Experiment." 6, No. 7 (1 Jly 1923), 49-55. Daytime Story.

8. "The Pain Thermometer." 6, No. 23 (1 Mar 1924), 46-50.
   Daytime Story.

ADLER, Harry

9. "The Impossible Murder." 6, No. 23 (1 Mar 1924), 9-38. "A
   Complete Novelette."

AITKEN, Donald S.

10. "All in a Night's Work." 22, No. 8 (Nov 1939), 105-109.

11. "The Same Old Oil." 23, No. 2 (Jun 1940), 90-101. Jack Gale,
    private dick.

ALLAN, Francis K.

12. "Model for Death." 36, No. 2 (Jly 1951), 86-92. Reprint; not from *BM*.

13. "That Second Answer." 25, No. 6 (Oct 1942), 10-43. Shamus Tim Hall of Hall & Branch, NYC; info on FKA, p. 8.

ALLENBY, Paul

14. "Overseer of the Poor." 23, No. 2 (Jun 1940), 87-89. Short-short.

ALTIMUS, Henry

15. "The Summons." 1, No. 5 (Aug 1920), 27-34.

AMBLER, J. Edgar

16. "The Buzzard." 10, No. 3 (May 1927), 112-119. The Buzzard & The Cracker, criminals.

ANTHONY, Wilder

17. "The Baffling Shadow." 1, No. 4 (Jly 1920), 35-44. Western.

ARTHUR, Robert

18. "The Coroner's Hand." 35, No. 3 (Jan 1951), 87-95. Reprint; not from *BM*.

19. "Too Much Static." 22, No. 10 (Jan 1940), 46-57. Patrol cop.

ASHER, Carl

20. **"And This Is How It is." 6, No. 22 (15 Feb 1924), 124-125. Short-short; "a satire."**

AYOTTE, John [Captain, USA]

21. "The Black Cracksman." 6, No. 13 (1 Oct 1923), 37-46. "A white Hawaiian thrill."

22. "Death's Rendezvous." 7, No. 9 (Oct 1924), 76-86. Hawaii.

23. "The Devil's Breath." 6, No. 10 (15 Aug 1923), 44-51. "Another of those fascinating Hawaiian tales."

24. "Hawaiian Driftage." 8, No. 8 (Oct 1925), 92-101. Opium ring in Honolulu; some characters from "The Puzzle of Hook Nam"; JA's last appearance in *BM*.

25. "Okolehao." 5, No. 13 (1 Mar 1923), 40-42. Short-short; "A Tragedy of Hawaii"; JA's debut in *BM*.

26. "Osaki's Revenge." 6, No. 12 (15 Sep 1923), 56-58. Short-short; 1st of 2 stories in issue by JA; see "The Puzzle of Hook Nam."

27. "A Pillar of Flame." 6, No. 3 (1 May 1923), 25-34.

28. "The Puzzle of Hook Nam." 6, No. 11 (1 Sep 1923), 62-74, Pt. 1; 6, No. 12 (15 Sep 1923), 75-86, Pt. 2. Chinese and death in Hawaii; 2d of 2 stories in issue by JA; see "Osaki's Revenge"; see also "Hawaiian Driftage."

29. "Rifles." 6, No. 21 (1 Feb 1924), 49-66. Capt. AYOTTE has departed Hawaii in fact & fiction.

30. "White Tents." 6, No. 15 (1 Nov 1923), 70-82. Col. Edwards.

AYRES, Don

31. "Marked for Murder." 20, No. 7 (Sep 1937), 76-99. Crooked politics & murder; 1st-person narrator.

B

BABCOCK, Dwight V.

32. "At the Bottom of Every Mess." 16, No. 11 (Jan 1934), 84-96. Private dick Maguire in L.A.; see also "Murder in Hell"; DVB's debut in *BM*.

33. "Blood in the Snow." 22, No. 9 (Dec 1939), 47-69. Beeker

("Beek"); last Beeker story & DVB's last appearance in *BM*.

34.   "Careless Killer." 21, No. 9 (Dec 1938), 58-79. Beeker.

35.   "Death Goes Free." 18, No. 7 (Sep 1935), 76-97. G-Man Chuck Thompson.

36.   "Death's Ransom." 18, No. 2 (Apr 1935), 68-96. Al, 1st person narrator, bodyguard to Beverly Hills woman, Hildred Kyle; 3d story in series.

37.   "Flight at Sunrise." 20, No. 5 (Jly 1937), 6-44. Chuck Thompson; last of 7 CT stories.

38.   "Free Ride to Rio." 19, No. 5 (Jly 1936), 101-127. Chuck Thompson with Kathleen Carnahan.

39.   " 'G-Man' Chuck Thompson." 18, No. 11 (Jan 1936), 75-96.

40.   "Hide-Out." 18, No. 4 (Jun 1935), 75-100. 1st G-Man Chuck Thompson story of 7; CT, Special Agent, FBI, in L.A.

41.   "Men of the F.B.I." 19, No. 7 (Sep 1936), 59-80. Chuck Thompson.

42.   "Murder After Midnight." 17, No. 12 (Feb 1935), 89-107. Al, bodyguard; 2d story in series.

43.   "Murder in Hell." 16, No. 12 (Feb 1934), 112-122. Maguire; "Hell" as in Hell Club, L.A. nightspot; see "At the Bottom of Every Mess."

44.   "Murder in the Family." 21, No. 2 (Apr 1938), 82-102. Beeker in San Joaquin Valley.

45.   "Murder on the Gayway." 22, No. 7 (Oct 1939), 6-30. Beeker; San Francisco World's Fair; Treasure Island Nude Ranch.

46.   "Murder on the Side." 19, No. 10 (Dec 1936), 40-63. Unemployed reporter; 1st-person narrator.

47. "Rat Bait." 18, No. 12 (Feb 1936), 83-108. Chuck Thompson.

48. "Renegade in Rio." 21, No. 12 (Mar 1939), 7-30. Beeker;
    see p. 31 for note on "Beek."

49. "Reward Chaser." 22, No. 3 (Jun 1939), 36-63. Beeker at
    San Francisco World's Fair.

50. "State Narcotic Dick." 19, No. 11 (Jan 1937), 72-106. Bromley &
    muggles (marijuana).

51. "Too Many Slips." 17, No. 10 (Dec 1934), 73-86. 1st Al,
    bodyguard, story.

52. "The Widow Regrets." 20, No. 11 (Jan 1938), 10-34. Beeker
    ("Beek"); 1st of 7 Beeker stories.

BAER, John

53. "Absolution." 4, No. 6 (Mar 1922), 49-56.

54. "The Campaign for Vengeance." 5, No. 1 (Apr 1922), 61-90.
    "Complete mystery novelette."

55. "Circumstantial Evidence and Guilt." 3, No. 5 (Aug 1921),
    63-84.

56. "Courage." 5, No. 3 (Jun 1922), 117-122. 2d story of 2 by JB in
    issue; see "The Vanishing Motive."

57. "The Dead Tell No Tales." 3, No. 6 (Sep 1921), 27-34. 1st of
    2 stories by JB in issue; see "Dr. Thorpe's Testimony."

58. "Dr. Thorpe's Testimony." 3, No. 6 (Sep 1921), 71-77. 2d
    of 2 stories by JB in issue; see "The Dead Tell No Tales."

59. "The Great Finale." 3, No. 3 (Jun 1921), 71-75.

60. "The Great Fur Robberies." 2, No. 6 (Mar 1921), 55-65.

61. "Have a Smoke?" 5, No. 4 (Jly 1922), 24-30.

62. "The Hole in the Alibi." 4, No. 4 (Jan 1922), 33-38.

63. "Murder in Haste." 5, No. 5 (Aug 1922), 37-43.

64. "The Murder of An Te-Hai." 2, No. 4 (Jan 1921), 99-102.
NYC's Chinatown; JB's debut in *BM*.

65. "The Murderer's Name and Address." 5, No. 6 (Sep 1922), 43-48.

66. "An Omen of Ill-Luck." 2, No. 5 (Feb 1921), 43-50.

67. "Partners in Crime." 3, No. 1 (Apr 1921), 88-92.

68. "The Pearl-Handled Revolver." 4, No. 5 (Feb 1922), 94-100.
2d of 2 stories by JB in issue; see "Written in Blood."

69. "The Second Trial." 4, No. 1 (Oct 1921), 3-30. "Complete
Mystery Novelette."

70. "The Silver Lining." 4, No. 2 (Nov 1921), 51-56.

71. "The Struggle in the Dark." 3, No. 2 (May 1921), 53-61.

72. "The Suicide's Murderer." 5, No. 2 (May 1922), 25-31.

73. "The Three Witnesses." 5, No. 14 (15 Mar 1923), 3-28.
"Complete Mystery Novelette"; set in Pittsburgh suburb.

74. "The Vanishing Motive." 5, No. 3 (Jun 1922), 39-45. 1st of
2 stories by JB in issue; see also "Courage."

75. "A Wholesaler in Crime." 6, No. 9 (1 Aug 1923), 7-31. "Complete
Mystery Novelette"; JB's last story in *BM*.

76. "Written in Blood." 4, No. 5 (Feb 1922), 29-35. 1st of 2 stories
in issue by JB; see "The Pearl-Handled Revolver."

BAIRD, Edwin

77.   "The Billion-Dollar Robbery." 6, No. 11 (1 Sep 1923), 116-118.

78.   "Keep It Dark." 6, No. 14 (15 Oct 1923), 117-118. Short-short.

79.   "This Way Out." 6, No. 9 (1 Aug 1923), 92-93. Short-short.

BAKAL, Rufe

80.   "The Random Kee-Whango." 34, No. 3 (May 1950), 99-104.

BAKER, Homer

81.   "Take It or Leave It." 17, No. 7 (Sep 1934), 78-79. Article;
        "Strange Events in the Field of Crime."

BALL, Eustace Hale

82.   "The City Slicker and the Dick." 6, No. 12 (15 Sep 1923), 47-55.

83.   "The Footprints of Doom." 6, No. 19 (1 Jan 1924), 87-99.
        The Scarlet Fox; last of a series.

84.   "Grandfather's Will." 6, No. 13 (1 Oct 1923), 101-109.

85.   "Little Miss Muffet—1923." 6, No. 14 (15 Oct 1923), 73-78.

86.   "The Old Gray Mouse." 11, No. 11 (Jan 1929), 109-114. Prison
        setting.

87.   "The Trail of the Scarlet Fox." 5, No. 10 (Jan 1923), 41-58,
        Pt. 1; 5, No. 11 ([1] Feb 1923), 98-114, Pt. 2; 5, No. 12 (15
        Feb 1923), 113-126, Pt. 3; 5, No. 13 (1 Mar 1923), 103-115, Pt.
        4; 5, No. 14 (15 Mar 1923), 110-123, Pt. 5; 6, No. 1 (1 (Apr
        1923), 105-120, Pt. 6. Debut (solo) of EHB and The Scarlet
        Fox in *BM*; serial has various subtitles.

88.   "A Vengeance of Death." 6, No. 22 (15 Feb 1924), 69-73.
        "A *Black Mask* Fantasy."

89.   "When 7539 Went Back." 6, No. 17 (1 Dec 1923), 89-96. 7539
        is a convict.

BALL, Eustace Hale and Earl DERBY

90.   "Dead Men Do Tell!" 5, No. 8 (Nov 1922), 63-76. "The first of the
             Black Mask Daytime Stories—not to be read at night by
             people with weak nerves"; EHB's debut in *BM*.

BALLARD, W[illis] T[odhunter]

91.   "After Breakfast." 18, No. 10 (Dec 1935), 101-122. Red Drake.

92.   "Blackmailers Die Hard." 19, No. 3 (May 1936), 98-121. Lennox.

93.   "Blood on the Moon." 19, No. 2 (Apr 1936), 36-62. Red Drake.

94.   "Call a Dead Man." 20, No. 3 (May 1937), 42-66. Red Drake.

95.   "The Colt and the Killer." 24, No. 10 (Feb 1942), 50-68.
             Bill Lennox.

96.   "Confession Means Death." 17, No. 12 (Feb 1935), 45-67.
             Jimmy DeHaven, "The People's Pal"; so named from radio
             show he runs; 1st of 2 DeH stories; see "Murder Makes a
             Difference."

97.   "The Con Man and the Cop." 25, No. 8 (Dec 1942), 100-106.
             Costello, LAPD plainclothesman.

98.   "Crime's Web." 17, No. 7 (Sep 1934), 42-60. Bill Lennox.

99.   "Death in the Zoo." 22, No. 4 (Jly 1939), 70-95.

100.   "Dressed to Kill." 26, No. 12 (May 1945), 29-41, 96.
             Sleepy Payne, gambler, 1st-person narrator; WTB's last
             story in *BM*.

101.   "Fortune Deals Death." 20, No. 5 (Jly 1937), 66-87. Lennox.

102.   "Friends Sometimes Kill." 20, No. 9 (Nov 1937), 75-93.
             Don Tomaso Sherman, narrator; 2d DTS story; see "Stones
             of Death."

103. "Fugitive for Justice." 19, No. 6 (Aug 1936), 72-91. Drake.

104. "Gamblers Don't Win." 18, No. 2 (Apr 1935), 45-67. Lennox.

105. "In Dead Man's Alley." 17, No. 9 (Nov 1934), 86-103. Lennox.

106. "The Lady with the Light Blue Hair." 23, No. 9 (Jan 1941), 60-77. Lennox.

107. "Lights, Action—Killer!" 25, No. 1 (May 1942), 11-36. Last Bill Lennox story.

108. "A Little Different." 16, No. 7 (Sep 1933), 83-101. Bill Lennox, trouble-shooter for Consolidated Films; 1st of 27 BL stories; WTB's debut in *BM*.

109. "A Million-Dollar Tramp." 16, No. 6 (Oct 1933), 38-53. Lennox.

110. "Murder Is a Swell Idea." 24, No. 7 (Nov 1941), 41-61. Lennox.

111. "Murder Isn't Legal." 17, No. 10 (Dec 1934), 10-51. Lennox.

112. "Murder Makes a Difference." 18, No. 4 (Jun 1935), 101-121. Jimmy DeHaven, "The People's Pal"; 2d of 2 DeH stories; see "Confession Means Death."

113. "Mobster Guns." 21, No. 8 (Nov 1938), 64-87. Lennox.

114. "Numbers with Lead." 18, No. 11 (Jan 1936), 97-122. Lennox.

115. "No Parole from Death." 21, No. 11 (Feb 1939), 9-33. Lennox; see p. 112 for letter from WTB about Lennox.

116. "Not in the Script." 24, No. 3 (Jly 1941), 10-31. Lennox.

117. "Only Proof Counts." 20, No. 10 (Dec 1937), 92-110. 7th & last Red Drake story.

118. "Pictures for Murder." 23, No. 5 (Sep 1940), 6-24. Lennox.

119. "Positively the Best Liar." 16, No. 9 (Nov 1933), 92-107. Lennox.

120. "A Ride in the Rain." 20, No. 8 (Oct 1936), 107-126. Drake.

121. "Scars of Murder." 22, No. 8 (Nov 1939), 6-30. Lennox; see p. 31 for letter from WTB about Lennox.

122. "Sing for Your Slaughter." 26, No. 7 (Jly 1944), 97-111.

123. "Snatching Is Dynamite." 17, No. 8 (Oct 1934), 62-92. Lennox & "The Secret Five" of Hollywood.

124. "Stones of Death." 20, No. 2 (Apr 1937), 80-103. Don Tomaso Sherman, "Border Adventurer"; 1st DTS story; see also "Friends Sometimes Kill."

125. "Tears Don't Help." 17, No. 2 (Apr 1934), 110-124. Lennox.

126. "That's Hollywood." 17, No. 3 (May 1934), 97-111. Lennox.

127. "There's No Excuse for Murder." 19, No. 7 (Sep 1936), 81-102; La Brea Tar Pits figure in story; Lennox.

128. "Thirty Miles to Albuquerque." 23, No. 11 (Mar 1941), 36-43.

129. "This Is Murder." 20, No. 1 (Mar 1937), 66-85. Lennox.

130. "Trouble-Hunted." 16, No. 11 (Jan 1934), 70-83. Lennox.

131. "Whatta Guy." 17, No. 5 (Jly 1934), 30-53. Lennox.

132. "Whipsawed." 19, No. 10 (Dec 1936), 64-85. Lennox.

133. "You Never Know About Women." 18, No. 8 (Oct 1935), 62-83; Red Drake, undercover man, State Racing Commission; 1st-person narrator; 1st of 7 RD stories.

BANKSON, Russell Arden

134. "The Ghost of Joe Speck." 5, No. 12 (15 Feb 1923), 48-56.

135. "Underground." 7, No. 4 (Jun 1924), 33-44. "The detective-sheriff of the Kaniksu country."

BARCELO, Ed

136.   "Suicidal Slay Ride." 33, No. 1 (May 1949), 114-124.

BARKER, S. Omar

137.   "Blood Is Quicker Than Water." 24, No. 1 (May 1941), 71-77.
           Old Hud Bateman, country character.

138.   "Two-Way Trick." 15, No. 12 (Feb 1933), 91-102. Sheriff
           John Lonsdale; modern Western.

139.   "The Way of a Westerner." 11, No. 11 (Jan 1929), 63-70.
           Pecos McKain; modern Western.

140.   "What Price Friendship?" 12, No. 1 (Mar 1929), 67-71. Western.

BARRETT, William E.

141.   "Behind the Star." 15, No. 12 (Feb 1933), 115-124. Black
           Bart Doyle, chief of detectives, & Michael Costigan,
           chief of police.

142.   "Snatch As Snatch Can." 35, No. 4 (Mar 1951), 70-83. Wrestler
           in Texas oil town; reprint; not from *BM*.

BARTLETT, Madeline

143.   "The Mutilated Masterpiece." 7, No. 4 (Jun 1924), 79-82.

144.   "Who Was Jake Kole?" 6, No. 12 (15 Sep 1923), 93-103. "A
           Strange Detective Case."

BEAM, Maurice [possible pseud. of Robert Leslie BELLEM?]

145.   "Death Swing." 22, No. 4 (Jly 1939), 31-45. Stunt flyers.

146.   "Ear-Witness." 32, No. 3 (Jan 1949), 92-95, 130. Malmin,
           lawyer.

147.   "The Fixer." 22, No. 12 (Mar 1940), 124-126. Short-short.

148.   "Flatfoot's Bullet." 20, No. 3 (May 1937), 67-76.

149.   "Ham Strung." 22, No. 10 (Jan 1940), 99-110. Small-town hardward store worker, 1st-person narrator.

150.   "Reprieve." 22, No. 8 (Nov 1939), 51-73. Chain-gang.

151.   "The White Lie." 22, No. 11 (Feb 1940), 30-55. See p. 29 for letter from MB about story.

BEARD, Walcott LeClear

152.   "Clara." 6, No. 17 (15 Jan 1924), 27-34. Action story set in Mexico.

BECERRA, M. Hernaiz

153.   "The Ordway Suicide Mystery." 5, No. 6 (Sep 1922), 85-100.

BECK, Allen

154.   "Long Live the Dead." 21, No. 9 (Dec 1938), 96-106. Magician.

BECK, Frances

155.   "Dig Down Deep." 27, No. 1 (Jly 1945), 74-78, 98.

BECKMAN, Charles J.

156.   "Satan's Step-Daughter." 34, No. 4 (Jly 1950), 90-103. Mike O'Connell, a cop.

BEDFORD-JONES, H[enry]

157.   "The Box in the Hold." 14, No. 12 (Feb 1932), 54-77. High-seas adventure; see p. 119 for note on HB-J.

BEFFEL, John Nicholas

158.   "Finger-Prints." 8, No. 3 (May 1925), 111-116. Article; can prints be forged?; this prompts answer from Dashiell

HAMMETT; see entry for Jun 1925; *cf.* under Jack WOODFORD.

BELL, J. M.

159. "The Blinking Eye." 19, No. 11 (Jan 1937), 126-127. Short-short.

160. "Deadline Murder." 19, No. 9 (Nov 1936), 64-87. Racing & state politics; Cochrane, reporter, 1st-person narrator.

BELLAMY, Harmon

161. "Shutterbug's Long Shot." 34, No. 4 (Jly 1950), 69-71, 129.

BENDER, John

162. "The High Cost of Lying." 34, No. 3 (May 1950), 105-109.

163. "Mayhem Patrol." 35, No. 2 (Nov 1950), 85-94. Prowl-car cop is 1st-person narrator.

BENDER, Russell

164. "Body-Guard to Death." 21, No. 7 (Oct 1938), 49-69. Jake Connolly.

165. "Copper's Moll." 23, No. 3 (Jly 1940), 92-105. McNulty, a young cop.

166. "Heat Target." 19, No. 8 (Oct 1936), 60-86. Mayor of small Maryland town.

BENSCOTER, Frank L.

167. "Gilligan and Co." 7, No. 4 (Jun 1924), 93-101. "Introducing a new character."

168. "Shola Al." 8, No. 2 (Apr 1925), 45-62. "A detective story."

169. "Two Tim's Idea." 8, No. 5 (Jly 1925), 87-92.

170.   "The Van Curl Affair." 8, No. 6 (Aug 1925), 59-75.

171.   "A Woman's Whim." 7, No. 7 (Sep 1924), 97-108. Concerns a cat.

BERTIN, Jack

172.   "Breed of Steel." 14, No. 2 (Apr 1931), 42-69. Western.

173.   "Desert Sentence." 17, No. 7 (Sep 1934), 80-107. Chip Huard; Western.

174.   "The Devil's Protége." 14, No. 11 (Jan 1932), 50-75. Chip Huard.

175.   "Rider in the Night." 18, No. 1 (Mar 1935), 72-100. Huard.

176.   "Sinful Cibola." 15, No. 9 (Nov 1932), 97-119. Huard.

177.   "Tequila." 16, No. 3 (May 1933), 80-102. Huard.

BEYERS, Meredith

178.   "The Dark Brown Dress." 4, No. 3 (Dec 1921), 91-101.

BISSON, Frank

179.   "The Betel." 9, No. 3 (May 1926), 93-101. South Seas.

BLACK MASK CRIME REVIEW

180.   "A Crime Expert's Review of the Hall-Mills Tragedy." 5, No. 13 (1 Mar 1923), 121-126. Article; anonymous; 1st segment in this irregular, short-lived Department; not Indexed beyond this point.

BLASSINGAME, Wyatt [see also William B. RAINEY]

181.   "The Bishop and the Tinkling Belle." 24, No. 3 (Jly 1941), 98-119, 128-129. The Bishop; young Eddie narrates.

182.   "Clothes Make the Corpse." 24, No. 8 (Dec 1941), 63-85. The

Bishop.

183.   "The Corpse Came Home." 24, No. 11 (Mar 1942), 77-97.
        Bishop; WB's last appearance in *BM*.

184.   "Killers in Glass Houses." 23, No. 9 (Jan 1941), 78-95. Bishop.

185.   "Murder Grows Fast." 20, No. 3 (May 1937), 26-41. Hotel
        in Deep South; WB's debut in *BM*.

186.   "Murder *Is* Bad Luck." 22, No. 12 (Mar 1940), 76-92. New
        Orleans racetrack; see p. 93 for letter from WB.

187.   "Some Call It Murder." 22, No. 10 (Jan 1940), 6-23. Bishop,
        political writer on Southern newspaper; known as "The
        Bishop"; sixtyish & peg-legged; 1st story in series.

188.   "10,001 Motives for Murder." 23, No. 4 (Aug 1940), 104-127.
        Bishop.

BLIGHTON, Frank

189.   "An Automatic Alibi." 2, No. 4 (Jan 1921), 27-39. Bank fraud;
        1st-person narrator.

190.   "The Hop on Hyperspace." 1, No. 2 (May 1920), 77-93.
        Hyperspace is a dog.

BONNELL, James Francis

191.   "Address Unknown." 19, No. 10 (Dec 1936), 126-127. Short
        short.

BONNETT, Hal Murray

192.   "Dynamite Deal." 21, No. 2 (Apr 1938), 69-81.

BOOTH, Charles G.

193.   "Lights Out." 6, No. 24 (15 Mar 1924), 31-40. Set near San
        Bernardino, California.

194.   "The Malevolent Bequest." 7, No. 1 (1 Apr 1924), 53-66.

195.   "One Shot." 8, No. 4 (Jun 1925), 42-52. "An impossible crime."

196.   "Raw Gold." 9, No. 6 (Aug 1926), 44-66. Western.

197.   "Sister Act." 15, No. 12 (Feb 1933), 103-114. Detective Blair
         & Joe Ricardo; reprinted, *The Hard-Boiled Omnibus*
         (1946).

198.   "Stag Party." 16, No. 9 (Nov 1933), 8-42. McFee of Blue Shield
         Detective Agency; crime & politics.

199.   "The Three Spiders." 6, No. 12 (15 Sep 1923), 7-24. "Complete
         Mystery Novelette."

BOOTH, Christopher B.

200.   "Candle Drip." 4, No. 6 (Mar 1922), 113-123. 2d of 2 stories in
         issue by CBB; see "The Oat Bin."

201.   "The Curse of Chester Whitaker." 2, No. 1 (Oct 1920), 95-101.

202.   "The Deviltry of Dr. Waugh." 1, No. 6 (Sep 1920), 49-60.

203.   "The Oat Bin." 4, No. 6 (Mar 1922), 39-48. 1st of 2 stories in
         issue by CBB; see "Candle Drip."

204.   "The Phelam Lodge Mystery." 4, No. 5 (Feb 1922), 3-27.
         "Complete Mystery Novelette."

BOUCHER, Anthony [pseud. of William Anthony Parker WHITE]

205.   "The Catalyst." 27, No. 1 (Jly 1945), 87-90, 92-97.

BRAND, Max [pseud. of Frederick FAUST]

206.   "Bulldog." 19, No. 11 (Jan 1937), 35-45.

207.   "The Silent Witness." 21, No. 1 (Mar 1938), 111-114.
         Short-short.

BRANDON, William E.

208.   "Danny, Once the Rat." 23, No. 5 (Sep 1940), 38-44. Danny the
        Rat, police-stoolie, & Nazi spies.

209.   "Handout." 21, No. 5 (Aug 1938), 105-114. Panhandler in
        trouble; WEB's debut in *BM*.

210.   "It's So Peaceful in the Country." 26, No. 3 (Nov 1943),
        73-79. Horse Luvnik, ex-con, goes to work for academic
        types; reprinted, *The Hard-Boiled Detective* (1977).

211.   "Modeled in Murder." 25, No. 12 (May 1943), 73-81. Shamus
        Ireland.

212.   "Stir-Bug." 25, No. 5 (Sep 1942), 37-40. A New Mexico jail.

213.   "Swing Low, Sweet Chariot." 21, No. 12 (Mar 1939), 98-107.
        Actually has sympathetic Black character.

214.   "Wake Up and Give!" 24, No. 10 (Feb 1942), 69-75. Skull-
        duggery & a college bequest.

BRAY, William Donald

215.   "A Call for Honor." 18, No. 3 (May 1935), 111-121. Britt
        Hardsley.

216.   "Death Dances." 18, No. 6 (Aug 1935), 112-122. Britt Hardsley.

217.   "Hot Gold." 18, No. 5 (Jly 1935), 103-113. Britt Hardsley.

218.   "An Interlude at Six Bit Flats." 10, No. 10 (Dec 1927), 108-115.
        Western.

219.   "A Keg of Muscatel." 18, No. 9 (Nov 1935), 112-122. Murder at
        a winery; WDB's last story in *BM*.

220.   "The Lost Hope." 10, No. 4 (Jun 1927), 100-106. Western
        mining story; WDB's debut in *BM*.

221.   "The Man Who Chased Himself." 14, No. 3 (May 1931), 103-112.
         "A suspected killer joins in the hunt to catch himself."

222.   "Penthouse Party." 18, No. 2 (Apr 1935), 111-120. Debut of
         Britt Hardsley, "man of murder and mystery"; 1st-person
         narrator; works for Carneal Construction Co.

223.   "The Red Mackinaw." 10, No. 7 (Sep 1927), 57-66. Mining yarn.

224.   "The Trap." 10, No. 8 (Oct 1927), 49-55. Western; Deputy
         Lee Tyndall.

225.   "The Trick Play." 11, No. 2 (Apr 1928), 102-111. Western.

226.   "The Tryst at Five-Mile Rock." 12, No. 1 (Mar 1929), 99-107.
         Gold-mining.

BRECK, Coleman

227.   "The Last Door." 5, No. 9 (Dec 1922), 95-101.

BREUKER, George W.

228.   "A Weapon of the Law." 5, No. 5 (Aug 1922), 44-46. Short-
         short.

BRIER, Royce

229.   "Black and Blue." 7, No. 7 (Sep 1924), 9-29. Set in Mexico.

230.   "Guilt-Edged Bonds." 7, No. 5 (Jly 1924), 87-94. $235,000
         in bonds stolen.

231.   "Hundred Thousand Cache." 6, No. 16 (15 Nov 1923), 43-48.

232.   "Other Worlds." 6, No. 11 (1 Sep 1923), 41-48. Western; Arizona.

233.   "The Thirteenth Tack." 6, No. 14 (15 Oct 1923), 88-95.
         Spider Klein, criminal.

BRIGGS, George

234.   " 'By His Own Hand—.' " 5, No. 4 (Jly 1922), 31-37.

235.   "The Too-Easy Alibi." 5, No. 1 (Apr 1922), 106-112.

BROCKLEBANK, Katherine

236.   "Bracelets." 11, No. 10 (Dec 1928), 86-94. Tex of the Border
        Service in Tia Juana; Tex is a woman!

237.   "The Canine Tooth." 12, No. 4 (Jun 1929), 108-117. Tex of
        the Border Service; Tia Juana & dog racing.

238.   "Hell-Bent for Tia Juana." 10, No. 2 (Apr 1927), 52-62.
        Wishbone, jockey; Hell-Bent, gelding; Tia Juana.

239.   "The Silver Horseshoe." 12, No. 5 (Jly 1929), 111-120.
        Tex of the Border Service; KB's last story in *BM*.

240.   "Snow-Birds." 10, No. 1 (Mar 1927), 76-87.

241.   "Tia Juana Red." 9, No. 1 (Mar 1926), 62-76. KB's debut in *BM*;
        very few women writers in magazine.

242.   "White Talons." 11, No. 11 (Jan 1929), 71-78. Tex of the
        Border Service.

BROWN, Fredric

243.   "Cry Silence." 32, No. 2 (Nov 1948), 100-103.

BROWN, Guthrie

244.   "Stalemate." 13, No. 7 (Sep 1930), 72-78. Western lynching.

245.   "Touchstone." 15, No. 5 (Jly 1932), 33-43. Western.

BROWN, Raymond J.

246.   "Phantom Bullets." 6, No. 1 (1 Apr 1923), 71-88, Pt. 1; 6,
        No. 2 (15 Apr 1923), 96-114, Pt. 2; 6, No. 3 (1 May 1923),
        71-84, Pt. 3; 6, No. 4 (15 May 1923), 60-76, Pt. 4; 6, No. 5

(1 Jun 1923), 99-118, Pt. 5. See pp. 127-128, last issue, for letter from RJB on how he writes.

BROWN, Walter C.

247.   "The Cat with Ten Lives." 26, No. 1 (Jly 1943), 100-110.
          Sgt. Dennis O'Hara, a.k.a. Sah-Jin; Chinatown Squad in NYC.

248.   "Dead Man's Shoes." 20, No. 12 (Feb 1938), 94-120. Laurence
          Sheldon, cop dick; WCB's debut in *BM*.

249.   "The House of Red Candles." 26, No. 4 (Jan 1944), 66-91.
          Last O'Hara story & last WCB story in *BM*.

250.   "The Macao Mark." 24, No. 5 (Sep 1941), 110-120, 122, 124, 126-
          130. Chinatown novelette with Chinese cast.

251.   "Mark Hoy's Death-Stick." 25, No. 12 (May 1943), 46-72.
          "Sah-Jin" O'Hara.

252.   "The Parrot That Wouldn't Talk." 24, No. 9 (Jan 1942),
          60-79. 1st O'Hara story of 4.

BRUEGGER, Frederick

253.   "The King of Spades." 2, No. 3 (Dec 1920), 85-95.

BUELL, Earl R.

254.   "Sign Reading at Yellow Dog." 11, No. 9 (Nov 1928), 103-108.
          Western.

BURKE, Joe

255.   "Who Shall Say?" 6, No. 20 (15 Jan 1924), 67-72. Western;
          letter from author, p. 126.

BURLESON, Terry O.K.

256.   "Killer Bait." 32, No. 1 (Sep 1948), 99-109, 128-129. Modern
          Western.

BURMAN, Ben Lucien

257.   "The Needle of Osiris." 9, No. 3 (May 1926), 63-76.

258.   "The Streaks in the Iris." 6, No. 20 (15 Jan 1924), 5-26. Boling, a Kentucky doctor, in "a complete murder-detective mystery novelette."

BURT, T.B.

259.   "Red Hot." 5, No. 4 (Jly 1922), 103-106.

260.   "The Spotter." 5, No. 2 (May 1922), 85-92.

BURTIS, Thomson

261.   "Deadline for Death." 28, No. 1 (Feb 1946), 10-42. Greg Sullivan, ex-USA intelligence officer, now police lieutenant.

262.   "The Death of a Deal." 15, No. 3 (May 1932), 82-92. Slats Kirke, minor boxing manager, 1st-person narrator.

263.   "Every Move a Picture." 14, No. 8 (Oct 1931), 48-76, Pt. 1; 14, No. 9 (Nov 1931), 83-103, Pt. 2. Dan Sloane, movie director, on location in Texas for $3,000,000 production.

264.   "Renegade." 15, No. 6 (Aug 1932), 86-101. George Groody, Texas Border Patrol.

265.   "They Don't Shake Hands in Arkansas." 15, No. 4 (Jun 1932), 64-75. Slats Kirke in Detroit; see also "The Death of a Deal"

BURTON, Walter E.

266.   "Shark Boat." 20, No. 6 (Aug 1937), 115-124.

267.   "The Stamp of Guilt." 21, No. 6 (Sep 1938), 116-127. Murder & philately.

BUTLER, John K.

268.   "Dark Return." 19, No. 3 (May 1936), 31-47. Mark Dana, ex G-man.

269.   "Dead Letter." 25, No. 5 (Sep 1942), 41-59. Rod Case; last (4th) RC story & JKB's last appearance in *BM*.

270.   "Death Has My Number." 24, No. 4 (Aug 1941), 10-40. Rod Case, trouble-shooter for General Pacific Telephone Co.; set against forest fire in Southern California; 1st RC story.

271.   "Don't Make It Murder." 23, No. 10 (Feb 1941), 30-49. McCarey of the D. A.'s staff.

272.   " 'G'—Heat." 18, No. 9 (Nov 1935), 87-111. R. T. "Brick" Hammond, G-man; JKB's debut in *BM*.

273.   "Guns for a Lady." 19, No. 1 (Mar 1936), 48-70. Ex-pug, 1st-person narrator; bodyguard for girl.

274.   "I Killed a Guy." 20, No. 2 (Apr 1937), 38-51. Fred, p.i., in L.A.

275.   "Murder for Nickels." 24, No. 8 (Dec 1941), 88-104, 106, 108, 110, 112, 114, 116-126, 128, 130. Rod Case.

276.   "Never Work at Night." 24, No. 11 (Mar 1942), 11-33. Rod Case.

277.   "No Rest for Soldiers." 19, No. 8 (Oct 1936), 14-37. WW I vets, bonuses, & Russ McGregor.

278.   "You Can't Bribe Bullets." 19, No. 6 (Aug 1936), 32-55. Marty Lewis, 1st-person narrator, & shady local politics.

C

CAIN, Paul [a.k.a Peter RURIC; né George Sims]

279.   "Black." 15, No. 3 (May 1932), 27-33. Black, 1st-person narrator, in Hollywood; see also "Trouble-Chaser."

280.   "Chinaman's Chance." 18, No. 7 (Sep 1935), 98-107. Johnny Gay, reporter, in Hollywood.

281. "The Dark." 15, No. 7 (Sep 1932), 84-101. Kells & Granquist; Pt. 5, *Fast One.*

282. "Death Song." 18, No. 11 (Jan 1936), 63-74. Pat Nolan, film studio trouble-shooter.

283. "Dutch Treat." 19, No. 10 (Dec 1936), 117-125. Emeralds; PC's last story in *BM.*

284. "Fast One." 15, No. 1 (Mar 1932), 8-26. Gerry Kells & S. Granquist; Pt. 1 (of 5), *Fast One* (pub. 1933); printed as separate stories rather than conventional serial; PC's debut in *BM.*

285. "The Heat." 15, No. 6 (Aug 1932), 65-85. Kells & Granquist; Pt. 4, *Fast One.*

286. "Hunch." 17, No. 1 (Mar 1934), 10-33. Brennan in NYC.

287. "Lead Party." 15, No. 2 (Apr 1932), 76-101. Kells & Granquist; Pt. 2, *Fast One;* see p. 120 for comment on PC.

288. "Murder Done in Blue." 16, No. 4 (Jun 1933), 86-104. Johnny Doolin, ex-stunt man.

289. "One, Two, Three." 16, No. 3 (May 1933), 103-114. Unnamed 1st-person narrator; agency 'tec in L.A.

290. "Parlor Trick." 15, No. 5 (Jly 1932), 83-87. Criminal narrator.

291. "Pigeon Blood." 16, No. 9 (Nov 1933), 77-91. Druse, "extra-legal" attorney.

292. "Pineapple." 19, No. 1 (Mar 1936), 71-87. Nick Green & Blondie Kessler, police-reporter.

293. "Red 71." 15, No. 10 (Dec 1932), 59-74. Dick Shane on fringes of Underworld; "71" is an NYC gambling-joint; reprinted, *The Hard-Boiled Omnibus* (1946).

294. "Trouble-Chaser." 17, No. 2 (Apr 1934), 60-71. Black; see also "Black."

295. "Velvet." 15, No. 4 (Jun 1932), 6-29. Kells & Granquist; Pt. 3, *Fast One.*

CALVIN, L.

296. "The Erstwhile Corpse of Patrick O'Flynn." 4, No. 1 (Oct 1921), 31-39.

CANNON, Millard H.

297. "For Customers Only." 36, No. 1 (May 1951), 82-84. Short-short.

CARLTON, Jack

298. "Bamboozled." 7, No. 6 (Aug 1924), 88-94. "A thrilling tale told in the refreshing slang of 'The Knights of the Road'" [headnote].

299. "Four Shots." 6, No. 4 (15 May 1923), 77-84. Cemetery Tale.

CARNES, Randal. J.

300. "Civilized." 6, No. 3 (1 May 1923), 85-88.

CARROLL, John D. [pseud. of Carroll John DALY]

301. "Roarin' Jack." 5, No. 9 (Dec 1922), 116-122.

CARTER, Hubert Raymond [prename also given as Herbert]

302. "His Thirteenth Wife." 5, No. 5 (Aug 1922), 89-97.

303. "The House with the Silver Shutters." 5, No. 6 (Sep 1922), 101-108.

CATTON, George L.

304. "That Laugh." 5, No. 10 (Jan 1923), 81-87.

AVE, Hugh B.

05. "Curtain Call." 21, No. 8 (Nov 1938), 88-102.

06. "Dead Dog." 20, No. 1 (Mar 1937), 113-123. Pooch Hanley,
      a cop who likes dogs.

07. "Front-Page Frame-Up." 23, No. 10 (Feb 1941), 80-99. Jeff
      Cardin, detective & former cop, narrator.

08. "Lost—and Found." 23, No. 1 (Apr 1940), 74-96. See p. 97
      for letter from HBC.

09. "The Missing Mr. Lee." 23, No. 7 (Nov 1940), 80-89.

10. "Shadow." 20, No. 2 (Apr 1937), 122-128.

11. "Smoke in Your Eyes." 21, No. 9 (Dec 1938), 28-50. Unusually
      well-plotted.

12. "Stranger in Town." 23, No. 12 (Apr 1941), 58-72. HBC's last
      appearance in *BM*.

13. "Too Many Women." 17, No. 3 (May 1934), 112-125. Gumshoe
      Bill Evans; HBC's debut in *BM*.

CHAMBERS, Whitman

14. "The Black Bottle." 19, No. 2 (Apr 1936), 104-126. Lt.
      Larry McMain, USN.

CHAMBLISS, John L.

15. "The Contact." 16, No. 10 (Dec 1933), 81-90. Schuyler Blake,
      private peep, in NYC.

CHAMPION, D. L.

16. "Blackmail Backfire." 33, No. 3 (Sep 1949), 56-72, 129.
      Rex Sackler & Joey Graham.

17. "Blood from a Turnip." 25, No. 1 (May 1942), 37-57. Sackler.

318.   "The Brand of Abel." 23, No. 7 (Nov 1940), 35-41. Desert
        setting.

319.   "Cash As Cash Can." 26, No. 8 (Sep 1944), 30-44. Sackler.

320.   "Come Out of the Grave." 25, No. 10 (Feb 1943), 12-35. Sackler.

321.   "A Corpse Can't Run." 32, No. 1 (Sep 1948), 30-50. Dan Morgan,
        private eye.

322.   "A Corpse Means Cash." 26, No. 10 (Jan 1945), 50-63, 92-93.
        Sackler.

323.   "The Corpse Pays Cash." 26, No. 6 (May 1944), 43-58. Sackler.

324.   "Dead As in Blonde." 26, No. 11 (Mar 1945), 37-48. Sackler.

325.   "Death for a Dollar." 26, No. 5 (Mar 1944), 66-84. Sackler;
        note same title for next entry.

326.   "Death for a Dollar." 34, No. 1 (Jan 1950), 52-66, 128-129.
        Sackler; different story, same title as above; last RS
        story & last DLC story in *BM*.

327.   "Death Stops Payment." 23, No. 3 (Jly 1940), 6-22. Introduces
        Rex Sackler, ex-cop turned p.i., known as the
        "Parsimonious Prince of Penny-Pinchers"; narrated by
        his assistant, Joey Graham; total of 26 RS stories &
        genuinely funny; DLC's debut in *BM*.

328.   "Down Payment on Death." 30, No. 4 (Nov 1947), 26-45.
        Sackler.

329.   "Extra Alibi." 32, No. 3 (Jan 1949), 104-124. Baxter Beamish,
        ex-con turned private eye; his card reads, "Set a Crook
        to Catch a Crook."

330.   "Heads—The Corpse Loses." 26, No. 2 (Sep 1943), 48-69.
        Sackler.

331.   "Infernal Revenue." 29, No. 2 (Nov 1946), 30-45. Sackler.

332. "Killer, Can You Spare a Dime?" 25, No. 4 (Aug 1942), 108-128. Sackler.

333. "Money Makes the Mare Go." 27, No. 3 (Nov 1945), 52-65, 91. Sackler, here dubbed "The Shylock of the Shamuses."

334. "Money to Burn." 23, No. 6 (Oct 1940), 48-68. Sackler.

335. "Murder By the Ears." 25, No. 6 (Oct 1942), 44-60. Sackler.

336. "Murder Pays 7 to 1." 24, No. 11 (Mar 1942), 59-76. Sackler.

337. "Padlocked Pockets." 30, No. 2 (Jly 1947), 100-118. Sackler.

338. "Pick Up the Marbles." 24, No. 7 (Oct 1941), 10-35. Sackler.

339. "Spend, Killer, Spend!" 27, No. 1 (Jly 1945), 8-23. Sackler.

340. "Split Fee." 24, No. 2 (Jun 1941), 108-130. Sackler.

341. "Too Mean to Die." 30, No. 1 (May 1947), 10-29. Sackler

342. "Two-Death Parlay." 28, No. 4 (Jly 1946), 25-39. Sackler.

343. "Vacation with Pay." 23, No. 12 (Apr 1941), 90-106. Sackler.

344. "What's Money?" 24, No. 9 (Jan 1942), 40-59. Sackler; see p. 8 for data on DLC.

345. "Who Took the Corpse?" 26, No. 4 (Jan 1944), 92-101. Villain is a professional magician, Marvelo.

CHANCE, Peter

346. "The Scarlet Scalpel." 6, No. 9 (1 Aug 1923), 33-39.

CHANDLER, Raymond

347. "Blackmailers Don't Shoot." 16, No. 10 (Dec 1933), 8-35. Mallory, private dick, in L.A.; RC's debut in *BM* & his 1st published 'tec story; see also "Smart-Aleck Kill."

348.   "The Curtain." 19, No. 7 (Sep 1936), 10-33. Carmady, p.i.

349.   "Finger Man." 17, No. 8 (Oct 1934), 8-38. Unnamed private
            eye in L.A. as 1st-person narrator.

350.   "Goldfish." 19, No. 4 (Jun 1936), 10-35. Carmady; see May
            1936 issue, p. 127, for comment on RC; reprinted, *The
            Hard-Boiled Detective* (1977); see also "The Curtain."

351.   "Guns at Cyrano's." 18, No. 11 (Jan 1936), 8-37. Ted Malvern.

352.   "Killer in the Rain." 17, No. 11 (Jan 1935), 8-33. Unnamed
            private dick in L.A. as 1st-person narrator.

353.   "The Man Who Liked Dogs." 19, No. 1 (Mar 1936), 10-33. 1st
            of 4 Carmady stories; reprinted, *The Hard-Boiled Omnibus*
            (1946).

354.   "Nevada Gas." 18, No. 4 (Jun 1935), 8-34. Johnny DeRuse.

355.   "Smart-Aleck Kill." 17, No. 5 (Jly 1934), 54-78. 2d Mallory
            story; see also "Blackmailers Don't Shoot."

356.   "Spanish Blood." 18, No. 9 (Nov 1935), 38-64. Delaguerra,
            an L. A. cop.

357.   "Try the Girl." 19, No. 11 (Jan 1937), 10-34. Last Carmady
            story & RC's last appearance in *BM*.

CHAPIN, C.

358.   "Room Rent." 8, No. 2 (Apr 1925), 96-103.

CHARLES, W. S.

359.   "Blue Gulch Joe Butts In." 11, No. 5 (Jly 1928), 103-119.
            Stagecoach Western with Lim Wang, a good Chinese for
            a change.

CHARTERIS, Leslie

360.   "The Invisible Millionaire." 21, No. 4 (Jun 1938), 6-41. The Sai

61.   "Murder Goes to Market." 26, No. 5 (Mar 1944), 8-48, 108.
        The Saint.

CHIDSEY, Donald Barr

62.   "Dead Heroes Don't Count." 36, No. 1 (May 1951), 93-112.
        DBC's last appearance in *BM*.

63.   "Let Me Tell It." 16, No. 11 (Jan 1934), 42-51. Police Capt.
        Mitchell; reprinted, 35, No. 4 (Mar 1951), 84-95.

64.   "The Man Who Turned Up Missing." 23, No. 6 (Oct 1940),
        72-76. Ed Wolfe, reporter.

65.   "A Man Who'll Talk." 16, No. 5 (Jly 1933), 84-98. Mahone of
        Homicide & Ed Marsh, "newsman *de luxe*"; DBC's debut
        in *BM*.

66.   "Plenty Tough." 16, No. 6 (Aug 1933), 112-126. State Trooper
        Kinlay.

67.   "Stage Fright." 24, No. 8 (Dec 1941), 86-87. Short-short.

CHRISTIE, Agatha

68.   "The Face of Helen." 36, No. 2 (Jly 1951), 37-48. Reprint;
        not from *BM*.

CLAFLIN, L. W.

69.   "Thunder in the Darkness." 15, No. 10 (Dec 1932), 114-125.
        Joe Stannard & road construction gang.

CLARK, Dale [see also Ronal KAYSER]

70.   "Booty and the Beast." 28, No. 4 (Jly 1946), 40-53. WW II
        vets running vacation camp.

71.   "The Brenneke Slug." 26, No. 2 (Sep 1943), 70-90. O'Hanna.

372.   "The Corpse with the Bloody Nose." 29, No. 4 (Mar 1947), 81-96. Last O'Hanna story (28th) & last DC story in *BM*.

373.   "Death Watch." 21, No. 11 (Feb 1939), 76-93. Scotland Y. Carr, undercover man; politics & murder.

374.   "The Early Corpse Gets the Worm." 28, No. 3 (May 1946) 60-71, 95-96. O'Hanna.

375.   "Five Who Killed." 24, No. 4 (Aug 1941), 41-57. O'Hanna.

376.   "Guy in the Sky." 25, No. 2 (Jun 1942), 71-87. O'Hanna.

377.   "Hands Down." 26, No. 5 (Mar 1944), 49-65, 109-110. O'Hanna.

378.   "Heavenly Homicide." 29, No. 3 (Jan 1947), 61-72. O'Hanna.

379.   "Heir in the Air." 27, No. 2 (Sep 1945), 49-61. O'Hanna.

380.   "Honeymoon in the Morgue." 20, No. 3 (May 1937), 78-95. Kensing, RR dick; DC's debut in *BM*.

381.   "Hot Towels." 24, No. 2 (Jun 1941), 39-55. O'Hanna.

382.   "I Ain't Got No Body." 27, No. 4 (Jan 1946), 37-47, 94-95. O'Hanna.

383.   "Killer in the Wind." 23, No. 5 (Sep 1940), 56-73. O'Hanna.

384.   "Monkey See." 26, No. 6 (May 1944), 82-96. "High" Price, private snoop; a.k.a. Highland Price.

385.   "Murder Had a Little Lamb." 26, No. 11 (Mar 1945), 49-60. O'Hanna.

386.   "Murder Is No Joke." 25, No. 1 (May 1942), 94-110. O'Hanna.

387.   "Murder Lode." 28, No. 1 (Feb 1946), 43-56. O'Hanna.

388.   "Murder o' Mine." 26, No. 4 (Jan 1944), 49-64. O'Hanna.

389.   "The Nip and the Bite." 26, No. 8 (Sep 1944), 45-57. O'Hanna.

390.   "Now I Slay Me—." 25, No. 7 (Nov 1942), 106-122, 124-128. O'Hanna.

391.   "Open and Shut." 27, No. 1 (Jly 1945), 38-52. O'Hanna.

392.   "Rhymes with Crimes." 23, No. 3 (Jly 1940), 106-126. 1st Mike O'Hanna story; house dick at San Alpa resort hotel; also in L.A. & environs; total of 28 O'H capers.

393.   "Rob and Kill." 23, No. 7 (Nov 1940), 64-79. O'Hanna.

394.   "San Quentin Quail." 24, No. 6 (Oct 1941), 103-114, 116, 118, 120-129. O'Hanna.

395.   "Say It with Murder." 25, No. 5 (Sep 1942), 60-76. O'Hanna.

396.   "Skin Game." 23, No. 10 (Feb 1941), 102-127. O'Hanna.

397.   "Slay As You Go." 25, No. 10 (Feb 1943), 46-65, 129. O'Hanna.

398.   "Slay on Sight." 26, No. 7 (Jly 1944), 46-61. O'Hanna.

399.   "The Sound of the Shot." 29, No. 1 (Sep 1946), 68-79, 97. O'Hanna with movie people & Hollywood beauty contest.

400.   "That's Murder for You." 26, No. 10 (Jan 1945), 64-91. O'Hanna.

401.   "This Will Slay You." 24, No. 8 (Dec 1941), 46-62. O'Hanna.

CLARK, Valma

402.   "A Little Matter of Chivalry." 8, No. 2 (Apr 1925), 76-88. "A Mystery of Real Life."

CLAUDY, C. H.

403.   "Out of the East." 5, No. 9 (Dec 1922), 22-32.

CLAUSEN, Carl

404.   "The Careful Alibi." 5, No. 8 (Nov 1922), 3-17. "Complete
            Novelette."

405.   "The Turquoise Ring." 9, No. 8 (Oct 1926), 83-102.

406.   "The Weight of a Feather." 5, No. 5 (Aug 1922), 81-88.

CLAY, M.C.

407.   "Finders, Takers." 24, No. 1 (May 1941), 78-81.

CLAY, Robert

408.   "The Man Who Hated Worms." 6, No. 1 (1 Apr 1923), 27-34.

CLUE CLUB

409.   "Clue Club Mystery Story Contest." 17, No. 12 (Feb 1935),
            122-126. Short-lived contest sponsored by Warner Bros. &
            BM with prizes, etc.; not indexed beyond this point.

CLUFF, Curtis

410.   "Leave Killings to the Cops." 31, No. 4 (Jly 1948), 6-34.
            Johnny Ford.

411.   "Overdose of Lead." 32, No. 2 (Nov 1948), 8-35, 128-130.
            Chuck Conrad, p.i., in NYC.

412.   "Snow at Waikiki." 31, No. 1 (Jan 1948), 96-124. Johnny Ford,
            private gumshoe, in Honolulu & 1st-person narrator;
            snow = heroin.

413.   "You'll Never Die Rich." 31, No. 3 (May 1948), 8-39. Ford
            earns a C-note.

COATES, Frederick Ames

414.   "The Accident." 5, No. 4 (Jly 1922), 80-86.

115.   "A Big Job." 4, No. 1 (Oct 1921), 113-123.

116.   "Bottled Judgment." 5, No. 8 (Nov 1922), 89-97.

117.   "A Double-Barreled Joke." 3, No. 3 (Jun 1921), 118-123.

118.   "In the Room of the Murder." 2, No. 3 (Dec 1920), 96-110.
            Wu Ling-Hsi, Chinese servant, avenger.

COCKRELL, Francis M.

119.   "Death by Appointment." 17, No. 2 (Apr 1934), 8-35. Hogan,
            private dick.

120.   "Ham-Strung." 16, No. 6 (Aug 1933), 31-53. Horse racing &
            gamblers.

COLE, William

421.   "Waiting for Rusty." 22, No. 7 (Oct 1939), 109-111. Short-
            short.

COLIN, Galen C.

422.   "Wrong Font Brands." 14, No. 1 (Mar 1931), 82-90. Pica Slim,
            tramp printer.

COLLINSON, Peter [pseud. of Dashiell HAMMETT]

423.   "Arson Plus." 6, No. 13 (1 Oct 1923), 25-36. 1st Continental
            Op story & billed as "full of fire"; see p. 127 for letter
            by DH.

424.   "The Road Home." 5, No. 9 (Dec 1922), 19-21. Short-short
            set in SE Asia; reprinted, *The Hard-Boiled Detective*
            (1977).

425.   "Slippery Fingers." 6, No. 14 (15 Oct 1923), 96-103. See p. 127 for
            letter by DH & discussion of story; 2d of 2 stories by DH
            in issue; see "Crooked Souls."

426.   "The Vicious Circle." 6, No. 6 (15 Jun 1923), 106-111. See

pp. 126-127 for letter by DH.

COLTON, Mel

427.   "Dead Men Can't Welsh." 32, No. 2 (Nov 1948), 104-121.
     Jimmy Rock, p.i.

428.   "Win, Lose—or Kill." 35, No. 4 (Mar 1951), 96-112.

CONDET, Peter

429.   "The Indorsed Check." 5, No. 8 (Nov 1922), 49-59. Baseball
     background.

430.   "Perfect Alibis." 6, No. 7 (1 Jly 1923), 29-37.

CONLY, Frank

431.   "A Bottle of Vinegar." 7, No. 5 (Jly 1924), 7-31. 1st-person
     narrator is Johnson of a 1-man 'tec agency; "A Complete
     Detective Novelette."

432.   "The Man Who Was Not." 6, No. 15 (1 Nov 1923), 93-100. "Can
     the dead be brought back to life....?"

CONMARR, Crowley

433.   "Fingers Clawing." 6, No. 10 (15 Aug 1923), 77-89.

434.   "Under the Hide of Tu Son." 5, No. 13 (1 Mar 1923), 29-39.
     A Weird Tale"; 1st-person narrator; Chinese character.

CONNELL, Richard

435.   "The Color of Honor." 6, No. 5 (1 Jun 1923), 49-58. KKK
     story in special KKK issue; see p. 127 for data on RC.

CONRAD, Cyril J.

     "A Breath of Suspicion." 9, No. 8 (Oct 1926), 113-122.

CONSTINER, Merle

437.   "Bury Me Not." 31, No. 1 (Jan 1948), 6-28. Luther McGavock;
        last (11th) in series & MC's last story in *BM*.

438.   "Dead on Arrival." 29, No. 4 (Mar 1947), 8-32. McGavock.

439.   "Hand Me Down My Thirty-Eight." 27, No. 4 (Jan 1946), 48-75,
        96-97. McGavock.

440.   "The Hound with the Golden Eye." 26, No. 6 (May 1944), 8-42.
        McGavock.

441.   "Killer Stay 'Way from My Door." 26, No. 9 (Nov 1944),
        66-96. McGavock.

442.   "Kill One, Skip One." 26, No. 3 (Nov 1943), 8-46. McGavock.

443.   "Let the Dead Alone." 25, No. 3 (Jly 1942), 44-77, 130.
        Luther McGavock, private detective; he works for
        Atherton Browne who heads a Memphis-based agency; 1st
        of 11 McG stories; usually with rural settings.

444.   "Let's Count Corpses." 25, No. 5 (Sep 1942), 77-111, 128,
        130. McGavock; see p. 8 for background data on story.

445.   "The Turkey Buzzard Blues." 26, No. 1 (Jly 1943), 62-99.
        McGavock; reprinted, *The Hard-Boiled Detective* (1977).

446.   "Until the Undertaker Comes." 26, No. 11 (Mar 1945), 10-36.
        McGavock.

447.   "Why Meddle with Murder?" 25, No. 9 (Jan 1943), 54-90, 129.
        McGavock.

448.   "The Witch of Birdfoot Ranch." 26, No. 12 (May 1945), 62-74.
        Sheriff Britten; hill-country setting.

CORCORAN, William

449.   "Manhattan Midnight." 16, No. 8 (Oct 1933), 74-82. Boland,
        NYC cabbie.

CORD, Barry

450.   "Shoot If You Must." 32, No. 1 (Sep 1948), 110-127. Steve
            Weston, shamus.

COREY, H. R.

451.   "Crusoe's Man Friday." 5, No. 3 (Jun 1922), 97-103.

CORRELL, A. Boyd

452.   "Blackmail, Theft & Murder, Inc." 23, No. 11 (Mar 1941),
            53-62. Jimmy Reed, Hollywood 'tec; see p. 6 for data on
            ABC.

453.   "The Shamus Called It Murder." 24, No. 4 (Aug 1941), 100-109.
            Jim Doyle, private shamus, in Hollywood & L.A.

COUEY, OWEN

454.   "Bring Your Own Body." 34, No. 4 (Jly 1950), 37-50.

COX, Charles E., Jr.

455.   "No Quarter." 15, No. 9 (Nov 1932), 120-122. In "Narrowest
            Escape" series, supposedly factual; offered as example;
            Italian front, WW I; see also under M.A. GUTSCHOW.

COX, William R.

456.   "Accounting in Blood." 22, No. 9 (Dec 1939), 102-109. A
            CCC bookkeeper.

457.   "Half a Crook." 21, No. 3 (May 1938), 117-126. Murder &
            politics.

COXE, George Harmon

458.   "Blood on the Lens." 25, No. 9 (Jan 1943), 11-44, Pt. 1; 25, No. 10
            (Feb 1943), 76-127, Pt. 2; 25, No. 11 (Mar 1943), 96-127,
            Pt. 3. Flashgun Casey; GHC's last appearance in *BM*;
            serial pub. as *Murder for Two* (1943).

459. "Buried Evidence." 18, No. 5 (Jly 1935), 72-90. Tom Wade with Casey.

460. "Casey and the Blonde Wren." 23, No. 4 (Aug 1940), 52-66. Casey; Wren = Women's Royal Naval Service.

461. "Casey—Detective." 17, No. 12 (Feb 1935), 68-88. Casey.

462. "Double or Nothing." 19, No. 9 (Nov 1936), 42-63. Paul Baron & sidekick, Buck O'Shea; last of 4 PB stories.

463. "Earned Reward." 18, No. 1 (Mar 1935), 101-121. Casey.

464. "Fall Guy." 19, No. 4 (Jun 1936), 62-81. Casey.

465. "Hot Delivery." 17, No. 5 (Jly 1934), 79-93. Casey.

466. "Killers Are Camera-Shy." 24, No. 5 (Sep 1941), 10-42, Pt. 1; 24, No. 6 (Oct 1941), 62-99, Pt. 2; 24, No. 7 (Nov 1941), 80-110, 121-129. Casey; pub. as *Silent Are the Dead* (1942); see p. 8 (Sep 1941) for letter from GHC on Casey.

467. "Letters Are Poison." 19, No. 2 (Apr 1936), 63-81. Baron.

468. "Mr. Casey Flashguns Murder." 18, No. 8 (Oct 1935), 32-61. Casey.

469. "Mixed Drinks." 17, No. 6 (Aug 1934), 88-106. Casey.

470. "Murder in the Red." 25, No. 2 (Jun 1942), 10-40. Casey; defense-plant boom town.

471. "Murder Mixup." 19, No. 3 (May 1936), 8-30. Casey; reprinted, *The Hard-Boiled Omnibus* (1946).

472. "Murder Picture." 17, No. 11 (Jan 1935), 73-97. Casey.

473. "Once Around the Clock." 24, No. 1 (May 1941), 48-70. Casey; reprinted, 36, No. 2 (Jly 1951), 59-85; reprinted, *The Hard-Boiled Detective* (1977).

474.   "Pinch-Hitters." 17, No. 7 (Sep 1934), 61-77. Casey.

475.   "Portrait of Murder." 18, No. 12 (Feb 1936), 58-82. Casey.

476.   "Push-Over." 17, No. 4 (Jun 1934), 83-101. Casey.

477.   "Return Engagement." 17, No. 1 (Mar 1934), 73-84. Debut of
        Flashgun Casey, news photographer, first with Boston
        Globe then with the *Express*; here he plays secondary role
        to young colleague, Tom Wade, who inevitably appears
        with FC; also GHC's debut in *BM*.

478.   "Special Assignment." 17, No. 2 (Apr 1934), 72-83. Casey.

479.   "Thirty Tickets to Win." 18, No. 4 (Jun 1935), 48-74. Casey
        at the race track.

480.   "Too Many Women." 19, No. 4 (Sep 1936), 34-58. Casey.

481.   "Trouble for Two." 19, No. 5 (Jly 1936), 57-81. Baron.

482.   "Two-Man Job." 17, No. 3 (May 1934), 43-61. Casey.

483.   "Women Are Trouble." 18, No. 2 (Apr 1935), 10-44. Casey.

484.   "You Gotta Be Tough." 19, No. 1 (Mar 1936), 34-47. 1st of 4
        Paul Baron stories.

CRAIG, Charles Hilan

485.   "The Wanderer." 6, No. 18 (15 Dec 1923), 65-70. Western; see
        6, No. 19 (1 Jan 1923), 127, for letter from CHC.

CRAIGIE, Hamilton

486.   "Above Suspicion." 2, No. 1 (Oct 1920), 91-94.

487.   "The Dead Ringer." 1, No. 3 (Jun 1920), 107-116.

488.   "The Lap of the Lady." 3, No. 1 (Apr 1921), 103-108. Shop
        lifting & female impersonator.

489.   "The Pendulum of Fate." 2, No. 4 (Jan 1921), 93-98.

490.   "A Question of Temperature." 2, No. 6 (Mar 1921), 49-54.

491.   "Receipted in Full." 1, No. 2 (May 1920), 3-17. Headnote is worth (partially) quoting from: "...Another typical *Black Mask* complete novelette...which represent[s] the very best mystery fiction...printed in America today. Novelty of plot, nervous suspense and ingenious solutions are the keynotes...;" HC's debut in *BM*; 1st of 3 stories in issue in which he figures; see entries below.

492.   "The Tell-Tale Band of Yellow." 2, No. 2 (Nov 1920), 77-84.

CRAIGIE, Hamilton and Walter GRAHAME

493.   "According to Specifications." 1, No. 2 (May 1920), 95-103. 2d story in issue by this tandem; *cf.* entry above.

494.   "The Jest Ironic." 1, No. 2 (May 1920), 38-43. See entry above.

CRAWFORD, Frank Hepburn

495.   Silver Bullets." 7, No. 11 (Jan 1925), 97-107. "A weird, unusual tale."

CRESSEY, Peter Ames

496.   "Do Your Stuff, Ranger." 12, No. 6 (Aug 1929), 89-98. Western with Carnes.

CREWE, David

497.   "Guilt Powder." 30, No. 4 (Mar 1951), 36-41. Reprint; not from *BM*.

CRITTENDEN, Anthony

498.   "Spike McCready's Exit." 6, No. 6 (15 Jun 1923), 119-122.

CROWELL, Ashton

499.   "The Prison Clock Strikes Nine." 1, No. 2 (May 1920), 31-37. Prison setting.

CSIDA, Joseph

500.   "Bank Night Kill." 21, No. 1 (Mar 1938), 115-126. Narrated by a "contest dick."

501.   "Strike Three." 21, No. 4 (Jun 1938), 88-99. Ball player killed on the field.

CUMMINGS, Ray[mond King]

502.   "The Mystery at Cragmoor." 8, No. 8 (Oct 1925), 7-52.

503.   "The System of T. McGuirk." 8, No. 2 (Apr 1925), 40-44. Timothy McGuirk.

504.   "T. McGuirk—Assistant Bank Robber." 7, No. 5 (Jly 1924), 79-86. McGuirk.

505.   "T. McGuirk—Burglary Adjuster." 7, No. 3 (May 1924), 47-54. McGuirk.

506.   "T. McGuirk Catches a Crook." 9, No. 7 (Sep 1926), 121-128. Last of 14 McG stories & RC's last appearance in *BM*.

507.   "T. McGuirk—Detective." 6, No. 9 (1 Aug 1923), 103-110. McGuirk.

508.   "T. McGuirk Enforces the Liquor Law." 6, No. 12 (15 Sep 1923), 44-46. Short-short McGuirk.

509.   "T. McGuirk Juggles a Diamond." 8, No. 4 (Jun 1925), 53-58. McGuirk.

510.   "T. McGuirk Juggles the Pawn Tickets." 6, No. 8 (15 Jly 1923), 111-117. McGuirk.

511.   "T. McGuirk—Klansman." 6, No. 5 (1 Jun 1923), 78-83.

McGuirk & KKK, alleged to be "humorous tale"; in special KKK issue.

512. "T. McGuirk Lends a Helping Hand." 8, No. 7 (Sep 1925), 91-99. McGuirk.

513. "T. McGuirk, Movie Actor." 6, No. 21 (1 Feb. 1924), 67-74. McGuirk.

514. "T. McGuirk Steals a Diamond." 5, No. 9 (Dec 1922), 57-63. 1st of 14 McG tales; billed as "the quaintest character in the underworld" & honest, more or less.

515. "T. McGuirk Tries the Luck Charms." 6, No. 13 (1 Oct 1923), 47-52. McGuirk.

516. "T. McGuirk Walks the Straight and Narrow." 5, No. 10 (Jan 1923), 36-40. McGuirk.

CUMMINGS, Ray and Gabrielle [2d wife]

517. "Haunted." 6, No. 2 (15 Apr 1923), 43-51.

CUMMINS, Ralph

518. "Ace King." 9, No. 7 (Sep 1926), 7-41. Western.

519. "The Fountain of Vengeance." 2, No. 3 (Dec 1920), 3-32. "A Complete Mystery Novelette"; set in L.A. on West Adams Blvd.

520. "The Gas Heater Mystery." 6, No. 3 (1 May 1923), 35-50.

CUNNINGHAM, Eugene

521. "An Old Spanish Custom." 17, No. 10 (Dec 1934), 52-72. Kerr.

522. "Bar Nuthin', Puzzle Buster." 12, No. 7 (Sep 1929), 112-134. Western; Bar Nuthin' is main character.

523. "Border Guns." 13, No. 9 (Nov 1930), 66-75. Western; Johnny

Hearne, Border patrolman.

524. "Chalk." 16, No. 10 (Dec 1933), 91-109. Cleve Corby.

525. "County Loop." 17, No. 6 (Aug 1934), 43-65. Corby & Vic Ruiz.

526. "Gunhands." 14, No. 4 (Jun 1931), 65-77. Western; Bob Burney.

527. "House Dick." 16, No. 7 (Sep 1933), 102-121. Cleve Corby, undercover Texas Ranger, here acting as house dick; 1st of 5 CC stories.

528. "If Murder Can Be Funny." 17, No. 5 (Jly 1934), 6-29. Corby.

529. "Information Received." 19, No. 9 (Nov 1936), 88-112. Border yarn with Detective Sergeant Bob Land, Border dick; EC's final story in *BM*; see also "Tough People."

530. "Over the River." 11, No. 10 (Dec 1928), 95-113. Western; Twistaway Smith of the Rangers; EC's debut in *BM*.

531. "Passing Through." 15, No. 10 (Dec 1932), 75-87. Western; Pony Kirk.

532. "Room Service." 17, No. 9 (Nov 1934), 104-113. Last Corby story.

533. "Singing Lead." 13, No. 6 (Aug 1930), 24-35. Western.

534. "Tough People." 18, No. 10 (Dec 1935), 60-79. Bob Land; see also "Information Received."

CUNNINGHAM, Captain Frank

535. "The Best New Books." 1, No. 2 (May 1920), 127-128. Regular column which reviewed new mystery & detective novels; also called "The New Mystery Books"; not indexed beyond this point.

CURRY, Tom

536. "Big Six." 10, No. 2 (Apr 1927), 41-51. Macnamara (Mac),

NYPD 1st-grade dick.

537. "Buck." 9, No. 3 (May 1926), 87-92. Mac; Buck, safecracker.

538. "Clancy Takes the Air." 16, No. 10 (Dec 1933), 110-121. Clancy another 1st-grade dick in NYC; TC's last appearance in *BM*.

539. "Crooks in Arcady." 11, No. 7 (Sep 1928), 122-128. Mac.

540. "Cul de Sac." 9, No. 2 (Apr 1926), 31-55. Jewel robbery on Long Island.

541. "The Dick-Killer." 9, No. 10 (Dec 1926), 101-118. Mac on the NY docks.

542. "Dumb-Bell." 8, No. 9 (Nov 1925), 96-103.

543. "The Frame-Up." 8, No. 8 (Oct 1925), 112-116. TC's debut in *BM*.

544. "The Gang." 11, No. 1 (Mar 1928), 82-97. DeVrite.

545. "The House of Jewels." 9, No. 4 (Jun 1926), 35-53.

546. "Jungle Thieves." 10, No. 1 (Mar 1927), 108-126. Venezuela & Federal agents on the chase.

547. "The Man from Headquarters." 12, No. 9 (Nov 1929), 121-128. Mac.

548. "The Master." 11, No. 6 (Aug 1928), 116-128. 7th & last DeVrite story; with Mac.

549. "Murder Cars." 10, No. 4 (Jun 1927), 58-65. Mac.

550. "Murder Chains." 10, No. 7 (Sep 1927), 38-56, Pt. 1; 10, No. 8 (Oct 1927), 113-128, Pt. 2. Gangster yarn; John Furnel, alias The Grand Street Kid; see p. 128 (Sep 1927) for data on & photo of TC.

551. "The Muscle Man." 11, No. 10 (Dec 1928), 114-128. Mac.

552. "Perfect Money." 10, No. 10 (Dec 1927), 121-128. Mac.

553. "The Peterman." 10, No. 5 (Jly 1927), 24-33. Mac; peterman = high explosives expert.

554. "The Price of a Rod." 15, No. 11 (Jan 1933), 106-122. Last Mac story.

555. "The Raiders." 10, No. 9 (Nov 1927), 45-51. Mac.

556. "The Reformation." 8, No. 11 (Jan 1926), 74-79. Mac.

557. "The Roper." 14, No. 8 (Oct 1931), 113-122. Mac.

558. "A Sense of Humor." 9, No. 1 (Mar 1926), 77-81. Mac.

559. "The Spies." 11, No. 4 (Jun 1928), 82-97. DeVrite.

560. "The Star." 12, No. 2 (Apr 1929), 95-101. Mac.

561. "The Stick-Up Club." 10, No. 3 (May 1927), 101-111. Mac.

562. "Stolen Justice." 13, No. 11 (Jan 1931), 101-122. Mac.

563. "The Stoolie." 9, No. 11 (Jan 1927), 18-24. Mac.

564. "Strong Men." 8, No. 12 (Feb 1926), 80-99. Mac; war between fur thieves & police.

565. "Supercrook." 11, No. 8 (Oct 1928), 35-46. Mac.

566. "The System." 11, No. 3 (May 1928), 81-93. DeVrite.

567. "The Taste of Blood." 11, No. 12 (Feb 1929), 86-102. Mac; smalltime crook develops into killer.

568. "The Terror." 12, No. 3 (May 1929), 90-106. Mac.

569. "Under Cover." 10, No. 12 (Feb 1928), 9-25. DeVrite, NYPD secret agent; 1st story in series of 7; subtitled "The Receiver."

570.　　　"The Water Rats." 12, No. 4 (Jly 1929), 91-110. Mac.

571.　　　"The Web." 12, No. 8 (Oct 1929), 110-116. John Flahertie,
　　　　　　the lone wolf; Mac, minor character.

572.　　　"Wheels Within Wheels." 11, No. 2 (Apr 1928), 112-128.
　　　　　　DeVrite.

573.　　　"The Woman." 11, No. 5 (Jly 1928), 81-95. DeVrite & Mac.

CURTIS, Ellis G.

574.　　　"Aces and Eights." 35, No. [1] (Sep 1950), 63-71.

CUSHING, Charles Phelps

575.　　　"A Tassel of Black Yarn." 5, No. 14 (15 Mar 1923), 45-58.
　　　　　　Mamie Skaggs, policewoman.

D

DABNEY, Thomas Ewing

576.　　　"The Drug of Ullua." 7, No. 10 (Dec 1924), 7-35. Hard-Boiled
　　　　　　Smith in Latin America.

577.　　　"Tom Shepherd and the Rat." 5, No. 8 (Nov 1922), 112-124.

DALE, Virginia

578.　　　"Alibi Bride." 20, No. 7 (Sep 1937), 125-127. Short-short.

DALY, Carroll John [see also John D. CARROLL]

579.　　　"Action! Action!" 6, No. 19 (1 Jan 1924), 25-56. Three-Gun
　　　　　　Terry Mack, 1st-person narrator; see also "Three Gun
　　　　　　Terry."

580.　　　"Alias Buttercup." 8, No. 8 (Oct 1925), 53-91. Race Williams
　　　　　　in Mexico.

581.　　　"The Amateur Murderer." 15, No. 2 (Apr 1932), 40-63, Pt. 1;
　　　　　　15, No. 3 (May 1932), 45-65, Pt. 2; 15, No. 4 (Jun 1932),

76-94, Pt. 3; 15, No. 5 (Jly 1932), 101-125, Pt. 4. Race Williams serial; pub. as novel (1933); see p. 119 (Apr 1932) for a CJD anecdote.

582. "Blind Alleys." 10, No. 2 (Apr 1927), 9-40. Race Williams.

583. "The Brute." 6, No. 20 (15 Jan 1924), 49-61. Buck Henderson in South Seas.

584. "Conceited, Maybe." 8, No. 2 (Apr 1925), 7-39. Race Williams.

585. "The Death Drop." 16, No. 3 (May 1933), 6-41. Race Williams out in the countryside.

586. "Death for Two." 14, No. 7 (Sep 1931), 8-32. Williams pinch-hits for his friend, Sergeant O'Rourke.

587. "Devil Cat." 7, No. 9 (Nov 1924), 7-36. Race Williams.

588. "Dolly." 5, No. 7 (Oct 1922), 57-65. 1st-person narrated mood piece; CJD's debut in *BM*; see p. 65 for editorial comment on story.

589. "The Egyptian Lure." 11, No. 1 (Mar 1928), 7-29. "The name of Race Williams stands for service."

590. "The Eyes Have It." 17, No. 9 (Nov 1934), 10-46. Last Race Williams caper in *BM* (wherein he had appeared "exclusively"); CJD not to pub. in *BM* until Mar 1938.

591. "The Face Behind the Mask." 7, No. 12 (Feb 1925), 9-34. Race Williams.

592. "The False Burton Combs." 5, No. 9 (Dec 1922), 3-18. 1st-person narrator in vernacular; reprinted, *The Hard-Boiled Detective* (1977).

593. "The False Clara Burkhart." 9, No. 5 (Jly 1926), 37-73. Race Williams.

594. "The Final Shot." 13, No. 6 (Aug 1930), 81-119. Race & The

Flame; Pt. 3 of loosely organized serial; see "Tainted Power" (Pt. 1) for data.

595. "Five Minutes for Murder." 23, No. 9 (Jan 1941), 8-32. 2d & last Pete Hines story; see also "No Sap for Murder."

596. " 'The Flame' and Race Williams." 14, No. 4 (Jun 1931), 34-64, Pt. 1; 14, No. 5 (Jly 1931), 90-120, Pt. 2; 14, No. 6 (Aug 1931), 88-119, Pt. 3. RW & The Flame; pub. as *The Third Murderer* (1931).

597. "Flaming Death." 17, No. 4 (Jun 1934), 24-59. Williams & The Flame; Pt. 2 of loosely organized serial; see "Six Have Died" (Pt. 1) for data.

598. "Framed." 13, No. 5 (Jly 1930), 76-110. Race & The Flame; Pt. 2 of loosely organized serial; see "Tainted Power" (Pt. 1) for data.

599. "Get Race Williams." 12, No. 3 (May 1929), 53-78. RW & introducing The Flame, a.k.a. Florence Drummond, The Girl with the Criminal Mind; Pt. 3 of loosely organized serial; see "Tags of Death" (Pt. 1) for data.

600. "Half-Breed." 9, No. 9 (Nov 1926), 5-36. Race Williams among the Oklahoma oil-rich Osage Indians.

601. "The Hidden Hand." 11, No. 4 (Jun 1928), 42-63. Williams vs. The Hidden Hand, i.e., Howard Travers; Pt. 1 of loosely organized 5-pt. serial; pub. as novel (1929).

602. "I Am the Law." 21, No. 1 (Mar 1938), 10-38. "Meet that implacable, coldly reckless manhunter, Satan Hall"; 1st of 2 SH stories; see also "Wrong Street."

603. "If Death Is Respectable." 16, No. 5 (Jly 1933), 26-48. Race Williams.

604. "I'll Tell the World." 8, No. 6 (Aug 1925), 3-41. Williams.

605. "It's All in the Game." 6, No. 2 (15 Apr 1923), 69-78. 1st-

person narrator, preying on "leading lights of the underworld," e.g., Ed, The Killer.

606. "Kiss-the-Canvas Crowley." 6, No. 11 (1 Sep 1923), 49-61. Prize-fight story.

607. "Knights of The Open Palm." 6, No. 5 (1 Jun 1923), 33-47. Debut of Race Williams; KKK story in special KKK issue; see p. 127 for letter from CJD on story; 1st of 53 RW stories; reprinted, *The Great American Detective* (1978).

608. "The Last Chance." 11, No. 7 (Sep 1928), 91-114. Race Williams vs. The Hidden Hand; Pt. 4 of loosely organized 5-pt. serial; see "The Hidden Hand."

609. "The Last Shot." 11, No. 8 (Oct 1928), 96-124. Pt. 5 of serial; see entry above; see p. 124 for word-sketch of Williams.

610. "The Law of Silence." 11, No. 2 (Apr 1928), 48-65, Pt. 1; 11, No. 3 (May 1928), 113-128, Pt. 2. Crime story; Charlie, 1st-person narrator; Pt. 2 subtitled "The Show-Down."

611. "Merger with Death." 15, No. 10 (Dec 1932), 88-113. Race Williams.

612. "Murder Book." 17, No. 6 (Aug 1934), 8-42. Williams & The Flame; Pt. 3 & finale of loosely organized serial; see "Six Have Died" (Pt. 1) for data.

613. "Murder by Mail." 14, No. 1 (Mar 1931), 10-41. Race Williams vs. Bull Lowery.

614. "Murder in the Open." 16, No. 8 (Oct 1933), 6-37. Williams.

615. "Murder Made Easy." 22, No. 2 (May 1939), 34-59. Clay Holt.

616. "Murder Theme." 26, No. 7 (Jly 1944), 29-44. WW II intrigue; CJD's last appearance in *BM*; Farrington.

617. "No Sap for Murder." 23, No. 7 (Nov 1940), 8-34. 1st of 2 Pete Hines stories; he is bodyguard; his motto: " 'It's better to be a live sap than a dead wise-guy' "; see also "Five Minutes for Murder."

618. "One Night of Frenzy." 7, No. 2 (15 Apr 1924), 23-47.

619. "Out of the Night." 9, No. 8 (Oct 1926), 5-39.

620. "A Pretty Bit of Shooting." 12, No. 2 (Apr 1929), 66-94. Race Williams; Pt. 2 of loosely organized 4-pt. serial; see "Tags of Death" for data & next entry.

621. "Race Williams Never Bluffs." 12, No. 4 (Jun 1929), 1-52. Pt. 4 & finale of loosely organized serial; see above entry.

622. "The Red Peril." 7, No. 4 (Jun 1924), 7-32. Race Williams.

623. "Rough Stuff." 11, No. 6 (Aug 1928), 62-86. Williams vs. The Hidden Hand; Pt. 3 of loosely organized 5-pt. serial; see "The Hidden Hand" for data.

624. "Say It with Lead!" 8, No. 4 (Jun 1925), 5-41. Race Williams.

625. "Shooting Out of Turn." 13, No. 8 (Oct 1930), 38-63. RW "goes out of town on a gun job."

626. "The Silver Eagle." 12, No. 8 (Oct 1929), 9-40, Pt. 1; 12, No. 9 (Nov 1929), 71-99, Pt. 2. Race Williams & The Flame; serial dropped after Pt. 2.

627. "Six Have Died." 17, No. 3 (May 1934), 8-42. Williams & The Flame; Pt. 1 of loosely organized 3-pt. serial; see also "Flaming Death" (Pt. 2) & "Murder Book" (Pt. 3); pub. as *Murder from the East* (1935).

628. "The Snarl of the Beast." 10, No. 4 (Jun 1927), 5-37, Pt. 1; 10, No. 5 (Jly 1927), 101-127, Pt. 2; 10, No. 6 (Aug 1927), 100-127, Pt. 3; 10, No. 7 (Sep 1927), 99-127, Pt. 4. Race Williams serial; pub. (1927) under same title.

629.   "South Sea Steel." 9, No. 3 (May 1926), 3-44. Williams in South Seas.

630.   "The Super Devil." 9, No. 6 (Aug 1926), 5-43. Race Williams.

631.   "Tags of Death." 12, No. 1 (Mar 1929), 7-34. Williams & introducing The Flame, The Girl with the Criminal Mind, a.k.a. Florence Drummond; Pt. 1 of loosely organized 4-pt. serial; pub. as *The Tag Murders* (1930).

632.   "Tainted Power." 13, No. 4 (Jun 1930), 5-40. Williams & The Flame; Pt. 1 of loosely organized 3-pt. serial; pub. as novel (1931) under same title.

633.   "Them That Lives by Their Guns." 7, No. 6 (Aug 1924), 5-30. Race Williams.

634.   "Three Gun Terry." 6, No. 4 (15 May 1923), 5-30. Terry Mack, Private Investigator; 1st TM tale; see also "Action! Action!"

635.   "Three Thousand to the Good." 6, No. 8 (15 Jly 1923), 31-42. Race Williams.

636.   "Twenty Grand." 9, No. 11 (Jan 1927), 25-44. Benny Slawson, "product of Delancey Street."

637.   "Under Cover." 8, No. 10 (Dec 1925), 9-29, Pt. 1; 8, No. 11 (Jan 1926), 110-126, Pt. 2. Race Williams.

628.   "Wanted for Murder." 11, No. 5 (Jly 1928), 5-27. Race Williams vs. The Hidden Hand; Pt. 2 of loosely organized 5-pt. serial; see "The Hidden Hand" for data.

639.   "Wrong Street." 21, No. 3 (May 1938), 6-35. Satan Hall in 2d & last story in *BM*; see also "I Am the Law."

DANIELS, Norman A.

640.   "Death Is No Stranger." 31, No. 1 (Jan 1948), 68-95. Rick Trent.

641.   "Dig Me a Deep Grave." 30, No. 1 (May 1947), 54-81. Rick

Trent, 1st-person narrator; ex-con (Sing Sing) & ex-shamus; 1st RT story.

642. "License to Kill." 31, No. 4 (Jly 1948), 35-43, 127-128. Stacy Tucker, private eye.

643. "My Dying Day." 30, No. 3 (Sep 1947), 58-84, 129-130. Rick Trent.

DARLING, Eric A.

644. "The Malachite Jar." 2, No. 4 (Jan 1921), 103-113.

645. "The Man in the Astrakhan Coat." 2, No. 1 (Oct 1920), 74-90. Dale Owen, amateur sleuth, in Paris.

646. "The Pigtail of Hi-Wing-Ho." 3, No. 1 (Apr 1921), 77-87. Chinese; diamond hidden in pigtail.

647. "That Thing on the Bed." 1, No. 3 (Jun 1920), 121-126.

648. "The Yellow Dog." 1, No. 6 (Sep 1920), 111-119.

DART, David

649. "The Held Up Hold-Up." 6, No. 1 (1 Apr 1923), 35-44.

650. "Parker Proves His Theory." 5, No. 7 (Oct 1922), 108-113.

DASH, Joseph E.

651. "Cass Munroe Plays a Hand." 11, No. 2 (Apr 1928), 95-101. Western.

DASHWOOD, Wyona

652. "Out of the Fog." 6, No. 6 (15 Jun 1923), 44-49. "Human weirdities."

DAVENPORT, H. B.

653. "Triggers of Justice." 6, No. 16 (15 Nov 1923), 59-63. Set in

Kentucky mountains.

654.   "Weapons." 6, No. 18 (15 Dec 1923), 30-52.

DAVIS, Frederick C[lyde]

655.   "All Roads Closed." 22, No. 5 (Aug 1939), 6-26. Kidnapping
           & amnesia.

656.   "All Things Considered." 6, No. 3 (1 May 1923), 102-109.
           FCD not to appear in *BM* again until Aug 1938.

657.   "Blind Witness." 22, No. 12 (Mar 1940), 94-112. James Teague,
           plainclothes Detective Sergeant.

658.   "The Blonde Who Wouldn't Die." 35, No. [1] (Sep 1950), 104-130.

659.   "Flaming Angel." 32, No. 4 (Mar 1949), 106-128. 1st-person
           narrator; psychopathic murderer.

660.   "Floating Pearls." 5, No. 9 (Dec 1922), 33-41.

661.   "Hide the Evidence." 22, No. 1 (Apr 1939), 6-27. Johnny
           Holland; politics & murder.

662.   "I Thought I'd Die." 26, No. 2 (Sep 1943), 96-128. Peter
           Trapp II, Wright Detective Agency; 2d PT yarn; see also
           "Save a Grave for Me."

663.   "Let Me Kill You, Sweetheart." 33, No. 3 (Sep 1949), 112-128.

664.   "The Living Dead." 5, No. 6 (Sep 1922), 49-56. FCD's debut
           in *BM*.

665.   "Save a Grave for Me." 25, No. 12 (May 1943), 8-35. Peter
           Trapp II; epistolary form, i.e., letter from PT to police
           inspector; 1st of 2 PT stories; see also "I Thought I'd Die."

666.   "Seven Knocks at My Door." 21, No. 5 (Aug 1938), 44-71.
           Dr. Joel Perry.

667.   "Stop the Presses." 21, No. 9 (Dec 1938), 7-27. Murray Gifford;

see p. 51 for data on how FCD writes; 2d MG story; see also "This Way to the Morgue."

668.   "Swing Low, Sweet Casket." 34, No. 2 (Mar 1950), 58-84.

669.   "This Way to the Morgue." 21, No. 8 (Oct 1938), 32-48.
            Murray Gifford, reporter; 1st MG story; see also "Stop
            the Presses."

670.   "Tonight I Must Die." 21, No. 11 (Feb 1939), 94-101.

DAVIS, Meredith

671.   "Beyond the Chair." 6, No. 6 (15 Jun 1923), 69-77.

672.   "The Lower Law." 5, No. 14 (15 Mar 1923), 29-36. Innocent
            victim burned at stake by lynch mob.

673.   "Velvet Tips." 5, No. 6 (Sep 1922), 68-72.

DAVIS, Norbert

674.   "Beat Me Daddy." 25, No. 7 (Nov 1942), 86-105. John Collins;
            California setting; 2d JC story; see "Don't You Cry for Me."

675.   "Bullets Don't Bother Me." 25, No. 4 (Aug 1942), 33-53. Sam
            Carey & Japanese agents in wartime San Francisco.

676.   "Don't You Cry for Me." 25, No. 1 (May 1942), 111-129. John
            Collins, piano man; Hollywood, etc.; 1st JC story; see also
            "Beat Me Daddy" & "Name Your Poison."

677.   "Hit and Run." 18, No. 2 (Apr 1935), 97-110. Private eye
            J.J. Tait.

678.   "Kansas City Flash." 16, No. 1 (Mar 1933), 77-87. Mark Hull,
            ex-stunt man, in Hollywood & L.A.; reprinted, *The Hard-
            Boiled Detective* (1977).

679.   "Medicine for Murder." 20, No. 8 (Oct 1937), 48-70. Dr. Bruce
            Gregory.

680. "Murder in Two Parts." 20, No. 10 (Dec 1937), 70-91. Brent.

681. "Name Your Poison." 25, No. 12 (May 1943), 90-106. Sergeant John Collins, Military Intelligence; 3d & last JC story & ND's last appearance in *BM*.

682. "The Price of a Dime." 17, No. 2 (Apr 1934), 100-109. Ben Shaley; see next entry.

683. "Red Goose." 16, No. 12 (Feb 1934), 87-99. Ben Shaley, private gumshoe, in Hollywood, etc.; title = stolen painting; reprinted, *The Hard-Boiled Omnibus* (1946).

684. "Reform Racket." 15, No. 4 (Jun 1932), 113-122. Dan Stiles, one-time gunman; ND's debut in *BM*.

685. "Walk Across My Grave." 24, No. 12 (Apr 1942), 45-53.

686. "You'll Die Laughing." 23, No. 7 (Nov 1940), 42-61. Dave Bly, loan-shark's legman.

DECOLTA, Ramon [pseud. of Raoul F. WHITFIELD]

687. "The Amber Fan." 16, No. 5 (Jly 1933), 99-109. Jo Gar; last (24th) JG story & RD's last appearance in *BM*.

688. "The Black Sampan." 15, No. 4 (Jan 1932), 95-105. Gar on banks of Pasig River, Manila.

689. "The Blind Chinese." 14, No. 2 (Apr 1931), 112-122. Jo Gar; 3d story in Rainbow Diamonds sequence.

690. "Blue Glass." 14, No. 5 (Jly 1931), 78-89. Jo Gar; 5th story in Rainbow Diamonds sequence.

691. "The Caleso Murders." 13, No. 10 (Dec 1930), 92-102. Jo Gar; 2d story (of 2) by RFW in issue; see "Murder in the Ring."

692. "China Man." 15, No. 1 (Mar 1932), 93-103. Jo Gar; reprinted, *The Hardboiled Dicks* (1965).

693. "Climbing Death." 15, No. 5 (Jly 1932), 88-100. Jo Gar;

aviation figures.

94. "Death in the Pasig." 13, No. 1 (Mar 1930), 49-56. Gar;
reprinted, *The Hard-Boiled Omnibus* (1946).

95. "Diamonds of Death." 14, No. 6 (Aug 1931), 46-54. Gar; 6th (&
last) story in Rainbow Diamonds sequence; 2d of 2 stories
in issue by RFW; see "The Sky Club Affair."

96. "Diamonds of Dread." 13, No. 12 (Feb 1931), 80-91. Jo Gar;
1st story (of 6) in Rainbow Diamonds sequence which
takes JG from Manila to San Francisco; 1st of 2 stories by
RFW in issue; see "About Kid Deth."

97. "Enough Rope." 13, No. 5 (Jly 1930), 25-36. Jo Gar.

98. "The Javanese Mask." 14, No. 10 (Dec 1931), 49-60. Jo Gar;
1st of 2 stories in issue by RFW; see "Unfair Exchange."

99. "The Magician Murder." 15, No. 9 (Nov 1932), 88-96. Jo Gar;
2nd of 2 stories by RFW in issue; see "Dead Men Tell
Tales."

00. "The Man from Shanghai." 16, No. 3 (May 1933), 115-124. Gar.

01 "The Man in White." 14, No. 1 (Mar 1931), 111-122. Gar; 2d
story in Rainbow Diamonds sequence.

702. "Nagasaki Bound." 13, No. 7 (Sep 1930), 103-114. Jo Gar;
see next entry for sequel.

703. "Nagasaki Knives." 13, No. 8 (Oct 1930), 26-37. Gar; see
entry above.

704. "Red Dawn." 14, No. 3 (May 1931), 113-122. Gar; 4th story
in Rainbow Diamonds sequence; 2d of 2 stories by RFW in
issue; see "Soft City."

705. "Red Hemp." 13, No. 2 (Apr 1930), 33-44. Jo Gar.

2d of 2 stories in issue by RFW; see "Steel Arena."

707.   "The Siamese Cat." 15, No. 2 (Apr 1932), 29-39. Jo Gar; 2d of 2 stories by RFW in issue; see "Man Killer."

708.   "Signals of Storm." 13, No. 4 (Jun 1930), 41-52. Jo Gar.

709.   "Silence House." 13, No. 11 (Jan 1931), 33-44. Gar; outside Manila.

710.   "West of Guam." 12, No. 12 (Feb 1930), 50-57. Debut of Jo Gar, Filipino p.i., with office in Manila; total of 24 JG stories.

DEFFENBAUGH, Walter

711.   "By the Print of a Thumb." 4, No. 4 (Jan 1922), 3-31. "Complete Mystery Novelette."

712.   "Fit for a King." 4, No. 3 (Dec 1921), 113-123. 2d of 2 stories by WD in issue; see also "Hear Not, See Not, Speak Not Evil."

713.   "Glass Jade." 3, No. 5 (Aug 1921), 113-123.

714.   "Hear Not, See Not. Speak Not Evil." 4, No. 3 (Dec 1921), 55-67. 1st of 2 stories by WD in issue; see also "Fit for a King."

715.   "Letter By Letter." 4, No. 1 (Oct 1921), 41-48.

716.   "The Lizard." 2, No. 5 (Feb 1921), 33-41. WD's debut in *BM*.

717.   "The Marching Ice." 3, No. 4 (Jly 1921), 75-83. 1st-person narrator.

718.   "The Persian Rug." 4, No. 6 (Mar 1922), 105-112.

719.   "The Second Safe." 3, No. 1 (Apr 1921), 61-75. Safe-cracker, narrator.

720.♪   "The Secret of Baldwin Castle." 5, No. 2 (May 1922), 76-84.

721.   "The Talking Wall." 4, No. 2 (Nov 1921), 116-123.

722.   "A Track-and-a-Half." 5, No. 1 (Apr 1922), 97-105.

723.   "The Turbans in the Forest." 5, No. 3 (Jun 1922), 104-110. WD's last appearance in *BM*.

724.   "24 Karat—But." 4, No. 5 (Feb 1922), 103-110.

DE LEON, Walter

725.   "Marked By the Moon." 3, No. 2 (May 1921), 110-117.

726.   "Smoked Out." 3, No. 3 (Jun 1921), 107-117.

DEMING, Richard

727.   "Big Shots Die Young." 33, No. 2 (Jly 1949), 8-33. Manville (Manny) Moon, 1st-person narrator.

728.   "Five O'Clock Shroud." 35, No. 2 (Nov 1950), 12-38, 129. Moon.

729.   "The Man Who Chose the Devil." 31, No. 3 (May 1948), 66-91, 128-130. Manville Moon, private 'tec; he wears artificial right leg as result of WW II wound; 1st of 6 MM stories.

730.   "No Pockets in a Shroud." 32, No. 3 (Jan 1949), 8-55. Moon.

731.   "Pay Up or Die." 36, No. 1 (May 1951), 53-81. Last Moon story.

732.   "A Shot in the Arm." 31, No. 4 (Jly 1948), 56-85. Moon.

DENNIS, Robert C.

733.   "Glitter Street Nightmare." 34, No. 3 (May 1950), 14-38. Set in Hollywood.

734.   "I Thee Kill." 35, No. 3 (Jan 1951), 26-39.

735.   "Murder in the Mails." 29, No. 2 (Nov 1946), 46-61. William (Willie) Carmody, Confidential Investigations, &

Margaret O'Leary, writer; Hollywood; WC is 1st-person narrator.

736.   "Murder's Little Helper." 35, No. [1] (Sep 1950), 10-48. Carmody.

737.   "Murder Tops the Cast." 31, No. 1 (Jan 1948), 40-67. Carmody & O'Leary in Hollywood.

738.   "An Oscar for O'Leary." 30, No. 1 (May 1947), 30-53. Carmody & O'Leary.

739.   "Out of This World." 29, No. 4 (Mar 1947), 42-61. Carmody & O'Leary.

740.   "Ride a Green Hearse." 36, No. 2 (Jly 1951), 93-112. Has the honor to be last (original) story published in *BM*.

741.   "The 7th Pallbearer." 33, No. 4 (Nov 1949), 10-49. Carmody.

742.   "Stop, You're Killing Me!" 34, No. 1 (Jan 1950), 32-44. Rhodes, shamus.

DENT, Lester

743.   "Angelfish." 19, No. 10 (Dec 1936), 12-30. Oscar Sail; reprinted, *The Hardboiled Dicks* (1965) & *The Hard-Boiled Detective* (1977).

744.   "Sail." 19, No. 8 (Oct 1936), 87-106. Oscar Sail in Miami; reprinted, *The Hard-Boiled Omnibus* (1946).

DE POLO, Harold

745.   "The Bass Lake Murder." 2, No. 6 (Mar 1921), 95-101.

746.   "For the Honor of Baronne's Corner." 7, No. 5 (Jly 1924), 95-103. Far North setting.

747.   "Mr. Dugan's Vocation." 7, No. 2 (15 Apr 1924), 91-98.

748.   "Old Dogs, Old Tricks." 6, No. 24 (15 Mar 1924), 67-74. Western.

749.   "Salted." 6, No. 22 (15 Feb 1924), 74-82.

750.   "There's Always Something Lacking." 2, No. 5 (Feb 1921), 113-118.

DERMODY, Richard

751.   "An Earful for Willie." 26, No. 6 (May 1944), 97-102, 107. Racetrack yarn.

DES ORMEAUX, J.—J [pseud. of Forrest ROSAIRE]

752.   "The Cross by Ximado." 14, No. 12 (Feb 1932), 78-101. Jack McGuire, Federal dick, 1st-person narrator; set in San Pedro; see also "The Devil Suit."

753.   "The Dago Trick." 13, No. 7 (Sep 1930), 115-121. Crook tale.

754.   "The Devil Suit." 15, No. 5 (Jly 1932), 6-32. Jack McGuire; reprinted, *The Hard-Boiled Omnibus* (1946); see also "The Cross by Ximado."

755.   "The Green and Ghastly Twig. 23, No. 11 (Mar 1941), 71-89. Dave Carr, p.i.; see p. 6 (Apr 1941) for data on poison used in story.

756.   "Murderers' Night." 13, No. 2 (Apr 1930), 71-83. Modern Western; 1st-person narrator; Des O's debut in *BM*.

DEVITT, Tiah

757.   "For a Million Dollars." 23, No. 3 (Jun 1939), 64-77. Joey narrates a crime to the Warden.

758.   "The Haunted Inn." 22, No. 7 (Oct 1939), 78-100.

DOLMAN, Alexis

759.   "An Admirable Man." 2, No. 5 (Feb 1921), 111-112. Short-short.

DONNEL, C. P., Jr.

760.   "Blood on the Book." 25, No. 6 (Oct 1942), 73-91. Colonel Walter (Doc) Rennie, USA Medical Corps.

761.   "Clues in the Night." 26, No. 5 (Mar 1944), 85-95, 111-112. Rennie.

762.   "Conspiracy in Sunlight." 25, No. 11 (Mar 1943), 87-95. Military Intelligence; set in WW II England.

763.   "Corpse-Eye View." 24, No. 12 (Apr 1942), 85-107. Doc Rennie.

764.   "Danger—Mind at Work!" 26, No. 1 (Jly 1943), 36-61. Doc Rennie back in Essexville.

765.   "Dead Ahead Lies Yesterday." 25, No. 4 (Aug 1942), 11-32. Psychiatrist-detective Doc Rennie has entered USA (Medical Corps); see p. 8 for note by CPD on story.

766.   "Death Do Us Part." 24, No. 2 (Jun 1941), 98-107. Rennie.

767.   "Death Draws the Shutter." 25, No. 12 (May 1943), 82-89. Tom Jenks, WW I vet, in civilian air defense, is 1st-person narrator.

768.   "Death of a Stout Fellow." 23, No. 11 (Mar 1941), 63-70. Doc Rennie.

769.   "The Death of the Party." 25, No. 1 (May 1942), 58-69. Doc Rennie.

770.   "Don't Stand Under the Blackjack Tree." 25, No. 9 (Jan 1943), 92-110. Rennie.

771.   "5 Shrieks at 10." 24, No. 9 (Jan 1942), 94-112, 114, 116,

118, 120-130. Rennie.

72.   "The Fourth Degree." 23, No. 10 (Feb 1941), 50-59. Rennie.

73.   "Funeral of a Small American." 24, No. 6 (Oct 1941), 36-61. Doc Rennie & Nazi spies.

74.   "Good Hunting." 26, No. 10 (Jan 1945), 41-49, 94-95. Last Doc Rennie story.

75.   "Keep the Killing Quiet." 31, No. 1 (Jan 1948), 29-31, 129-130. 1st-person narrator; CPD's last story in *BM*.

76.   "The Man Who Knew Fear." 23, No. 9 (Jan 1941), 51-57. 1st (of 16) Doc Rennie stories & CPD's debut in *BM*.

77.   "So Red the Ruby." 26, No. 3 (Nov 1943), 80-116. Privates Maguire & Caldwell on 3-day leave in NYC.

78.   "The Sunday That Came on a Thursday." 24, No. 4 (Aug 1941), 83-99. Doc Rennie.

79.   "The White Walker." 26, No. 8 (Sep 1944), 10-29. Rennie.

DONOHO, Mary Browne

80.   "Man, Woman and the Iceman." 5, No. 7 (Oct 1922), 49-56.

DOUGLAS, Ford

781.   "Accordin' to Hoyle." 3, No. 6 (Sep 1921), 51-57.

782.   "The Checkered Cap." 3, No. 4 (Jly 1921), 45-53.

783.   "The Mardi Gras Souvenir." 3, No. 1 (Apr 1921), 3-21. "Complete Mystery Novelette"; 1st-person narrator.

784.   "The 'Plant.' " 3, No. 5 (Aug 1921), 3-26.

DOUGLAS, Marjory Stoneman

785.   "White Midnight." 6, No. 23 (1 Mar 1924), 51-71, Pt. 1; 6, No. 24
         (15 Mar 1924), 95-109, Pt. 2; 7, No. 1 (1 Apr 1924), 110-126,
         Pt. 3; 7, No. 2 (15 Apr 1924), 116-126, Pt. 4. South Seas
         setting.

DOWNEY, Fairfax

786.   "Blood or Wine." 6, No. 3 (1 May 1923), 89-93.

787.   "Girl or Gold?" 6, No. 7 (1 Jly 1923), 56-60. Conquistadoes
         in the Canaries.

DRAKE, Samuel

788.   "Blind Man's Bluff." 23, No. 1 (Apr 1940), 30-35.

DREW, Gaius

789.   "Murder Magic." 3, No. 1 (Apr 1921), 109-116. Benson, the
         houseman.

790.   "The Perfect Flaw." 3, No. 3 (Jun 1921), 77-83.

DUDLEY, Elizabeth (Bessie)

791.   "Ananias Ltd." 4, No. 3 (Dec 1921), 21-29. A Chinese among
         the characters.

792.   "The Baron's Otter." 3, No. 4 (Jly 1921), 115-123.

793.   "The Blonde Shadow." 4, No. 2 (Nov 1921), 27-32.

794.   "The Case of the 'Red' Mulcahy." 4, No. 4 (Jan 1922),
         39-45. Cop story.

DUNCAN, James

795.   "Crook Bait." 18, No. 6 (Aug 1935), 57-75. Ivor Small.

796.   "A Deal in Coconuts." 21, No. 3 (May 1938), 46-68. The Parson;
         lives on mythical isle, Cariba.

797.   "Delayed Snatch." 20, No. 8 (Oct 1937), 8-30. The Parson; Caribbean locale.

798.   "Double Trouble." 20, No. 1 (Mar 1937), 34-56. The Parson in Havana; 1st of 5 TP stories.

799.   "Heir to Murder." 19, No. 6 (Aug 1936), 115-127. Jerry Blaze.

800.   "Ice and Snow." 16, No. 12 (Feb 1934), 8-36. Ivor Small— Investigations; "He was fat without being fat enough to gain a livelihood as a professional fat man"; 1st of 3 IS stories; JD's debut in *BM*.

801.   "Murder for Pennies." 21, No. 10 (Jan 1939), 40-62. The Parson; JD's last appearance in *BM*.

802.   "The Parson Tells a Lie." 20, No. 4 (Jun 1937), 8-29. The Parson.

803.   "Runaround Murder." 18, No. 7 (Sep 1935), 108-124. Ivor Small; final IS story.

804.   "Thoroughbred." 19, No. 10 (Dec 1936), 107-116. Jerry Breton, 1st-grade dick, & Florida Racing Commission.

DUNCAN, Thomas W.

805.   "The Cat and the Corpses." 20, No. 11 (Jan 1938), 52-74. Dan Macey.

DUNN, Dorothy

806.   "Dead-End Darling." 34, No. 3 (May 1950), 110-127. Double-crosser's comedown.

DUNSTER, Drayton

807.   "Aided and Abetted by Law." 6, No. 14 (15 Oct 1923), 119-123.

808.   "Behind the Agreement." 6, No. 12 (15 Sep 1923), 87-92.

809.   "The Conscientious Grave-Digger." 5, No. 12 (15 Feb 1923), 40-47.

810.   "The Fruit of the Tomb." 6, No. 2 (15 Apr 1923), 53-58. A
            Cemetery Tale.

811.   "The Funeral Offering." 6, No. 20 (15 Jan 1924), 61-66. Chinese;
            "A novelty of life—and death—in a small town setting";
            DD's last appearance in *BM*.

812.   "Her Gold and Her Pearls." 5, No. (11 [1] Feb 1923), 52-55.

813.   "Sabotage." 6, No. 6 (15 Jun 1923), 78-92. A Cemetery Tale.

814.   "The Sexton." 5, No. 10 (Jan 1923), 19-22. Billed as "short
            and vivid"; DD's debut in *BM*.

815.   "The Tombstone of Babette." 5, No. 14 (15 Mar 1923), 74-80.
            A Cemetery Tale.

DU SOE, Bob

816.   "All Over a Pup." 11, No. 1 (Mar 1928), 109-116. Waterfront
            bum takes on hijackers because of dog.

817.   "The Kid on Number Twenty." 10, No. 7 (Sep 1927), 93-98.

818.   "A Score Settled." 11, No. 2 (Apr 1928), 88-94. Action in
            NYC night clubs.

E

EDSON, George Alden

819.   "Hot Lead." 17, No. 11 (Jan 1935), 111-122.

EDSTROM, Ed

820.   "Never Call the Cops." 30, No. 2 (Jly 1947), 119-122.

EDWARDS, H. Stephen

821.   "Detective Alias Thief." 2, No. 4 (Jan 1921), 85-91. Con

men outwit banker, *et al.,* in small Montana town.

EISENBRANDT, Marie

822.   "The Breaking Point." 5, No. 8 (Nov 1922), 83-88.

ELSTON, Allan Vaughan

823.   "Conscience Money." 28, No. 4 (Jly 1946), 85-95.

ENDELL, Gregor

824.   "Murder Suspected." 21, No. 2 (Apr 1938), 103-123.

ENGLAND, George Allen

825.   "The Heel of Achilles." 3, No. 3 (Jun 1921), 94-106.

826.   "Pound for Pound." 5, No. 2 (May 1922), 3-24. "Complete Novelette"; Pod Slattery & Pittsburgh Bender, con men.

EPSTEIN, Harry

827.   "The Case of the Mind-Reading Seal." 28, No. 3 (May 1946), 87-94.

ETTINGER, Edward

828.   "The Mystery of Perkins Farm." 7, No. 2 (15 Apr 1924), 99-103.

829.   "The Widow." 6, No. 24 (15 Mar 1924), 88-94. Woman's lover wanted for policeman's murder in upstate New York.

EVANS, Dean

830.   "Frame for a Dame." 32, No. 4 (Mar 1949), 64-73.

831.   "Hot-Rod Homicide." 34, No. 2 (Mar 1950), 108-122.

832.   "Scandal-Time Gal." 35, No. 3 (Jan 1951), 2-25.

EVERMAN, Paul

833.   "A Call at Carnagy's." 3, No. 2 (May 1921), 33-36. Short-short.

834.   "Devil's Choice." 2, No. 3 (Dec 1920), 111-118.

835.   "The Heart on the Mantle." 1, No. 6 (Sep 1920), 72-76.

836.   "The Stealing Scent." 4, No. 4 (Jan 1922), 67-74.

EYTINGE, Louis Victor

837.   "His Last Pete Job." 10, No. 10 (Dec 1927), 67-71. Paul Prentiss; see next entry.

838.   "When Fingerprints Lied." 10, No. 11 (Jan 1928), 101-106. Paul Prentiss, former pete-man (safe blower).

F

FAGIN, N. Bryllion

839.   "Mrs. Frye Captures a Highwayman." 6, No. 5 (1 June 1923), 119-122.

FAIRMAN, Paul W.

840.   "Big-Time Operator." 31, No. 4 (Jly 1948), 117-120. Young guy (1st-person narrator) getting into the rackets; reprinted, *The Hard-Boiled Detective* (1977).

FARLEY, Alan [pseud. of (Mrs.) W. Lee HERRINGTON]

841.   "Buttered on Both Sides." 25, No. 9 (Jan 1943), 45-53.

842.   "How Big Is the Bucket?" 25, No. 7 (Nov 1942), 38-49. Her 1st pub. story; see p. 8 for brief biographical note.

FAUS, Joseph and James Bennett WOODING

343.   "The Object in the Handkerchief." 3, No. 6 (Sep 1921), 106-110.

FAYERWEATHER, Grover

344.   "When Two Plus Two Equals Five." 4, No. 2 (Nov 1921), 79-88.

FEAK, Donald

345.   "Black Commandments." 6, No. 13 (1 Oct 1923), 63-73. South
            Seas tale.

346.   "Emeralds!" 6, No. 18 (15 Dec 1923), 92-103. Pirates.

347.   "The Reaper of Regret." 6, No. 7 (1 Jly 1923), 39-47. "A Tale
            of the Sea."

FETTER, Arthur

348.   "The Treachery of Spike McGuire." 6, No. 9 (1 Aug 1923),
            111-115. "A Queer Glimpse of the Underworld."

FIELD, Anthony

349.   "Fallen Angel." 20, No. 5 (Jly 1937), 98-125. The Angel—who
            is male.

FIRANZE, Harold C.

350.   "The Crime Circle." 10, No. 10 (Dec 1927), 102-107.

351.   "The Scented Crime." 11, No. 5 (Jly 1928), 71-80. Detective
            Emil Quinton.

FISCHER, Bruno

352.   "Five O'Clock Menace." 33, No. 1 (May 1949), 82-88. 1st-
            person narrator in barber's chair; reprinted, *The Hard-
            Boiled Detective* (1977).

353.   "Kill Without Murder." 26, No. 4 (Jan 1944), 102-122. Fred
            Hammond.

854.   "A Killer in the Crowd." 30, No. 2 (Jly 1947), 55-57, 130.
        1st-person narrator; homicide lieutenant, NYPD.

855.   "The Lady Grooms a Corpse." 34, No. 1 (Jan 1950), 76-90.

856.   "Middleman for Murder." 30, No. 4 (Nov 1947), 116-126.
        Willie, narrator, is blackmailer, etc.

FISHER, Henry W.

857.   "Executioners I Have Met." 6, No. 15 (1 Nov 1923), 120-125;
        6, No. 16 (15 Nov 1923), 119-125; 6, No. 17 (1 Dec 1923),
        121-125; 6, No. 18 (15 Dec 1923), 120-126; 6, No. 19 (1
        Jan 1924), 120-126; 6, No. 20 (15 Jan 1924), 120-125. Six
        "true" articles with various subtitles.

858.   "Odd Bits." 6, No. 9 (1 Aug 1923), 116-117. Short-lived
        feature; not indexed beyond this point.

859.   "The Truth About the Belgrade Assassinations." 5, No.
        7 (Oct 1922), 91-96. Murders of King Alexander & Queen
        Dragna of Serbia in 1903.

FISHER, Steve [Stephen Gould]

860.   "Death of a Dummy." 20, No. 12 (Feb 1938), 121-127. Edmund
        Peterson, ventriloquist, & Lou Shane, his dummy.

861.   "Flight to Paris." 21, No. 11 (Feb 1939), 34-43.

862.   "Hollywood Party." 21, No. 4 (Jun 1938), 42-57. Tony Key;
        see also "Murder at Eight."

863.   "Jake and Jill." 21, No. 10 (Jan 1939), 89-97. Honolulu
        setting.

864.   "Latitude Unknown." 22, No. 1 (Apr 1939), 99-111. Treachery
        on the high seas; SF's last appearance in *BM*.

865.   "Murder at Eight." 20, No. 6 (Aug 1937), 93-114. Tony Key
        in Hollywood; see also "Hollywood Party"; SF's debut in
        BM.

866. "No Gentleman Strangles His Wife." 20, No. 11 (Jan 1938), 75-84. Kip I. Muldane, p.i. in Hawaii.

867. "Wait for Me." 21, No. 3 (May 1938), 69-77. Murder & intrigue in Shanghai.

868. "You'll Always Remember Me." 21, No. 1 (Mar 1938), 39-51. Young punk murderer; psychopathic narrator.

FLEMING-ROBERTS, G. T.

869. "The Creeps." 26, No. 12 (May 1945), 10-28, 97. William Payne, clumsy oaf; the town has "the creeps."

870. "Don't Look Behind You." 30, No. 3 (Sep 1947), 28-57.

871. "Invitation to Murder." 24, No. 7 (Nov 1941), 111-114, 116-120.

872. "Legitimately Dead." 32, No. 3 (Jan 1949), 68-91. Fells.

873. "The Paper Doll." 36, No. 2 (Jly 1951), 2-36.

874. "Pattern for Shrouds." 31, No. 3 (May 1948), 40-65. Red Morgan, newspaper editor; politics & murder.

875. "Rats Breed Rats." 23, No. 4 (Aug 1940), 95-103. Detective Sergeant Bill Teed, tough cop, & Pop Walker, sentimental reporter; GTF-R's debut in *BM*.

876. "Something Dead Has Been Added." 32, No. 4 (Mar 1949), 42-63. John Anthony Gwinn, Indianapolis reporter.

FLETCHER, J. S. [Joseph Smith]

877. "Exterior to the Evidence." 5, No. 1 (Apr 1922), 3-18, Pt. 1; 5, No. 2 (May 1922), 51-75, Pt. 2; 5, No. 3 (Jun 1922), 59-74, Pt. 3; 5, No. 4 (Jly 1922), 43-70, Pt. 4; 5, No. 5 (Aug 1922), 55-71, Pt. 5. Serial re-run of novel 1st pub. in London (1920) under same title.

878. "The Skene-Dhu of Inverikie." 8, No. 4 (Jun 1925), 59-69. "A Family Mystery."

FORAN, John P.

879.   "Copper, Come Back to Me." 33, No. 1 (May 1949), 48-57.

880.   "Epitaph for an Eager Beaver." 34, No. 2 (Mar 1950), 96-106.

FOSTER, Geoffrey

881.   "Bedlam." 6, No. 9 (1 Aug 1923), 78-80. Short-short.

FOSTER, Henry Clay

882.   "The Klan As It Was." 6, No. 5 (1 Jun 1923), 59-62. "Who started it and why"; article in special KKK issue.

FOWLER, B. B.

883.   "A Frame Should Stick." 18, No. 5 (Jly 1935), 114-122. Red Candless, reporter.

884.   "A Sucker Has to Learn." 22, No. 1 (Apr 1939), 82-98. Rick Sadler, lawyer, born on wrong side of tracks.

FOWLER, Kenneth A.

885.   "Escape." 21, No. 12 (Mar 1939), 108-110. Short-short.

FOY, Clinton

886.   "The Fatal Sin." 6, No. 10 (15 Aug 1923), 109-112. Insane 1st-person narrator.

FROST, Walter Archer [Captain]

887.   "Cal Hatfield's Spirit." 1, No. 4 (Jly 1920), 119-126. Spiritualism, etc.

FUESSLE, Kenneth

888.   "Superstition." 6, No. 9 (1 Aug 1923), 94-102. "Adventure in Weird Surroundings.

FUESSLE, Newton A.

889.   "Hoodwinked." 6, No. 6 (15 Jun 1923), 50-68. KKK story
        but not in special KKK issue (1 Jun 1923).

890.   "The Purple Mask." 6, No. 13 (1 Oct 1923), 7-24. N. B.
        KF & NAF may be one & same.

G

GANNETT, S. S.

891.   "Invisible Fingers." 8, No. 4 (Jun 1925), 89-92.

GARBETT, Arthur S.

892.   "Something Lingering." 3, No. 6 (Sep 1921), 89-94.

893.   "The Time Speeder." 7, No. 2 (15 Apr 1924), 48-75. Amateur
        sleuth, 1st-person narrator; novelette.

894.   "The Wax Witness." 3, No. 5 (Aug 1921), 105-112.

895.   "The Wet Hand." 4, No. 5 (Feb 1922), 37-41.

GARDNER, Erle Stanley [see also Charles M. GREEN]

896.   **"Above the Law." 18, No. 10 (Dec 1935), 12-35. Ed Jenkins,**
        The Phantom Crook.

897.   "Accommodatin' a Lady." 7, No. 7 (Sep 1924), 84-96. Bob
        Larkin, 1st-person narrator; 1st of 10 BL stories;
        ESG's 1st appearance in *BM* under his name.

898.   "According to Law." 8, No. 11 (Jan 1926), 41-58. Ed Jenkins.

899.   "All the Way." 12, No. 5 (Jly 1929), 5-28. Bob Larkin.

900.   "Among Thieves." 20, No. 7 (Sep 1937), 8-34. Pete Wennick, undercover man; 1st PW story.

901.   "Beating the Bulls." 19, No. 3 (May 1936), 48-72. Jenkins.

902.   "Beyond the Law." 7, No. 11 (Jan 1925), 42-63. Ed Jenkins, The Phantom Crook, 1st-person narrator; 1st of 73 EJ stories; a.k.a. Bob Sabin, private detective; full name; Edward Gordon Jenkins; more often than not, stories take place in Chinatown, San Francisco.

903.   "Big Shot." 13, No. 5 (Jly 1930), 37-64. Ed Jenkins in last (of 3) Crime Crusher stories; see also "The Crime Crusher" & "Hell's Kettle."

904.   "Black and White." 15, No. 7 (Sep 1932), 57-83. Jenkins.

905.   **"Blackmail with Lead." 16, No. 6 (Aug 1933), 93-111. 6th** & last Ken Corning story.

906.   "Bracelets for Two." 11, No. 12 (Feb 1929), 68-85. Jenkins & Helen Chadwick—their love.

907.   "Brass Tacks." 12, No. 9 (Nov 1929), 100-120. Jenkins & Chadwick, his wife, in L.A.; see "Triple Treachery."

908.   "Burnt Fingers." 17, No. 4 (Jun 1934), 102-124. Jenkins, masquerading as Bob Sabin; with Ngat T'oy (Little Sun) & her father, Soo Hoo Duck.

909.   "Buzzard Bait." 9, No. 8 (Oct 1926), 40-65. Black Barr; 2d story in series.

910.   "The Cat-Woman." 9, No. 12 (Feb 1927), 60-86. Jenkins.

911.   "A Chance to Cheat." 18, No. 3 (May 1935), 54-77. Jenkins.

912.   "Chinatown Murder." 16, No. 2 (Apr 1933), 73-94. Jenkins,

Ngat T'oy, & Soo Hoo Duck; Chinese frequently spoken.

913. "The Chinese People..." 24, No. 1 (May 1941), 8-47. Jenkins, Soo Hoo Duck, *et al*; "title" in Chinese characters; in full (literal translation): "The Chinese people have the best relationship with me [which I] never can forget."

914. "Close Call." 15, No. 11 (Jan 1933), 31-50. Ken Corning, lawyer.

915. "Come and Get It." 10, No. 2 (Apr 1927), 63-87. Jenkins & his 2d "thrilling" adventure with The Girl with the Mole; Helen Chadwick, present; see p. 87 for ESG's depiction of EJ; see also "This Way Out" & "In Full Account."

916 "Cooking Crooks." 15, No. 4 (Jun 1932), 45-63. Jenkins with Norma Gay.

917. "Cop Killers." 17, No. 1 (Mar 1934), 50-72. Jenkins, with Ngat T'oy & Soo Hoo Duck.

918. "Crash and Carry." 18, No. 8 (Oct 1935), 8-31. Jenkins, Ngat T'oy; **ESG's return to** *BM* **heralded by announcement Sep 1935, p. 9.**

919. "The Crime Crusher." 13, No. 3 (May 1930), 73-92. Jenkins & wife, Helen Chadwick, in 1st of 3-pt. Crime Crusher series; see also "Hell's Kettle" & "Big Shot."

920. "Curse of the Killers." 11, No. 9 (Nov 1928), 78-96. Black Barr, "known along the Border as the Executioner of Fate"; last BB tale.

921. "Dark Alleys." 22, No. 6 (Sep 1939), 6-32. Jenkins; spy story with Ngat T'oy & Soo Hoo Duck; Soo has name for EJ: Sai Yan Pang Yeu (Man of the West Who Is My Friend).

922. "Dead Men's Letters." 9, No. 10 (Dec 1926), 9-38. Jenkins & Lois Lambert, rich, young flapper.

923.   "Dead Men's Shoes." 16, No. 10 (Dec 1933), 36-59. Jenkins in Chinatown with Ngat T'oy.

924.   "The Devil's Deputy." 11, No. 7 (Sep 1928), 43-70. Black Barr; Chinese, Wing Lee, is Deputy.

925.   "Devil's Fire." 16, No. 5 (Jly 1933), 61-83. Corning.

926.   "Double or Quits." 12, No. 11 (Jan 1930), 64-87. Jenkins; last episode in his fight with Ramsay; Arthur Hemington also around.

927.   "Face Up." 14, No. 11 (Jan 1932), 87-109. Ed Jenkins, Sammy the Snitch, & Lui Sing Fong, known in Chinatown as "The Master," EJ's friend, "he whom I called '*Sin Sahng*,' or first born, the saluation which is given to a Master" (p. 95).

928.   "A Fair Trial." 7, No. 4 (Jun 1924), 102-108. Pub. anonymously; authorship established in Hughes, *Gardner* (1978), p. 312.

929.   "Fangs of Fate." 11, No. 6 (Aug 1928), 7-37. Black Barr.

930.   "Feet First." 15, No. 1 (Mar 1932), 54-76. Ed Jenkins.

931.   "Forget 'Em All." 9, No. 4 (Jun 1926), 9-34. Jenkins.

932.   "The Girl Goes with Me." 8, No. 9 (Nov 1925), 74-95. Debut of Black Barr; 1st of 7 BB stories.

933.   "Goin' Into Action." 8, No. 12 (Feb 1926), 9-31. Bob Larkin.

934.   "The Gong of Vengeance." 26, No. 2 (Sep 1943), 8-47. Last (73d) Ed Jenkins story; with Ngat T'oy; ESG's last appearance in *BM*.

935.   "Grinning Gods." 10, No. 10 (Dec 1927), 79-101. Jenkins in Chinatown with Soo Hoo Duck, Ngat T'oy, & Helen Chadwick; headnote to story provides excellent background to series.

936.   "A Guest of the House." 16, No. 11 (Jan 1934), 8-27. Jenkins as

Bob Sabin, p.i.; with Soo Hoo Duck, *et al.*

937.   "Hairy Hands." 14, No. 6 (Aug 1931), 28-45. The "Hairy Hands" reach for Ed Jenkins; see p. 45 for statement on ESG's knowledge of Chinese language & people.

938.   "Ham, Eggs, an' Coffee." 8, No. 6 (Aug 1925), 76-90. Bob Larkin & prohibition in Tia Juana.

939.   "Hanging Friday." 12, No. 7 (Sep 1929), 43-60. Larkin.

940.   "Hard As Nails." 8, No. 1 (Mar 1925), 49-62. Ed Jenkins.

941.   "The Heavenly Rat." 17, No. 7 (Sep 1934), 8-41. Jenkins, Ngat T'oy, & Soo Hoo Duck in Chinatown.

942   "Hell's Kettle." 13, No. 4 (Jun 1930), 101-118. Jenkins as Dr. Chew, Chinese herbalist, & Colonel Grayson; 2d of 3 Crime Crusher stories; see also "Crime Crusher" & "Big Shot."

943.   "Honest Money." 15, No. 9 (Nov 1932), 69-87. 1st appearance of Ken Corning, honest, fighting attorney in NYC; prototype of Perry Mason.

944.   "Hooking the Crooks." 12, No. 1 (Mar 1929), 74-89. Jenkins & wife, Helen Chadwick.

945.   "Hot Cash." 17, No. 9 (Nov 1934), 47-61. Jenkins as Bob Sabin.

946.   "The Hot Squat." 14, No. 8 (Oct 1931), 77-99. Jenkins.

947.   "The Hour of the Rat." 15, No. 12 (Feb 1933), 40-60. Jenkins, Ngat T'oy, Soo Hoo Duck; the "hour" is 11 p.m. (Chinese time cycle).

948.   "The Incredible Mister Smith." 25, No. 11 (Mar 1943), 10-44. Ed Jenkins, Soo Hoo Duck, & Ngat T'oy.

949.   "In Full of Account." 10, No. 3 (May 1927), 63-92. Last of 3

EJ tales with The Girl with the Mole; see also "This Way Out" & "Come and Get It."

950. "Jade Sanctuary." 23, No. 8 (Dec 1940), 6-39. Jenkins; reader points out discrepancy in story, Feb 1941, p. 29.

951. "Laugh That Off." 9, No. 7 (Sep 1926), 42-75. Jenkins & Helen Chadwick are engaged.

952. "Leg Man." 20, No. 12 (Feb 1938), 10-33. 2d Pete Wennick caper; reprinted, *The Hard-Boiled Detective* (1977).

953. "Making the Breaks." 16, No. 4 (Jun 1933), 25-42. Ken Corning.

954. "Money, Marbles and Chalk." 9, No. 9 (Nov 1926), 98-128. Jenkins—still a "crook."

955. "The Murder Push." 16, No. 8 (Oct 1933), 105-120. Jenkins as Bob Sabin.

956. "Muscle Out." 21, No. 2 (Apr 1938), 8-30. Jenkins, Ngat T'oy & Soo Hoo Duck.

957. "New Twenties." 17, No. 2 (Apr 1934), 36-59. Jenkins & Ngat T'oy.

958. "The Next Stiff." 11, No. 10 (Dec 1928), 9-28. Jenkins, Big Bill Delano, & gang war; see sequel, "One Crook to Another."

959. "No Questions Asked." 12, No. 2 (Apr 1929), 102-128. Jenkins & Helen Chadwick.

960. "Not So Darned Bad." 8, No. 4 (Jun 1925), 70-82. Jenkins, The Phantom Crook again.

961. "On Two Feet." 15, No. 8 (Oct 1932), 86-104. Bob Larkin on the Border; last BL story; 1st since Sep 1929.

962. "One Crook to Another." 11, No. 11 (Jan 1929), 20-37. Ed

Jenkins; sequel to "The Next Stiff."

963.   "Out of the Shadows." 11, No. 3 (May 1928), 9-36. EJ in
       Chinatown with Helen Chadwick, Soo Hoo Duck, & Ngat
       T'oy.

964.   "Painless Extraction." 8, No. 3 (May 1925), 83-98. Bob
       Larkin in Mexico.

965.   "Promise to Pay." 14, No. 7. (Sep 1931), 83-104. Jenkins &
       his friend, Lui Sing Fong, patriarchal master of
       Chinatown; see also "Tommy Talk" & "Strictly Personal."

966.   "Rain Check." 24, No. 8 (Dec 1941), 11-45. Jenkins.

967.   "Red Jade." 16, No. 1 (Mar 1933), 6-29. EJ, Ngat T'oy, &
       Soo Hoo Duck; see p. 5 for letter from ESG to JTS.

968.   "Register Rage." 9, No. 2 (Apr 1926), 9-30. Jenkins in & around
       L.A. & Hollywood.

969.   "Rough Stuff." 15, No. 5 (Jly 1932), 64-82. Jenkins; see pp.
       124-125, Aug 1932, for note on authenticity of Chinese
       background in EJ tales.

970.   "Scum of the Border." 12, No. 4 (Jun 1929), 81-97. Bob Larkin.

971.   "Snow Bird." 11, No. 2 (Apr 1928), 5-29. Jenkins, Ngat T'oy
       Paul Boardman, et al.

972.   "Spawn of the Night." 12, No. 6 (Aug 1929), 27-52. Larkin; TofC
       p. gives incorrect title, "Hanging Friday."

973.   "Straight Crooks." 15, No. 2 (Apr 1932), 102-118. Jenkins &
       2 crooks: The Cracker & Norma Gay.

974.   "Straight from the Shoulder." 12, No. 8 (Oct 1929), 84-98.
       Jenkins, Helen Chadwick, & Arthur Hemington, here &
       elsewhere; cf. "Triple Treachery."

975.   "Strictly Personal." 14, No. 10 (Dec 1931), 8-31. EJ & Lui
       Sing Fong; see also "Promise to Pay" & "Tommy Talk."

976. "Take It or Leave It." 21, No. 12 (Mar 1939), 32-59. 3d & last Pete Wennick story.

977. " 'Thisissosudden!' " 9, No. 3 (May 1926), 45-62. Jenkins.

978. "This Way Out." 10, No. 1 (Mar 1927), 7-32. "The first of of Ed Jenkins' thrilling adventures with The Girl with the Mole"; see also "Come and Get It" & "In Full of Account"; see pp. 127-128 for info on ESG; see next entry for same title, different story.

979. "This Way Out." 20, No. 1 (Mar 1937), 12-33. Jenkins as Bob Sabin; with Ngat T'oy.

980. "Three O'Clock in the Morning." 8, No. 5 (Jly 1925), 32-46. Ed Jenkins, The Phantom Crook.

981. "Tommy Talk." 14, No. 5 (Jly 1931), 6-30. Jenkins' return after death of his wife, Helen, which had broken him; out of hospital & in Chinatown with Lui Sing Fong; see also "Promise to Pay" & "Strictly Personal."

982. "Tong Trouble." 23, No. 2 (Jun 1940), 6-39. Jenkins, Soo Hoo Duck, & Ngat T'oy.

983. "The Top Comes Off." 15, No. 10 (Dec 1932), 38-58. 2d appearance of Ken Corning, fighting young lawyer.

984. "The Triple Cross." 8, No. 10 (Dec 1925), 49-63. Jenkins.

985. "Triple Treachery." 12, No. 10 (Dec 1929), 103-117. EJ vs. Ramsay in L.A.; with Helen Chadwick; sequel to "Brass Tacks."

986. "Two Dead Hands." 24, No. 12 (Apr 1942), 10-44. Jenkins.

987. "Under the Guns." 15, No. 3 (May 1932), 93-114. Jenkins.

988. "The Wax Dragon." 10, No. 9 (Nov 1927), 52-77. Jenkins, Helen Chadwick, & Soo Hoo Duck.

989.   "The Weapons of a Crook." 16, No. 3 (May 1933), 42-58.
         EJ as Bob Sabin in Chinatown with usual cast.

990.   "Where the Buzzards Circle." 10, No. 7 (Sep 1927), 9-30.
         Black Barr.

991.   "Whispering Feet." 11, No. 1 (Mar 1928), 47-73. Jenkins,
         Soo Hoo Duck, & Ngat T'oy; see endnote, p. 73, for data
         on series.

992.   "Whispering Justice." 16, No. 7 (Sep 1933), 46-64. Jenkins.

993.   "Whispering Sand." 9, No. 11 (Jan 1927), 78-106. Black Barr.

994.   "Winged Lead." 17, No. 11 (Jan 1935), 48-72. Bald Pete.

995.   "Without No Reindeer." 7, No. 10 (Dec 1924), 36-54. 2d Bob
         Larkin story.

996.   "Yellow Shadows." 10, No. 12 (Feb 1928), 35-59. Ed Jenkins in
         Chinatown with Helen Chadwick & Ngat T'oy; headnote
         to story provides valuable data (background).

GAULT, William Campbell

997.   "The Bloody Bokhara." 32, No. 2 (Nov 1948), 36-66, 127. The
         carpet business!

998.   "The Case of the Sleeping Beauty." 30, No 4 (Nov 1947),
         8-25. Mortimer Jones.

999.   "The Cold, Cold Ground." 29, No. 3 (Jan 1947), 8-26, 98. Jones.

1000.   "The Constant Shadow." 30, No. 2 (Jly 1947), 6-27, 129.

1001.   "Dead-End for Delia." 35, No. 2 (Nov 1950), 50-59, 127. WCG's
         last story in *BM*.

1002.   "Don't Bet on Death." 31, No. 4 (Jly 1948), 44-55, 129-130.
         Cary Vaughn & Ned Orlow, private eyes.

1003.   "Hot-House Homicide." 29, No. 1 (Sep 1946), 10-34, 98. Debut of Mortimer Jones (Jonesy), private cop, narrator; drives a Duesenberg; WCG's 1st story in *BM*.

1004.   "A Murder for Mac." 29, No. 4 (Mar 1947), 62-80. Mortimer Jones.

1005.   "Red Runaround." 31, No. 2 (Mar 1948), 64-84. Jones.

GERRY, Bill

1006.   "Autoposies Tell." 22, No. 6 (Sep 1939), 86-107.

1007.   "You Can't Ration Murder." 25, No. 3 (Jly 1942), 78-105. Walsh, private dick, 1st-person narrator.

GIBSON, Erle Dana

1008.   "The Ardwicke Mystery." 8, No. 11 (Jan 1926), 88-98, Pt. 1; 8, No. 12 (Feb 1926), 112-126, Pt. 2.

GIBSON, Livingston

1009.   "Traffic Light." 20, No. 2 (Apr 1937), 120-121. Short-short.

GILBERT, Gene

1010.   "Set for Life." 20, No. 4 (Jun 1937), 127-128. Short-short.

GLENDINNING, Richard E.

1011.   "Die, Gypsy, Die!" 35, No. 2 (Nov 1950), 76-84. Lt. Oscar Daniels, homicide.

GLICK, Carl

1012.   "In the Grey Dawn." 6, No. 4 (15 May 1923), 49-59.

1013.   "The Shot in the Dark." 2, No. 5 (Feb 1921), 88-94.

GLUCK, Sinclair

1014.   "Double for Danger." 18, No. 7 (Sep 1935), 10-50. Ted
            Murray, reporter in Hollywood, 1st-person narrator.

GODWIN, K.

1015.   "Conscience." 6, No. 9 (1 Aug 1923), 81-84. Billed as *BM*'s
            "first one-act play."

GOLDTHWAITE, Eaton K.

1016.   "Black Is for Widows." 24, No. 12 (Apr 1942), 54-65. Duke Brian.

1017.   "Falling Star." 24, No. 4 (Aug 1941), 110-119, 122, 124-127.
            Duke Brian.

1018.   "The Frame That Didn't Fit." 23, No. 4 (Aug 1940), 82-93. Duke
            Brian & Franny Steinmetz, "ex-felons from Philly," now
            private dicks, more or less; Brian narrates.

1019.   "Murder Set to Music." 23, No. 6 (Oct 1940), 33-43. Duke
            Brian & Franny Steinmetz.

1020.   "The Veiled Vampire." 23, No. 8 (Dec 1940), 100-115, 128.
            Duke Brian.

GOLLOMB, Joseph

1021.   "The Man Who Stole a Palace." 8, No. 7 (Sep 1925), 85-90. Study
            of Paris police methods; article.

1022.   "A Pass Key to Scotland Yard." 8, No. 8 (Oct 1925), 117-122.
            Article.

1023.   "Pinkerton and the Express Murder." 8, No. 9 (Nov 1925),
            120-127(?). The Manhunters; for this series, see chiefly
            under Charles SOMERVILLE.

1024.   "Tell-Tale Ears." 8, No. 5 (Jly 1925), 126-128. Article on identification.

1025.   "Thomas Furlong and the Torn Check." 8, No. 11 (Jan 1926), 80-87. Article.

1026.   "Vienna's Scholarly Detectives." 8, No. 10 (Dec 1925), 91-97. Article

GORDON, Frank

1027.   "Last Kill and Testament." 33, No. 4 (Jly 1949), 104-106. Alphonse Bertillon.

GOTTLIEB, Jack J.

1028.   "The Blunt Fingers of Hate." 5, No. 3 (Jun 1922), 29-38. 1st of 2 stories by JJG in issue; see also "On Page 119."

1029.   "Crimsoned Baubles." 5, No. 4 (Jly 1922), 117-122.

1030.   "Eyes That See Not." 5, No. 6 (Sep 1922), 115-122. North, a criminal, & poetic justice.

1031.   "Ling the Lucky." 5, No. 7 (Oct 1922), 66-71. Chinese gunman Ling Yar in San Francisco.

1032.   "On Page 119." 5, No. 3 (Jun 1922), 75-79. 2d of 2 stories by JJG in issue; see also "The Blunt Fingers of Hate."

1033.   "The Poisoned Pencil." 5, No. 2 (May 1922), 41-50. JJG's debut in *BM*.

1034.   "The Strength of the Weak." 5, No. 21 (15 Feb 1923), 103-112.

1035.   "With His Enemies' Aid." 5, No. 13 (1 Mar 1923), 43-53. "A Mystery of the D.A.'s office"; JJG's last story in *BM*.

GOULDEN, Graham

1036.	"Moonlight 'n' Murder." 33, No. 4 (Nov 1949), 63-71, 128-129.

GOULDNER, D. Westcott

1037.	"All Work and No Slay." 34, No. 4 (Jly 1950), 104-105, 130.

GRADY, Preston

1038.	"Massacre." 18, No. 8 (Oct 1935), 107-121. Ned Price, p.i., in
	South Carolina, 1st-person narrator; smuggling &
	Chinese villain.

GRAHAM, John

1039.	"Murder Crate." 17, No. 5 (Jly 1934), 112-123. Ambulance crew;
	NYC setting.

1040.	"Too Tough." 23, No. 4 (Aug 1940), 67-81. Vic Smail, kidnapper.

GRAVATT, Glenn G.

1041.	" 'The Million Dollar Robbery.' " 8, No. 7 (Sep 1925), 116-128.
	The Manhunters; for this series, see chiefly under Charles
	SOMERVILLE.

GRAY, Westmoreland

1042.	"Box V's Night of Mystery." 10, No. 5 (Jly 1927), 34-56.
	Western.

1043.	"Guns of Silence." 10, No. 11 (Jan 1928), 50-77. Vic Cammack,
	reporter, & Jerry the Yegg, crook, vs. bandits.

1044.	"Slayer's Finesse." 9, No. 11 (Jan 1927), 61-69. Wallace
	McNeel, private 'shoe, & a police captain.

GREEN, Charles M. [pseud. of Erle Stanley GARDNER]

1045.	"The Serpent's Coils." 6, No. 19 (1 Jan 1924), 76-83. A
	Daytime Story.

1046.	"The Shrieking Skeleton." 6, No. 18 (15 Dec 1923), 7-29.

"A Novelette of Mystery and Thrill"; ESG's debut in *BM*.

1047.   "The Verdict." 6, No. 21 (1 Feb 1924), 45-48.

GREGORY, Francis F.

1048.   "A Pile of Dust." 5, No. 7 (Oct 1922), 72-78.

GREGORY, Jackson

1049.   "Dusty Death." 21, No. 10 (Jan 1939), 107-112.

1050.   "Indian Gift." 35, No. 4 (Mar 1951), 60-69. Reprint; not
             from *BM*.

GRUBER, Frank

1051.   "Ask Me Another." 20, No. 4 (Jun 1937), 61-71. Oliver Quade,
             The Human Encyclopedia; 1st OQ story in *BM*, but not
             1st in series; earlier stories pub. in *Thrilling Detective;*
             FG's debut in *BM*.

1052.   "Candid Witness." 20, No. 5 (Jly 1937), 126-127. Short-
             short.

1053.   "Death on Eagle's Crag." 20, No. 10 (Dec 1937), 111-126.
             Oliver Quade; reprinted, *The Hardboiled Dicks* (1965).

1054.   "Death Sits Down." 21, No. 3 (May 1938), 98-115. Quade.

1055.   "Dog Show Murder." 21, No. 1 (Mar 1938), 78-110. Quade.

1056.   "Forced Landing." 21, No. 7 (Oct 1938), 8-30. Quade; see p. 128
             for letter from FG on Oliver Q.

1057.   "Funny Man." 22, No. 2 (May 1939), 6-33. Quade in Holly-
             wood; see p. 5 for letter from FG on OQ.

1058.   "No Motive." 21, No. 2 (Apr 1938), 31-42.

1059.   "Oliver Quade at the Races." 22, No. 8 (Nov 1939), 32-50.

Profit & murder at the track.

060.   "Rain, the Killer." 20, No. 7 (Sep 1937), 100-116. Quade.

061.   "The Ring and the Finger." 21, No. 5 (Aug 1938), 34-43. 1st-person narrator.

062.   "The Sad Serbian." 21, No. 12 (Mar 1939), 83-97. Small-time con man in Chi.

063.   "State Fair Murder." 21, No. 11 (Feb 1939), 62-75. Quade.

064.   "Words and Music." 22, No. 12 (Mar 1940), 4-26. Last Quade story & FG's final appearance in *BM*.

GRUMBLE, Peter

065.   "What Happened at Flanders." 6, No. 6 (15 Jun 1923), 33-43. Western yarn.

GUERNSEY, H. W.

066.   "The Last Pin." 22, No. 11 (Feb 1940), 123-126. Short-short.

067.   "Late Harvest." 20, No. 9 (Nov 1937), 112-122. Mushrooms, e.g., morel (nightshade):

068.   "The Razzberry." 20, No. 6 (Aug 1937), 125-127.

069.   "A Thousand Iron Men." 21, No. 10 (Jan 1939), 31-39. Iron man = $1.

GUILLAUME, Eugene

070.   "The Choice." 1, No. 6 (Sep 1920), 28-?

GUTSCHOW, M.A.

071.   "The Wild Rose Hermit." 19, No. 4 (Jun 1936), 123-126. Another example of "Narrowest Escape" series; see under Charles E. COX, Jr.

H

HAGAR, Richard Frank

1072.   "In Sea Bats' Craws." 8, No. 4 (Jun 1925), 93-104. Mystery of the sea.

HALL, Emmett Campbell

1073.   " 'When the Wind Blows.' " 1, No. 4 (Jly 1920), 89-92.

HALL, Ennen Reaves

1074.   "Dead Men Don't Ask Questions." 26, No. 7 (Jly 1944), 62-81, 112-113. Ed Fellows, construction worker.

HALL, James

1075.   "Back Door to Hell." 33, No. 3 (Sep 1949), 104-111.

HALL, M. P.

1076.   "Ad Lib." 21, No. 9 (Dec 1938), 107-109. Short-short; radio broadcasting.

HALL, Marshall R.

1077.   "Shagtown Learns the Law." 10, No. 2 (Apr 1927), 92-101. Western story; Sled Drury.

HALLIDAY, Brett [pseud. of Davis Dresser]

1078.   "Dead Man's Diary." 27, No. 2 (Sep 1945), 10-48. Mike Shayne.

1079.   "A Taste for Cognac." 26, No. 9 (Nov 1944), 30-54. Mike Shayne.

HAMILTON, Gertrude Brooke

080.   "The Dead and the Quick." 1, No. 1 (Apr 1920), 109-121.

HAMILTON, H. M.

081.   "The Fall of the Bastile." 4, No. 1 (Oct 1921), 107-112.

082.   "Vanishing Gold." 6, No. 2 (15 Apr 1923), 59-68.

HAMILTON, Schuyler

083.   "Run to Earth." 1, No. 3 (Jun 1920), 55-61.

084.   "The Silvered Sentinel." 1, No. 2 (May 1920), 56-65.

HAMLIN, Curt

085.   "Killer Come Home." 31, No. 2 (Mar 1948), 85-89. Mr. Teel
            & unfaithful wife; reprinted, *The Hard-Boiled Detective*
            (1977).

HAMMETT, Samuel Dashiell [see also Peter COLLINSON]

086.   "Afraid of a Gun." 6, No. 23 (1 Mar 1924), 39-45. Set in Kootenai
            River country (Montana); 1st of 2 stories by DH in issue;
            see also "Zigzags of Treachery"; see pp. 127-128 for
            2 letters from DH.

087.   "The Assistant Murderer." 8, No. 12 (Feb 1926), 57-79. Billed
            as "The best story of its kind ever written."

088.   "The Big Knock-Over." 9, No. 12 (Feb 1927), 7-38. The
            Continental Op; see "$106,000 Blood Money" for sequel.

089.   "Black Honeymoon." 11, No. 11 (Jan 1929), 38-62. The Op: Pt. 3
            (of 4 pts.), *The Dain Curse* (pub. 1929); printed as
            separate stories rather than conventional serial; *e.g.*, see
            next entry.

090.   "Black Lives." 11, No. 9 (Nov 1928), 41-67. The Op; Pt. 1
            (of 4 pts.), *The Dain Curse;* see entries above and
            following.

1091.   "Black Riddle." 11, No. 12 (Feb 1929), 40-67. The Op; Pt. 4
         (of 4 pts.), *The Dain Curse;* see 2 previous entries.

1092.   "Bodies Piled Up." 6, No. 17 (1 Dec 1923), 33-42. The Op.

1093.   "The Cleansing of Poisonville." 10, No. 9 (Nov 1927),
         9-37. The Op; Pt. 1 (of 4 pts.), *Red Harvest* (pub 1929);
         printed as separate stories rather than conventional serial.

1094.   "Corkscrew." 8, No. 7 (Sep 1925), 4-36. The Op in Arizona;
         billed as "A Western Detective Novelette."

1095.   "Creeping Siamese." 9, No. 1 (Mar 1926), 38-47. The Op.

1096.   "Crime Wanted—Male or Female." 10, No. 10 (Dec 1927),
         9-33. The Op; Pt. 2 (of 4 pts.), *Red Harvest.*

1097.   "Crooked Souls." 6, No. 14 (15 Oct 1923), 35-44. The Op; 1st of
         2 stories by DH in issue; see "Slippery Fingers"
         (COLLINSON); 1st story by DH under his name in *BM.*

1098.   "The Cyclone Shot." 13, No. 2 (Apr 1930), 45-70. Ned
         Beaumont; Pt. 2 (of 4 pts.), *The Glass Key* (pub. 1931);
         printed as separate stories rather than conventional
         serial; see next entry.

1099.   "Dagger Point." 13, No. 3 (May 1930), 50-72. Beaumont; Pt.
         3 (of 4 pts.), *The Glass Key;* see previous entry.

1100.   "Dead Yellow Women." 8, No. 9 (Nov 1925), 9-39. The Op;
         "A story of San Francisco's Chinatown."

1101.   "Death and Company." 13, No. 9 (Nov 1930), 60-65. Last Op
         story & DH's final appearance in *BM.*

1102.   "Dynamite." 10, No. 11 (Jan 1928), 7-26. The Op; Pt. 3 (of
         4 pts.), *Red Harvest.*

1103.   "The Farewell Murder." 12, No. 12 (Feb 1930), 9-30. The Op.

1104. "Finger-Prints." 8, No. 4 (Jun 1925), 127-128. Letter to ed.; see entry under John Nicholas BEFFEL.

1105. "Fly Paper." 12, No. 6 (Aug 1929), 7-26. The Op & arsenical fly paper; reprinted, *The Hard-Boiled Omnibus* (1946).

1106. "The Girl with the Silver Eyes." 7, No. 4 (Jun 1924), 45-70. The Op, referred to in *BM* as "Hammett's San Francisco detective"; sequel to "The House in Turk Street"; there is a letter from DH on story in issue.

1107. "The Golden Horseshoe." 7, No. 9 (Nov 1924), 37-62. The Op; see p. 128 for autobiographical sketch by DH.

1108. "The Gutting of Couffignal." 8, No. 10 (Dec 1925), 30-48. The Op; reprinted, *The Hard-Boiled Detective*, (1977).

1109. "The Hat Trick." 13, No. 1 (Mar 1930), 7-30. Ned Beaumont; Pt. 1 (of 4 pts.), *The Glass Key*.

1110. "The Hollow Temple." 11, No. 10 (Dec 1928), 38-64. The Op; Pt. 2 (of 4 pts.), *The Dain Curse*.

1111. "The House in Turk Street." 7, No. 2 (15 Apr 1924), 9-22. The Op; see "The Girl with the Silver Eyes" for sequel.

1112. "It." 6, No. 15 (1 Nov 1923), 45-53. Private detective, 1st person narrator; not an Op tale.

1113. "The Main Death." 10, No. 4 (Jun 1927), 44-57. The Op.

1114. "The Maltese Falcon." 12, No. 7 (Sep 1929), 7-28, Pt. 1; 12, No. 8 (Oct 1929), 41-64. Pt. 2; 12, No. 9 (Nov 1929), 31-52, **Pt. 3; 12, No. 10 (Dec 1929), 69-91, Pt. 4; 12, No. 11** (Jan 1930), 29-54, Pt. 5. Sam Spade; serialization of novel (pub. 1930); see 15, No. 12 (Feb 1933), 125, for important letter from reader on *TMF*.

1115. "The Man Who Killed Dan Odams." 6, No. 20 (15 Jan 1924), 35-41. Crime story.

1116. "Mike or Alec or Rufus." 7, No. 11 (Jan 1925), 87-96. The Op.

1117.   "The Nails in Mr. Cayterer." 8, No. 11 (Jan 1926), 59-73.
        Robin Thin; billed as "A new kind of detective at work."

1118.   "The New Racket." 6, No. 22 (15 Feb 1924), 34-37. Billed
        as a "tip for judges and lawyers."

1119.   "Night Shots." 6, No. 21 (1 Feb 1924), 33-44. The Op, or,
        as *BM* calls him, "Mr. Hammett's nameless detective."

1120.   "The 19th Murder." 10, No. 12 (Feb 1928), 69-96. The Op;
        Pt. 4 (of 4 pts.), *Red Harvest.*

1121.   "One Hour." 7, No. 1 (1 Apr 1924), 44-52. The Op; in previous
        issue, 15 Mar 1924, there is letter from DH, pp. 127-128.

1122.   "$106,000 Blood Money." 10, No. 3 (May 1927), 9-34. The Op;
        sequel to "The Big Knock-Over."

1123.   "Our Own Short Story Course." 7, No. 6 (Aug 1924), 127-128.
        Letter to ed. from DH; in part, re *BM*'s rejection of
        "Women, Politics and Murder."

1124.   "The Scorched Face." 8, No., 3 (May 1925), 9-31. The Op,
        called here "The Continental Sleuth" by ed.

1125.   "The Second-Story Angel." 6, No. 16 (15 Nov 1923), 110-118.

1126.   "The Shattered Key." 13, No. 4 (Jun 1930), 53-91. Ned
        Beaumont; Pt. 4 (of 4 pts.), *The Glass Key;* see pp. 119-120
        for ed. note on DH.

1127.   "The Tenth Clew." 6, No. 19 (1 Jan 1924), 5-23. The Op; see
        p. 127 for letter from DH on character in story, Creda
        Dexter.

1128.   "The Whosis Kid." 8, No. 1 (Mar 1925), 7-32. The Op.

1129.   "Women, Politics and Murder." 7, No. 7 (Sep 1924), 67-83.
        The Op; see "Our Own Short Story Course."

1130.   "Zigzags of Treachery." 6, No. 23 (1 Mar 1924), 80-102. The

Op; 2d of 2 stories in issue by DH; see "Afraid of a Gun"; see pp. 127-128 for 2 letters from DH.

HAMMOND, Gilbert

131.   "Psycho-Whatchamacallit." 6, No. 10 (15 Aug 1923), 63-72.

HANLEY, Thomas A.

132.   "The Mysterious Terror." 2, No. 1 (Oct 1920), 111-117. Horror tale, featuring a beast, The Unnamable.

HANLON, John

133.   "Christmas Eve." 5, No. 10 (Jan 1923), 23-35. Billed as *BM's* "Christmas Story."

134.   "The Door." 5, No. 13 (1 Mar 1923), 27-28. "A Skit with Spirits."

135.   "A Shred of Yellow Paper." 5, No. 8 (Nov 1922), 18. Short-short less than ½-p.

HANNAN, Robert

136.   "The Thirteenth Victim." 5, No. 6 (Sep 1922), 32-34. Short-short.

HARCOURT, Clinton [a.k.a. Charles]

137.   "The Chest of Delicious Curves." 1, No. 5 (Jun 1920), 38-44.

138.   "The Gorilla." 2, No. 2 (Nov 1920), 91-96.

139.   "The Hold-Up on Napoleon Boulevard." 3, No. 1 (Apr 1921), 117-123. Barney Fagan, thief.

140.   "The Necklace of the Pharaohs." 1, No. 2 (May 1920), 118-126.

141.   "The Reflection in the Mirror." 3, No. 2 (May 1921), 37-42.

1142.   "The White Face at the Cellar Window." 2, No. 4 (Jan 1921),
            121-126.

HARPER, Mark [pseud. of Joseph T. SHAW]

1143.   "Death Rides Double." 22, No. 7 (Oct 1939), 69-77. Motor-
            cycle cop.

HARPER, Thomas de V.

1144.   "A Melanesian Holiday." 6, No. 18 (15 Dec 1923), 111-112.
            Short-short.

HARRIMAN, David E. and John Irving PEARCE, Jr.

1145.   "The Mysterious Package." 1, No. 1(Apr 1920), 79-90.

HARRINGTON, Joseph

1146.   "Footloose Goes Astray." 13, No. 7 (Sep 1930), 24-34.
            Western.

HARRIS-BURLAND, J.B.

1147.   "Barbour's New Book." 3, No. 5 (Aug 1921), 53-61.

HART, John B.

1148.   "In Full Payment." 4, No. 3 (Dec 1921), 102-106.

HARVEY, Eliza Mae

1149.   "The Last Snow." 5, No. 11 ([1] Feb 1923), 92-95.

HAWARD, H. W.

1150.   "Who Killed Challoner?" 2, No. 5 (Feb 1921), 119-123. The
            name may be HARWARD; in any case, possibly pseud. of
            Harold WARD.

HAWKINS, John

1151.   "The Mercy Shot." 22, No. 12 (Mar 1940), 66-75.

HAWLEY, J.B.

1152.   "The Extra Dozen Eggs." 5, No. 1 (Apr 1922), 51-56. JBH's
        final appearance in *BM*.

1153.   "The Feel of the Place." 3, No. 6 (Sep 1921), 58-69.

1154.   "Footprints." 3, No. 5 (Aug 1921), 27-34.

1155.   "The Fornahan Murder." 1, No. 4 (Jly 1920), 107-118.
        JBH's debut in *BM*.

1156.   "The Hallowell Murder." 4, No. 5 (Feb 1922), 111-118.

1157.   "The Man O'Leary Couldn't catch." 2, No. 1 (Oct 1920),
        41-48. Inspector O'Leary, NYPD, & jewel thief.

1158.   "The Murder at Greycourt." 4, No. 6 (Mar 1922), 19-24.

1159.   "The Mysterious Shot." 2, No. 3 (Dec 1920), 33-42.

1160.   "The Mystery of the One-Legged Man." 4, No. 3 (Dec 1921),
        49-54.

1161.   "The Revolving Chair." 4, No. 1 (Oct 1921), 49-55.

1162.   "The Tell-Tale Cigarette." 4, No. 4 (Jan 1922), 75-81.

1163.   "The Unbelievable." 2, No. 2 (Nov 1920), 27-41.

HAWTHORNE, Christopher

1164.   "The King Condor." 1, No. 4 (Jly 1920), 81-88. Baja Cali-
        fornia setting.

1165.   "The Triple Murder in Mulberry Bend." 1, No. 5 (Aug 1920),
        71-80.

HEATH, William H.

1166.   "Motive Missing." 6, No. 20 (15 Jan 1924), 81-86. Crime story; see pp. 126-127 for letter from WHH.

HEISER, Robert Lee

1167.   "The Armchair Detective." 6, No. 12 (15 Sep 1923), 120-126. Puzzle-column as feature; not indexed beyond this point.

1168.   " 'Devil Dan' Hewett." 6, No. 5 (1 Jun 1923), 90-98. KKK story in special KKK issue; see p. 128 for data on RLH & his stories.

1169.   "Fifty Dollars a Peep." 6, No. 14 (15 Oct 1923), 109-116. Alleged to be true.

1170.   "How Lightning Dropped Out." 6, No. 7 (1 Jly 1923), 61-70. Lightning Todd, crook.

1171.   "The Norris Case." 7, No. 10 (Dec 1924), 117-126. The Manhunters; for this series, see chiefly under Charles SOMERVILLE.

1172.   "Where the Road Ends." 6, No. 16 (15 Nov 1923), 9-36. "Complete Novelette."

1173.   "The World's Greatest Mystery." 6, No. 9 (1 Aug 1923), n.p. True account of murder of Clare Stone, a child, in Baltimore; would occupy readers for some time; not indexed beyond this point.

HELLMAN, Sam

1174.   "Where the Span Splits." 1, No. 5 (Aug 1920), 95-99.

HENDERSON, Arthur Floyd

1175.   "A Matter of Gallantry." 6, No. 1 (1 Apr 1923), 89-95.

HENDERSON, George C.

1176.   "Who Shot?" 6, No. 15 (1 Nov 1923), 9-36. "Complete novelette."

HEPLER, Hartley H.

1177.   "Justice at Dawn." 3, No. 4 (Jly 1921), 73-74. Short-short.

HERRINGTON, W. Lee [see also under Alan FARLEY]

1178.   "Bury Me Last." 31, No. 4 (Jly 1948), 96-116. Barney Moffatt, D.A.'s office.

1179.   "Die, Die Again." 33, No. 2 (Jly 1949), 45-56.

1180.   "Middle Man for Murder." 28, No. 4 (Jly 1946), 76-84, 96. "Long" Lane, p.i. & frustrated photographer.

1181.   "Your Funeral—Not Mine." 31, No. 2 (Mar 1948), 90-101.

HERRON, Edward A.

1182.   "Death's 43 Days." 33, No. 2 (Jly 1949), 107-109. Yukon short-short.

HERVEY, Harry C., Jr.

1183.   "The Black Menace." 1, No. 3 (Jun 1920), 3-37.

1184.   "Can This Thing Be?" 2, No. 5 (Feb 1921), 95-110.

1185.   "Daughter of the Pigeon." 1, No. 6 (Sep 1920), 61-71.

1186.   "The Devil at the Helm." 5, No. 4 (Jly 1922), 3-23. "Complete Mystery Novelette."

1187.   "Mr. Sin." 2, No. 6 (Mar 1921), 3-42. "Complete Mystery Novelette."

1188.   "More Deadly Than the Viper." 1, No. 5 (Aug 1920), 49-64. Set in Tibet.

1189.   "Piracy." 1, No. 1 (Apr 1920), 65-78. Set in Burma.

1190.   "Two Bells." 2, No. 2 (Nov 1920), 97-113.

HEWES, Robert E.

1191.   "The Murder at Lost Creek." 2, No. 2 (Nov 1920), 85-90.

1192.   "Red Jade." 5, No. 10 (Jan 1923), 70-72. Short-short.

HICKEY, Charles T.

1193.   "Lefty Helps the Cops." 10, No. 12 (Feb 1928), 111-116.
             Lefty McRae, crook.

HILL, Clif

1194.   "Water." 6, No. 16 (15 Nov 1923), 49-58. Western.

HILL, Grimes [pseud. of Frederick Lewis NEBEL]

1195.   "The Kill." 14, No. 1 (Mar 1931), 72-81. Polk, private eye;
             1st of 2 stories by FLN in issue; see also "Junk" (NEBEL).

1196.   "The Spot and the Lady." 14, No. 3 (May 1931), 55-58. Short-
             short; 1st of 2 stories by FLN in issue; see also "Beat the
             Rap" (NEBEL).

HILLEARY, Cecil F.

1197.   "The Lost Bullet." 9, No. 4 (Jun 1926), 116-126.

1198.   "Suspended Justice." 8, No. 11 (Jan 1926), 31-40. "Padlock
             Holmes solves a mystery."

HILTON, Francis W.

1199.   "The Kid Wrangler." 11, No. 7 (Sep 1928), 115-121.

HOBART, Richard L.

1200.   "Penny Pim—Accidental Detective." 35, No. 4 (Mar 1951),
             42-59. Reprint; not from *BM*.

HODGKINS, Fred

201.   "Crime at the Crossing." 22, No. 1 (Apr 1939), 48-56. Death
        of a little girl.

202.   "The Hunters' Prey." 23, No. 1 (Apr 1940), 113-124. Madman.

203.   "Strangle-Hold." 22, No. 7 (Oct 1939), 101-108.

OFFLUND, Stanley R.

204.   "The Third Rider." 6, No. 15 (1 Nov 1923), 37-44. Yarn
        set in Mexico.

OLDEN, John

205.   "The Perfect Plan." 5, No. 13 (1 Mar 1923), 67-74. Gerald
        Drago, embezzler.

OLLEY, Helen

206.   "Down Where the Glades Begin." 8, No. 12 (Feb 1926), 32-56,
        Pt. 1; 9, No. 1 (Mar 1926), 112-127, Pt. 2. Billed as "A
        Florida mystery-detective story."

OLMES, W.H.

207.   "Creeping Death." 5, No. 11 ([1] Feb 1923), 3-21. "A Complete
        Mystery Novelette."

208.   "The House in Boney Hollow." 6, No. 12 (15 Sep 1923), 110-119.
        "A weird detective mystery."

209.   "Scrambled Motives." 6, No. 6 (15 Jun 1923), 5-31. "A Complete
        Mystery Novelette."

OOD, Arthur H.

210.   "Trailing Trouble." 13, No. 11 (Jan 1931), 46-76. Western,
        with Jerry Fox, a woman.

ORN, R. de S.

1211.   "Tubby Gower Collects His Dues." 5, No. 9 (Dec 1922), 102-115.

HOTCHKISS, Chauncey C.

1212.   "The Wrong Box." 2, No. 5 (Feb 1921), 63-72.

HOWARD, Eric

1213.   "Copper, Have a Heart." 20, No. 10 (Dec 1937), 61-69.

1214.   "The Doc and the Dame." 21, No. 10 (Jan 1939), 98-106.

1215.   "Fifty Grand Frail." 21, No. 8 (Nov 1938), 103-112. Tim
             Ryan, private snoop, 1st-person narrator.

1216.   "Mary, Mary, the Secretary." 20, No. 4 (Jun 1937), 30-38.

1217.   "The Mugg from Frisco." 20, No. 1 (Mar 1937), 103-112.
             Kelly, 1st-person narrator, & some shady politics.

1218.   "Racket Buster." 20, No. 5 (Jly 1937), 88-97. Corrupt
             politics; narrated by D.A.'s assistant; see entry above.

HOWARD, H. F.

1219.   "The Corpse Takes a Wife." 22, No. 11 (Feb 1940), 113-122.

HOWARD, Harvey

1220.   "Red Friday." 23, No. 8 (Dec 1940), 95-99, 116-127. Entirely
             possible HH & HFH (previous entry) one and same.

HOWE, Frank, Jr.

1221.   "The Vernacular at the Night Court." 7, No. 4 (Jun 1924), 78.
             No data.

HOWELL, Haughton

1222.   "The Hunch." 4, No. 6 (Mar 1922), 61-74. "Complete Mystery
             Novelette."

HOYT, Vance

1223.   "The Silent Law." 6, No. 16 (15 Nov 1923), 96-102.

HUNGERFORD, James Edward

1224.   "By Fast Freight." 2, No. 4 (Jan 1921), 75-83. Embezzlement
             in & around San Francisco.

HYDE, John B.

1225.   "The Black Fin." 6, No. 3 (1 May 1923), 51-59.

HYNE, [Charles John] Cutcliffe

1226.   "The Escape." 10, No. 1 (Mar 1927), 66-75. Captain Kettle.

1227.   "Fortunes Adrift." 9, No. 12 (Feb 1927), 50-59. Kettle.

1228.   "The Guns for Cuba." 9, No. 9 (Nov 1926), 47-67. 1st Captain
             Kettle yarn & CH's debut in *BM*.

1229.   "The Liner and the Iceberg." 10, No. 3 (May 1927), 93-100.
             Kettle.

1230.   "The Pearl Poachers." 10, No. 2 (Apr 1927), 102-112. Kettle.

1231.   "The Pilgrim Ship." 9, No. 11 (Jan 1927), 118-128. Kettle.

1232.   "The Raiding of Donna Clotilde." 10, No. 4 (Jun 1927), 66-76.
             8th & last Kettle tale & CH's last story in *BM*.

1233.   "The War-Steamer of Donna Clotilde." 9, No. 10 (Dec 1926),
             119-128. Kettle.

I

IGNATIEFF, Ivan

1234.   "Jungle Shadows." 7, No. 5 (Jly 1924), 32-46. Marlow narrates
             adventure in Philippines.

J

JACKSON, Frederick

1235.   "Risky Whiskey." 9, No. 4 (Jun 1926), 66-78.

JACOBS, Gottlieb

1236.   "Two Letters." 4, No. 4 (Jan 1922), 59-60. Short-short.

JAMES, Francis

1237.   "The Art Killer." 7, No. 3 (May 1924), 9-46. Prentice.

1238.   "The Green Enigma." 7, No. 9 (Nov 1924), 63-77, Pt. 1; 7, No. 10 (Dec 1924), 96-116, Pt. 2. Prentice & Chief of Police Shannon; see p. 128 (Nov 1924) for letter from FJ with small photo.

1239.   **"The Laughing Death." 6, No. 17 (1 Dec 1923), 43-60, Pt. 1;** 6, No. 18 (15 Dec 1923), 71-91, Pt. 2; 6, No. 19 (1 Jan 1924), 106-119, Pt. 3; 6, No. 20 (15 Jan 1924), 102-117, Pt. 4. Prentice & Shannon; *cf.* serial by Raoul F. WHITFIELD using same title.

1240.   "The Long Hand of Middleton." 7, No. 7 (Sep 1924), 45-66. Prentice.

1241.   "The Phantom Hi-Jacker." 8, No. 12 (Feb 1926), 100-111.

1242.   "The Saldetta Mystery." 5, No. 10 (Jan 1923), 3-18. "Complete Novelette "; Prentice.

1243.   "The Sand Devil." 5, No. 7 (Oct 1922), 3-30. Billed as "A Complete Novelette of Mystery and Action... This weird story should be read by daylight"; debut of Prentice, Harvard-trained criminologist, turned policeman, & FJ's debut in *BM*.

1244.   "The Scroll of Death." 6, No. 11 (1 Sep 1923), 7-40. Prentice.

1245.　　　"Sinister Images." 5, No. 11 ([1] Feb 1923), 63-76, Pt. 1;
　　　　　　5, No. 12 (15 Feb 1923), 75-85, Pt. 2; 5, No. 13 (1 Mar
　　　　　　1923), 75-87, Pt. 3; 5, No. 14 (15 Mar 1923), 90-109, Pt. 4.
　　　　　　Prentice, the young Central Office Man.

1246.　　　"Spark of Death." 6, No. 1 (1 Apr 1923), 5-25. Prentice (?)

1247.　　　"The Steel Avenger." 10, No. 8 (Oct 1927), 56-69. Timothy
　　　　　　O'Toole, bodyguard to Peter Holt; FJ's last story in *BM*.

1248.　　　**"The Were-Demon." 6, No. 8 (15 Jly 1923), 5-30. "A Complete
　　　　　　Novelette"; Prentice.**

1249.　　　"Yellow Roses." 8, No. 11 (Jan 1926), 5-30. Prentice.

JENKINS, George B., Jr.

1250.　　　"Appearances Are Deceiving." 5, No. 1 (Apr 1922), 27-34.

1251.　　　"The Bug of Ambition." 5, No. 2 (May 1922), 105-112.

1252.　　　"Business and Pleasure." 5, No. 12 (15 Feb 1923), 57-64.

1253.　　　"Two Faultless Crimes." 5, No. 4 (Jly 1922), 73-79.

1254.　　　"Two Minutes Alone." 5, No. 3 (Jun 1922), 111-116.

JENKINS, George, *et al.*

1255.　　　"The Day of the Dead." 3, No. 4 (Jly 1921), 3-36. Mystery
　　　　　　novelette in which "six suspects give their version of this
　　　　　　peculiar crime."; each chapter by different writer, viz.,
　　　　　　Jenkins (1), Cynthia Woolford (2), Leslie Burton Blades (3),
　　　　　　Helen Hysell (4), Rosalind Blades (5), & Murray
　　　　　　LEINSTER (6); TofC p. gives authorship as "In Collabora-
　　　　　　tion"; this is LEINSTER'S debut in *BM*.

JESTINGS, Charles E.

1256.   "Jim Gregg: A Prison Poem." 23, No. 4 (Aug 1940), 128.

1257.   " 'Soapy' Slater: A Prison Poem." 23, No. 3 (Jly 1940), 127.
         Con is killed in attempted crash-out.

JOHANSEN, Margaret Alison

1258.   "Mrs. Vandam's Diamonds." 6, No. 15 (1 Nov 1923), 83-92.

JOHNSON, Leslie N.

1259.   "The Killing of Antone Mulvaney." 11, No. 2 (Apr 1928),
         82-87. Ex-con attempts vengeance.

1260.   "The Show-Down." 11, No. 4 (Jun 1928), 64-71. Western.

JONES, Hiawatha

1261.   "Murder Express." 33, No. 3 (Sep 1949), 47-54.

JONES, Jones

1262.   "The Talented Burglar." 6, No. 14 (15 Oct 1923), 29-34.

JONES, Marc Edmond

1263.   "Death's Bridegroom." 3, No. 1 (Apr 1921), 41-54.

JONES, Marvin J.

1264.   "Sing a Song of Murder." 32, No. 4 (Mar 1949), 33-41. Jimmy
         Bell, cop.

JORDAN, Charles T.

1265.   "Felton Celebrates Egg-Day." 6, No. 16 (15 Nov 1923), 87-95.

1266.   "A Matter of Postage." 6, No. 4 (15 May 1923), 31-39.

JORGENSEN, Nels Leroy

1267.   "Against Evidence." 14, No. 12 (Feb 1932), 32-53. Black Burton;
         prename: Stuart; see p. 119 for data on NLJ.

1268.   "Black Burton." 8, No. 6 (Aug 1925), 53-58. 1st Black Burton
         story, the square-shooting gambler from the Southwest,
         often entangled with Law; NLJ's debut in *BM*.

1269.   "Black Burton Hits Back." 12, No. 12 (Feb 1930), 109-118.
         Burton.

1270.   "Black Burton Sits In." 9, No. 4 (Jun 1926), 54-65. Burton.

1261.   "Black Burton Visits Frisco." 14, No. 2 (Apr 1931), 70-78.
         Burton has excellent Chinatown connections.

1272.   "Black Sheep's Return." 11, No. 8 (Oct 1928), 11-34. Flash
         Powell; Western.

1273.   "Blood in the Fog." 20, No. 11 (Jan 1938), 113-127. Black
         Burton in London.

1274.   "Boom Town." 13, No. 1 (Mar 1930), 57-75. Burton.

1275.   "Crooks Assorted." 12, No. 2 (Apr 1929), 25-35. Burton.

1276.   "The Dark Pack." 13, No. 8 (Oct 1930), 7-25. Western.

1277.   "Death Drinks Champagne." 20, No. 2 (Apr 1937), 104-119.
         Black Burton.

1278.   "The Faith o' MacGown." 10, No. 11 (Jan 1928), 78-87. Rio
         Kennedy of Customs Service in Santo Domingo; 1st of 3
         RK stories; see also "Lone Hand Tactics" & Racketeers'
         Reef."

1279.   "Gambling in Yellow." 12, No. 3 (May 1929), 42-52. Black
         Burton.

1280.   "Gambling Men." 17, No. 6 (Aug 1934), 107-126. Burton;

his wife, Vivian, appears briefly.

1281.   "Get Burton." 10, No. 9 (Nov 1927), 114-128. Burton.

1282.   "Homicide Cue." 19, No. 6 (Aug 1936), 92-114. Burton.

1283.   "Immunity Murders." 17, No. 8 (Oct 1934), 93-108. Burton
         & Vivian, his wife.

1284.   "I.O.U.—One Life." 9, No. 10 (Dec 1926), 39-50. Burton.

1285.   "Lone Hand Tactics." 13, No. 9 (Nov 1930), 39-59. 2d Rio
         Kennedy story; see also "The Faith o' MacGown"
         & "Racketeers' Reef."

1286.   "The Man from Monaco." 18, No. 10 (Dec 1935), 80-100.
         Black Burton.

1287.   "Monte Carlo Merry-Go-Round." 20, No. 8 (Oct 1937), 71-89.
         Burton.

1288.   "Murder Can Multiply." 19, No. 2 (Apr 1936), 82-103.
         Burton.

1289.   "Murder Cruise." 20, No. 4 (Jun 1937), 94-111. Burton.

1290.   "Murder Masquerade." 21, No. 6 (Sep 1938), 92-109. Last
         (32d) Black Burton adventure & NLJ's final appearance
         in *BM*.

1291.   "New Boss." 15, No. 5 (Jly 1932), 44-63. Burton; reprinted
         as "Patsy in Slaughter-Land," 35, No. [1] (Sep 1950),
         72-90.

1292.   "Purple Canyon." 14, No. 9 (Nov 1931), 104-118. Dan Clinton;
         Western.

1293.   "Racketeers' Reef." 13, No. 10 (Dec 1930), 47-61. 3d & last
         Rio Kennedy story; see also "The Faith o' MacGown"
         & "Lone Hand Tactics."

1294.   "The Reformation of Ace Brand." 9, No. 11 (Jan 1927), 45-54.
          Border story.

1295.   "Salon Piece." 18, No. 3 (May 1935), 96-110. Black Burton
          & wife, Vivian; they do not cohabit.

1296.   "Showdown Hands." 13, No. 3 (May 1930), 93-117. Burton.

1297.   "Shylock Is Murdered." 18, No. 12 (Feb 1936), 109-124.
          Burton.

1298.   "The Sound of Guns." 14, No. 7 (Sep 1931), 106-122. Burton;
          set in NYC.

1299.   "The Stolen Rancho." 9, No. 12 (Feb 1927), 39-49. Border tale.

1300.   "Stud Tactics." 10, No. 5 (Jly 1927), 9-23. Burton.

1301.   "Surprise Party." 17, No. 1 (Mar 1934), 98-110. Burton returns
          after long absence; with wife, Vivian.

1302.   "Tax Plus." 10, No. 4 (Jun 1927), 77-87. Burton.

1303.   "Two Tickets to Trinidad." 19, No. 4 (Jun 1936), 104-122.
          Burton.

1304.   "Unlisted Cargo." 10, No. 6 (Aug 1927), 65-74. Burton.

1305.   "Yellow Smoke." 10, No. 7 (Sep 1927), 67-74. Burton.

1306.   "Your Play, Gentlemen!" 13, No. 2 (Apr 1930), 84-106.
          Burton in NYC; story features Kyoto Kara, a Japanese.

JOSEPH, John

1307.   "Jazz Water—By Special Delivery." 7, No. 3 (May 1924), 77-88.
          Advertised as "the romance of hooch."

JOSES, R.M.F.

1308.   "And Death Did Them Part." 30, No. 1 (May 1947), 110-130. Hollywood private snoop, Duane, 1st-person narrator.

1309.   "Mum's the Corpse." 35, No. [1] (Sep 1950), 95-102, 130.

1310.   "Red Pearls." 30, No. 4 (Nov 1947), 72-95, 127-128. Duane.

1311.   "Side Bet on Death." 32, No. 1 (Sep 1948), 64-87. Duane in Las Vegas.

JOYCE, Harold

1312.   "Death in a Homburg Hat." 25, No. 8 (Dec 1942), 35-43, 128. Shamus Marty Flynn & military secrets in WW II.

K

KANDEL, A.

1313.   "Eulogy on a Rare Theme." 5, No. 11 ([1] Feb 1923), 114. Brief-brief.

KARNEY, Jack

1314.   "Shake Well and Kill." 29, No. 2 (Nov 1946), 62-78. Garfield Dolan, red-headed private cop in NYC, 1st-person narrator.

KATKOV, Norman

1315.   "The Fix." 28, No. 4 (Jly 1946), 54-59.

KAYSER, Ronal [pseud. of Dale CLARK]

1316.   "Murder in Haste." 24, No. 6 (Oct 1941), 100-102. Short-short; desert setting.

KEARNS, Arthur

1317.   "A Born Thief." 8, No. 2 (Apr 1925), 89-95.

1318.   "That Grahame Gem Robbery." 8, No. 4 (Jun 1925), 83-88.
            Touted as "A Compressed Novelette."

KEENAN, Lillian W.

1319.   "The Lost Glove Needle." 8, No. 3 (May 1925), 99-110.
            Described as "shrewd detective work."

KEENE, Day

1320.   "No Match for Murder." 31, No. 3 (May 1948), 116-124.

1321.   "Sauce for the Gander." 25, No. 12 (May 1943), 36-45. John
            Cansdale, schoolteacher murderer.

KENDRICK, Baynard H[ardwick]

1322.   "Arson." 21, No. 10 (Jan 1939), 9-30. Miles Standish Rice;
            see p. 63 for note by BHK on story.

1323.   "Burial Mound." 20, No. 9 (Nov 1937), 52-74. Rice.

1324.   "Clear As Crystal." 22, No. 9 (Dec 1939), 70-87. Rice.

1325.   "Death Plays Seventeen." 22, No. 3 (Jun 1939), 78-101. Rice.

1326.   "The Death Pool." 21, No. 7 (Oct 1938), 70-99. Rice.

1327.   "Fish to Fry." 19, No. 12 (Feb 1937), 14-43. Debut of Miles
            Standish (Stan) Rice, "The Hungry"; 1st of 14 MSR stories;
            all set in Florida; also debut of BHK in *BM*.

1328.   "Fisherman's Luck." 22, No. 11 (Feb 1940), 86-112. Rice in
            South Florida.

1329.   "The Gorgon's Head." 22, No. 1 (Apr 1939), 28-47. Rice.

1330.   "Headless Angel." 22, No. 6 (Sep 1939), 34-59. Rice; Florida
            swamp.

1331.   "Hot Trail." 20, No. 12 (Feb 1938), 34-58. Rice.

1332.   "Plumes of Slaughter." 20, No. 6 (Aug 1937), 38-66. Rice in & around Miami.

1333.   "A Short Cut to Murder." 22, No. 12 (Mar 1940), 113-123. Last (14th) Rice story & final appearance of BHK in *BM*.

1334.   "Venom." 21, No. 4 (Jun 1938), 58-86. Rice.

1335.   "White Birds." 20, No. 2 (Apr 1937), 52-78. Rice.

KENNER, Thomas Clarence

1336.   "The Man from Helldorado." 12, No. 4 (Jun 1929), 118-126. Western.

KENT, Seer

1337.   "The Striped Suit." 4, No. 4 (Jan 1922), 118-123.

KENT, W.H.B.

1338.   "Framing the Killer." 12, No. 12 (Feb 1930), 120-128. Killer Blake; Western mystery.

1339.   "The Killer." 10, No. 8 (Oct 1927), 91-97. Western; 1st of 6 Killer Blake stories; KB is deputy sheriff & agent of Stock Association.

1340.   "The Killer Comes In." 11, No. 2 (Apr 1928), 40-47. Blake.

1341.   "The Killer Finds a Horseshoe." 11, No. 3 (May 1928), 108-112. Blake.

1342.   "The Lost Hand." 13, No. 5 (Jly 1930), 111-118. Last Killer Blake story.

1343.   "Pirate Blood." 11, No. 5 (Jly 1928), 28-37. Blake.

KETCHUM, Philip

1344. "Coffin Number Three." 25, No. 11 (Mar 1943), 54-86. Death of army officer; WW II.

1345. "Mind Over Murder." 24, No. 5 (Sep 1941), 93-109. 1st-person narrator is private eye who has been kicked out of D.A.'s office on trumped-up charge; married with sick child.

1346. "One Sunk Punk." 34, No. 1 (Jan 1950), 91-99.

KILMAN, Julian

1347. "The Case of Renlaw." 1, No. 4 (Jly 1920), 49-52.

1348. "The Fugitive." 3, No. 2 (May 1921), 118-123.

1349. "The Peculiar Affair at the Axminster." 1, No. 1 (Apr 1920), 53-58. JM's debut in *BM*.

1350. "Playing a Hunch." 2, No. 4 (Jan 1921), 41-49. Dave Lacey, just out of prison.

1351. "The Snare." 10, No. 10 (Dec 1927), 34-39. Far North; JM's last tale in *BM*.

1352. "Twenty-Four Hours Ashore." 2, No. 3 (Dec 1920), 119-126. Lake Erie & Buffalo.

KILPATRICK, Lewis H.

1353. "The Pyre of Wrath." 2, No. 3 (Dec 1920), 77-83. Kentucky mountains as setting; there is excellent chance that LHK & Lewis H. MOULTON are one & the same.

KING, Harrison

1354. "One Million Dollars." 6, No. 8 (15 Jly 1923), 88-100. Bank "robbery."

KJELGAARD, Jim

1355. "Backfire." 23, No. 8 (Dec 1940), 67-69. Short-short; wilderness setting.

1356. "Curse of the Beaver." 24, No. 3 (Jly 1941), 120-127. Again, the wilderness.

1357.   "Hangman's Mark." 23, No. 6 (Oct 1940), 69-71. Short-short.

1358.   "Hounded." 24, No. 4 (Aug 1941), 120-121, 128-129. Wilderness
             yet again; see p. 8 for biographical data on JK.

1359.   "The Man They Couldn't Break." 25, No. 3 (Jly 1942), 41-43.
             Short-short; JK's final piece in *BM*.

1360.   "So Skulks the Weasel." 23, No. 3 (Jly 1940), 23-25. Short-
             short; JK's debut in *BM*; rural scene after prison
             break.

KNIGHT, K. M.

1361.   "Without Benefit of Camera." 26, No. 8 (Sep 1944), 58-88,
             92-97. Hollywood actor involved in war effort; Mexico.

KNOX, John H.

1362.   "Goodbye, Enemy." 32, No. 1 (Sep 1948), 52-63.

KOEHL, Herbert

1363.   "See See Drops In." 17, No. 9 (Nov 1934), 114-124. C.C. Cane,
             private investigator, 1st-person narrator.

KOFOED, J.C.

1364.   "Black Shadows." 1, No. 6 (Sep 1920), 3-27. "Complete
             Novelette."

1365.   "Brothers-of-the-Coast." 1, No. 5 (Aug 1920), 122-126.
             Port Royal, Jamaica.

1366.   "Fear." 2, No. 5 (Feb 1921), 83-87.

1367.   "The Mountains of Madness." 1, No. 4 (Jly 1920), 65-80.
           Debut of JCK in *BM*; 1st of 2 stories by him in issue; see
           also "Pirate Stuff."

1368.   "The Mystery of the Marseilles Express." 2, No. 2 (Nov 1920),
           115-126. Possible connection between JCK & William H.
           KOFOED who appears in same issue.

1369.   "The Odd Case of Mr. Hanka." 2, No. 6 (Mar 1921), 103-108.
           Hanka, forger.

1370.   "Pirate Stuff." 1, No. 4 (Jly 1920), 101-106. High seas; 2d
           of 2 stories by JCK in issue; see also "The Mountains of
           Madness."

1371.   "The Puzzling Affair in the Rue Tilsit." 2, No. 4 (Jan 1921),
           59-74. Complete Novelette; fired NYC cop murdererd in
           Paris.

1372.   "The Singular Murder of Darrel Weymouth, 3d." 3, No. 4 (Jly
           1921), 95-113. "Complete Mystery Novelette"; JCK's
           final appearance in *BM*.

KOFOED, William H.

1373.   "The Foot on the Skylight." 3, No. 2 (May 1921), 65-75.

1374.   "The Half-Asleep Girl." 2, No. 2 (Nov 1920), 61-76. Possible
           **connection between WHK & J.C. KOFOED who appears
           in same issue.**

1375.   "The Scarlet Mask." 1, No. 3 (Jun 1920), 81-94.

KOLTON, Paul

1376.   "Don't Kill, My Love." 35, No. [1] (Sep 1950), 49-62.

KOMISARUK, Paul

1377.   "Shot From In Close." 29, No. 2 (Nov 1946), 10-29. Harry
           Nyland, Consolidated Detective Agency, narrates.

KORNBLUTH, C[yril] M.

1378.   "Beer-Bottle Polka." 29, No. 1 (Sep 1946), 35-43. Tim Skeat, private cop, 1st-person narrator, in NYC.

1379.   "The Brooklyn Eye." 29, No. 2 (Nov 1946), 79-94. Tim Skeat.

KRAMER, Edgar Daniel

1380.   "The Long Arm of Malfero." 1, No. 1 (Apr 1920), 122-126.

KRIER, H.J.

1381.   "Bad Penny." 11, No. 5 (Jly 1928), 96-102. Penny Dutro, that is.

KRILL, John

1382.   "Make with a Wake." 33, No. 4 (Nov 1949), 89-96.

KU KLUX KLAN

1383.   6, No. 5 (1 Jun 1923). Special KKK Issue. See under Herman PETERSEN, Carroll John DALY, Henry Clay FOSTER, Christopher SANDSTONE, Charles SOMERVILLE, Ray CUMMINGS, & Robert Lee HEISER.

KULL, George F.

1384.   "Death Is No Bargain." 31, No. 3 (May 1948), 92-115. Eddie Gates, private eye, 1st-person narrator; wears glasses.

1385.   "Red Christmas." 31, No. 1 (Jan 1948), 32-39. In Reno.

L

L'AMOUR, Louis

1386.   "Collect from a Corpse." 33, No. 3 (Sep 1949), 73-82, 130.

LANE, Fred

1387.   "Slayer at Sea." 34, No. 2 (Mar 1950), 10-43.

LANE, Jeremy

1388.   "Deep Water." 5, No. 2 (May 1922), 32-40.

LARSON, Charles

1389.   "Eye for an Eye." 36, No. 1 (May 1951), 33-39. Reprint; not
         from *BM*.

LA SPINA, Greye

1390.   "The Seventh Step." 1, No. 2 (May 1920), 69-75.

LAURISTON, Victor

1391.   "The Dead Man's Letters." 4, No. 2 (Nov 1921), 3-26.

1392.   "Six Shots." 7, No. 5 (Jly 1924), 47-78. "Complete Mystery
         Novelette."

LA VARRE, William

1393.   "The Golden Head." 8, No. 7 (Sep 1925), 100-106. A Daytime
         Story.

LAWRENCE, John

1394.   "Body of Evidence." 23, No. 2 (Jun 1940), 71-86. Al Hackett,
         Broadway Squad (plainclothes), 1st-person narrator.

1395.   **"Broadway Babe." 18, No. 6 (Aug 1935), 8-33. King Carrick,
         ex-G-Man.**

1396.   "Club Fighter." 20, No. 10 (Dec 1937), 10-41. Barron Hargraft
         & boxing in Detroit & NYC; see also "Deed of Gift."

1397.   "Death in the Pluperfect." 23, No. 5 (Sep 1940), 25-37.
         Ace McGuire, Broadway Squad, 1st-person narrator; see
         also "Murder Done in Gold."

1398. "Death to Spare." 22, No. 6 (Sep 1939), 60-72.

1399. "Deed of Gift." 21, No. 5 (Aug 1938), 6-34. Barron Hargraft;
       see also "Club Fighter."

1400. "Detour to Death." 25, No. 6 (Oct 1942), 61-72. JL's final
       appearance in *BM*.

1401. **"Iron Cure." 24, No. 5 (Sep 1941), 62-92. Haley, M.D.,**
       railroaded into prison.

1402. "Murder Done in Gold." 23, No. 12 (Apr 1941), 29-57. Ace
       McGuire, Broadway Squad, 1st-person narrator; see also
       "Death in the Pluperfect."

1403. "Murder, Maestro, Please." 24, No. 10 (Feb 1942), 10-49.
       Jamie Harrod, Maestro of Swing, 1st-person narrator,
       framed for murder; set in Detroit.

1404. "My Body Lies Over the Ocean." 25, No. 2 (Jun 1942), 41-70.
       Disbarred attorney, Larssen T. (Larceny) Kyne; see
       also "Treasonable Facsimile."

1405. **"Picture Killer." 23, No. 10 (Feb 1941), 6-28. Broadway Squad;
       Big Johnny Berthold, 1st person narrator.**

1406. "Scarlet Stakes." 16, No. 4 (Jun 1933), 60-85. Kirk Carney,
       big-time gambler; JL's debut in *BM*.

1407. "Treasonable Facsimile." 25, No. 4 (Aug 1942), 54-79. Larceny
       Kane; see also "My Body Lies Over the Ocean."

LAWRENCE, Raymond Emery

1408. "Gold Is Where You Find It." 11, No. 4 (Jun 1928), 126-132.
       Mining.

1409. "Riker Accomodates." 10, No. 9 (Nov 1927), 105-113. Aviator.

LEE, Albert and Harford POWEL, Jr.

1410. "Cold Hands," 6, No. 8 (15 Jly 1923), 57-70. N.B. See also
       under POWEL.

LEE, Thorne

1411.   "The Mad Dog of Lame Creek." 28, No. 2 (Mar 1946), 47-51, 95.

LEHMAN, Paul Evan

1412.   "Lead Medicine." 14, No. 6 (Aug 1931), 75-86. Western.

LEINSTER, Murray [pseud. of Will F. Jenkins]

1413.   "The Ending of El Jefe." 10, No. 8 (Oct 1927), 24-31. Western
            bandits; ML's final story in *BM*.

1414.   "The Frankenstein Twins." 5, No. 3 (Jun 1922), 80-86.

1415.   "One Small Smudge of Soot." 4, No. 6 (Mar 1922), 25-32.
            ML's solo debut in *BM* but see under George JENKINS, *et
            al.*

1416.   "Pink Ears." 5, No. 1 (Apr 1922), 113-119.

1417.   "Third Man's It." 7, No. 3 (May 1924), 98-108. Payroll bandits.

1418.   "The Vault." 5, No. 5 (Aug 1922), 30-36.

1419.   "The Wallet That Weighed Too Much." 5, No. 7 (Oct 1922),
            97-107.

LENNOX, Robert K.

1420.   "The Price of Vanity." 3, No. 2 (May 1921), 95-103.

LEVEL, Maurice

1421.   "The Confession." 1, No. 3 (Jun 1920), 103-106.

1422.   "In the Light of the Red Lamp." 1, No. 2 (May 1920), 66-68.
            Short-short.

LEVEQUE, James Howard

1423.   "Nigger Loon." 13, No. 8 (Oct 1930), 72-79. Bayou tale.

LEVERAGE, Henry

1424.   "The Clue Upstairs." 11, No. 1 (Mar 1928), 38-45. Big Scar,
             yegg, just out of stir.

1425.   "The Gopher." 11, No. 3 (May 1928), 102-107. Tony Fishera,
             alias The Crawler, a.k.a. The Gopher—gangster.

LEWIS, Ken

1426.   "Suicide Soup." 26, No. 8 (Sep 1944), 89-91. Secret explosive;
             short-short.

LIEBE, Hapsburg

1427.   "Alias Kid Buck." 11, No. 4 (Jun 1928), 36-41. Western.

1428.   "Red Dice." 13, No. 4 (Jun 1930), 92-100. Blaze Hanson in
             in Florida cattle country; see p. 120 for HL's comment on
             story.

1429.   "The Regeneration of John Carter." 12, No. 11 (Jan 1930),
             55-63. Western.

1430.   "The Wolf of Rowdy Horse." 15, No. 3 (May 1932), 115-123.
             Western.

LINKLATER, J. Lane

1431.   "Five Gray Seeds." 23, No. 11 (Mar 1941), 44-52.

1432.   "Killer in Camp." 23, No. 6 (Oct 1940), 77-85.

1433.   "The Shadowy Line." 24, No. 9 (Jan 1942), 80-93.

LISH, L.M.

1434.   "Poker." 7, No. 2 (15 Apr 1924), 113-115. Short-short.

LITTEN, F.N.

1435.   "The Ninth Life." 10, No. 5 (Jly 1927), 70-80. Gangster story.

LIVINGSTON, Don

1436.   "The Awakening of Bash Langley." 9, No. 9 (Nov 1926), 37-46. Modern-day Western.

1437.   **"No Grandstand Play." 10, No. 1 (Mar 1927), 92-100. Western.**

LOFTUS, J. Burton

1438.   "At the Expense of James Cathew." 4, No. 5 (Feb 1922), 101-102. Short-short.

LONERGAN, Lloyd

1439.   "The Disappearing Judge." 4, No. 5 (Feb 1922), 43-57.

1440.   "An Eye for an Eye." 4, No. 6 (Mar 1922), 3-18. "Complete Mystery Novelette"; 1st of 2 stories in issue by LL; see also "A Shot in the Dark."

1441.   "The Hunch." 3, No. 2 (May 1921), 77-94. LL's debut in *BM*.

1442.   "In the Grip of the Everglades." 5, No. 4 (Jly 1922), 87-97.

1443.   "The Monolith Hotel Mystery." 5, No. 5 (Aug 1922), 47-54. LL's final *BM* story.

1444.   "A Shot in the Dark." 4, No. 6 (Mar 1922), 75-88. 2d of 2 stories by LL in issue; see also "An Eye for an Eye."

1445.   "The Six Suspects." 5, No. 3 (Jun 1922), 3-18. "Complete Mystery Novelette"; 1st of 2 stories in issue by LL; see next entry.

1446.   "State's Exhibit A." 5, No. 3 (Jun 1922), 92-96. 2d of 2 stories by LL in issue; see previous entry.

LONG, James Parker

1447.   "Twice to Make Sure." 7, No. 12 (Feb 1925), 55-80. "Cautious, conservative business man" as sleuth.

LONG, Julius

1448.   "Blind Bogey." 26, No. 9 (Nov 1944), 55-65. Ben Corbett.

1449.   "Call in the Coroner." 30, No. 4 (Nov 1947), 46-71. Last (17th) Corbett story in *BM*.

1450.   "Carnie Kill." 26, No. 12 (May 1945), 78-95. Corbett.

1451.   "Crime Is Bustin' Out All Over." 28, No. 4 (Jly 1946), 60-75. Corbett.

1452.   "Date with Dynamite." 27, No. 4 (Jan 1946), 76-93. Corbett.

1453.   "The Devil's Jack-Pot." 26, No. 3 (Nov 1943), 118-129. Addison Secore, criminal lawyer, is villain.

1454.   "Don't Ration Murder." 26, No. 6 (May 1944), 66-81. Black market shenanigans in WW II; 1st-person narrator.

1455.   "Flowers for Flanagan." 28, No. 1 (Feb 1946), 60-71. Corbett.

1456.   "Forgive Not Our Trespassers." 28, No. 2 (Mar 1946), 35-46. Corbett.

1457.   "Goon My Way?" 26, No. 11 (Mar 1945), 78-97. Corbett.

1458.   "Her Favorite Alibi." 33, No. 4 (Nov 1949), 72-88. "Daring Crime-Adventure Novelette"; JL's final curtain in *BM*.

1459.   "I Remember Murder." 29, No. 3 (Jan 1947), 27-41, 97 Corbett.

1460.   "Keyed for a Killing." 25, No. 12 (May 1943), 117-124, 126-129. Dan Kincaid, ex-criminal lawyer, Phi Beta Kappa, 1st-person narrator; JL's debut in *BM*.

1461. "Leave Your Killing Card." 26, No. 10 (Jan 1945), 30-40, 96. Corbett.

1462. "Loser Take All." 26, No. 1 (Jly 1943), 118-127. Attorney Hyre, 1st-person narrator.

1463. "Merely Murder." 26, No. 7 (Jly 1944), 82-96. Ben Corbett, D.A.'s chief investigator, 1st-person narrator; 1st BC caper in *BM*.

1464. "Murder By the Carton." 28, No. 3 (May 1946), 8-25. Corbett.

1465. "Never Kid a Killing." 27, No. 3 (Nov 1945), 33-44, 88. Corbett.

1466. "No Match for Murder." 26, No. 2 (Sep 1943), 91-95, 129. Jake Manders, attorney; see p. 6 for biographical note on JL.

1467. "One Life to a Customer." 30, No. 1 (May 1947), 82-109. Ben Corbett.

1468. "Over My Dead Booty." 27, No. 2 (Sep 1945), 80-97. Corbett.

1469. "This Is Murder." 29, No. 1 (Sep 1946), 80-96. Corbett.

1470. "The Witch of Endor County." 27, No. 1 (Jly 1945), 24-37. Corbett.

LOPEZ, Roy

1471. "The Murder's All Mine." 34, No. 1 (Jan 1950), 100-103, 126-127.

LORD, Mindret

1472. "The Tattooed Tramp." 22, No. 5 (Aug 1939), 27-38.

LUNDIE, Hugh

1473. "A Farewell to Strife." 17, No. 10 (Dec 1934), 112-125.

LYBECK, Ed

1474.   "Dead Evidence." 15 No. 1 (Mar 1932), 41-53. Harrigan;
         see p. 121 for note on EL.

1475.   "Kick-Back." 14, No. 11 (Jan 1932), 35-49. Harrigan; re-
         printed, *The Hard-Boiled Omnibus* (1946).

1476.   "Leaded Ink." 14, No. 10 (Dec 1931), 32-48. Debut of Francis
         St. Xavier Harrigan, reporter on *Leader*, & EL's debut in
         BM.

1477.   "Silent Heat." 16, No. 12 (Feb 1934), 100-111. Last Harrigan
         story & EL's final appearance in *BM*.

M

McCAIG, Robert J.

1478.   **"Trouble on Circuit 13." 32, No. 3 (Jan 1949), 56-67. Marty**
         Cullane, telephone lineman.

McCARDELL, John W.

1479.   "The Return of Gun Eagen." 10, No. 9 (Nov 1927), 38-44.
         Western.

1480.   "Warren of Granite Canyon." 11, No. 8 (Oct 1928), 89-95.
         Western.

McCARDELL, Roy L.

1481.   "A Million a Year." 5, No. 8 (Nov 1922), 29-39, Pt. 1; 5, No. 9
         (Dec 1922), 82-94, Pt. 2; 5, No. 10 (Jan 1923), 95-103,
         Pt. 3; 5, No. 11 ([1] Feb 1923), 115-125, Pt. 4.

1482.   Pieces of Men." 5, No. 13 (1 Mar 1923), 55-66. Daytime Story.

McCARTHY, J.R.

1483.   "Payment As Promised." 5, No. 8 (Nov 1922), 60-62.
         Short-short.

McCOLL, John

484. "Beside Three Tables." 5, No. 9 (Dec 1922), 32. Short-short.

485. "But She Looked Lovely." 5, No. 8 (Nov 1922), 21. Poem.

486. "For Value Received." 5, No. 10 (Jan 1923), 110-111. Short-short.

McCOY, Horace

487. "The Devil Man." 10, No. 10 (Dec 1927), 72-78. South Pacific setting; HMcC's debut in *BM*.

488. "Dirty Work." 12, No. 7 (Sep 1929), 29-42. Debut of Captain Jerry Frost, Texas (Air) Rangers.

489. "Flight at Sunrise." 17, No. 3 (May 1934), 84-96. Frost.

490. "Frost Rides Alone." 13, No. 1 (Mar 1930), 76-95. Frost.

491. "The Golden Rule." 15, No. 4 (Jun 1932), 30-44. Frost.

492. "The Gun-Runners." 13, No. 6 (Aug 1930), 57-75. Frost & Hell's Stepsons stage a "hold-up."

493. "Headfirst into Hell." 14, No. 3 (May 1931), 35-54. Frost & Eddie Giles in Mexico ("Mañana land").

494. "Hell's Stepsons." 12, No. 8 (Oct 1929), 65-83. Frost.

495. "The Little Black Book." 12, No. 11 (Jan 1930), 107-128. Frost.

496. "The Mailed Fist." 13, No. 10 (Dec 1930), 103-119. Frost & Stepsons have go at "The Big Shot."

497. "The Mopper-Up." 14, No. 9 (Nov 1931), 26-42. Captain Tom Bender, Texas Ranger, in oil country.

498. "Murder in Error." 15, No. 6 (Aug 1932), 48-64. Compton,

private shamus.

1499.   "Renegades of the Rio." 12, No. 10 (Dec 1929), 7-26. Frost.

1500.   "Somebody Must Die." 17, No. 8 (Oct 1934), 39-61. Last
         Jerry Frost adventure & HMcC's last story in *BM*.

1501.   "Somewhere in Mexico." 13, No. 5 (Jly 1930), 3-24. Frost &
         Texas Air Patrol smash border gang.

1502.   "The Trail to the Tropics." 15, No. 1 (Mar 1932), 27-40.
         Forst in Rigaria, a Central American republic.

1503.   **"Wings over Texas." 15, No. 8 (Oct 1932), 28-53. Frost.**

MacCRAY, Albert

1504.   "In the Shadows of the Jungle." 2, No. 1 (Oct 1920), 122-127.
         Set in Borneo; Chinese, *et al.*

McCULLY, Anderson

1505.   "The Masked Trail." 11, No. 1 (Mar 1928), 117-128. Story
         of the Far North.

1506.   "The Rajah's Bracelet." 11, No. 11 (Jan 1929), 79-92.
         "Crime involving a group of socially prominent people."

MacDONALD, John D[ann]

1507.   "The Case of the Carved Model." 32, No. 1 (Sep 1948), 88-98,
         130. Sam Dermott, police dick.

1508.   "Heritage of Hate." 33, No. 2 (Jly 1949), 34-44.

1509.   "Jukebox Jungle." 34, No. 4 (Jly 1950), 52-68. MacD's last
         BM story.

1510.   "Killing All Men!" 32, No. 4 (Mar 1949), 10-32.

1511.   "Manhattan Horse Opera." 30, No. 3 (Sep 1947), 115-122.

MacD's 1st *BM* piece.

1512.   "Murder in One Syllable." 33, No. 1 (May 1949), 58-80.

MacDONALD, William Colt

1513.   "Romney Gets the Dope." 9, No. 5 (Jly 1926), 3-36. Western.

McDONELL, Charles

1514.   "The Crimson Scars." 2, No. 1 (Oct 1920), 102-109.

1515.   "The Strange Case of Nathaniel Broome." 1, No. 6 (Sep 1920), 81-92.

MacDOWD, Kennie

1516.   "Lottery Tickets." 11, No. 9 (Nov 1928), 97-102. Criminal in San Francisco.

McDOWELL, J. E.

1517.   "The True Story of the Benders." 8, No. 1 (Mar 1925), 123-126. Short-lived Department of Investigations; not indexed beyond this point.

MacGREGOR, Donald

1518.   "The Dancer in the East." 8, No. 8 (Oct 1925), 102-111.

1519.   "Full Speed Ahead." 9, No. 8 (Oct 1926), 74-82. MacG's last *BM* yarn.

1520.   "The House of Flashing Lights." 8, No. 10 (Dec 1925), 85-90. Concerning a vaudeville actor.

1521.   "The Literary Failings of Robber Bill." 8, No. 1 (Mar 1925), 101-108.

1522.   "New Styles in Criminals." 9, No. 1 (Mar 1926), 104-111. "Factual" article.

1523.   "The One-Dollar Bandit." 7, No. 10 (Dec 1924), 88-95.

1524.   "The Sheriff Lends a Hand." 8, No. 9 (Nov 1925), 111-119.
             Set in small town.

1525.   "Ten Stories Up." 8, No. 5 (Jly 1925), 109-117.

1526.   "West Rides East." 9, No. 2 (Apr 1926), 69-80. Wild West
             show comes to NYC.

1527.   "Winged Blackmail." 7, No. 8 (Oct 1924), 99-109. MacG's
             debut in *BM*.

MACKAY, Bentley B.

1528.   "Bullfrogs." 11, No. 1 (Mar 1928), 98-108. Louisiana tale.

MACKENDER, H.T.

1529.   "The Coward." 1, No. 3 (Jun 1920), 117-120.

McKENNA, James R.

1530.   "Caliente." 26, No. 12 (May 1945), 75-77. Short-short; horse
             racing; 1st person narrator.

MACKLIN, Foreman

1531.   "Buffalo Burke's Prayer." 6, No. 12 (15 Sep 1923), 25-32.
             Western.

McLAUGHLIN, Fred

1532.   "The White Streak." 6, No. 16 (15 Nov 1923), 64-69.

McLAUREN, Hamish

1533.   "The Basket Trick." 5, No. 9 (Dec 1922), 42-49. Set in India.

MacLEAN, Robinson

1534.   "Somebody for the Wolves." 32, No. 3 (Jan 1949), 96-103.
           Eddie O'Meara, shoestring Hollywood producer.

MAJOR, William Wallace

1535.   "The Georgetown Mystery." 2, No. 2 (Nov 1920), 43-54.

MANKIEWICZ, Don M.

1536.   "Odds on Death." 32, No. 2 (Nov 1948), 92-99.

MANN, Fred B.

1537.   "An Affair of Honor." 5, No. 4 (Jly 1922), 71-72. Short-short.

MARCUS, Larry J.

1538.   "A Matter of Timing." 35, No. [1] (Sep 1950), 91-94.

1539.   "Through the Murder Glass." 33, No. 2 (Jly 1949), 97-103.

MARKHAM, Roylston

1540.   "The Scar of the Gibbering Imp." 2, No. 1 (Oct 1920), 49-50.
           Short-short.

MARQUIS, George Bruce

1541.   "The Phantom Check." 5, No. 5 (Aug 1922), 19-29.

MARSH, Howard R.

1542.   "Checkmate." 6, No. 8 (15 Jly 1923), 53-56.

1543.   "The Sign at No. 278." 6, No. 10 (15 Aug 1923), 73-76.
           Billed as a "ten-minute story"; set in Chinatown,
           San Francisco.

MARTIN, Carl L.

1544.   "The Discard." 11, No. 11 (Jan 1929), 115-126. Deputy Lon
           Havens.

1545.   "Figgerin' Roughly." 10, No. 5 (Jly 1927), 81-87. Debut of
             Lon Havens (Drew County) in Bayou country & CLM's
             debut in *BM*.

1546.   "Pore Pickin's." 10, No. 11 (Jan 1928), 27-39. Havens; bank
             robbery & Mississippi R. flood; dialect used.

1547.   "Purging Purgatory." 11, No. 5 (Jly 1928), 52-70. Havens,
             Caleb Cooper, & Sid Rathbone.

1548.   "Still Buzzards." 11, No. 12 (Feb 1929), 103-118. Havens &
             friends in the Delta.

1549.   "Trackless Trails." 12, No. 1 (Mar 1929), 108-126. Last (6th)
             Havens story & final appearance of CLM in *BM*.

MARTIN, J. F.

1550.   "Strong Arm Stuff." 8, No. 9 (Nov 1925), 104-110. Hatred
             between father & son.

MARTIN, J. L.

1551.   "The Tip on the Market." 3, No. 5 (Aug 1921), 41-51.

MARTIN, Robert

1552.   "Death's Glass Slipper." 33, No. 1 (May 1949), 90-113.
             Dr. Clint Colby.

1553.   "Dirge in Bolero Time." 34, No. 1 (Jan 1950), 8-30. Colby.

1554.   "For Better or For Death." 35, No. 4 (Mar 1951), 2-25. See
             headnote, p. 2, for data on RM; final appearance by RM in
             BM & last (6th) Colby story.

1555.   "Hanging Is Too Good." 31, No. 2 (Mar 1948), 40-63, 128-129.
             Lee Fiske, p.i., 1st-person narrator; story set in small
             Ohio town.

1556.   "Let's All Swing Together." 32, No. 4 (Mar 1949), 78-99.

Debut of Dr. Clint Colby, medical detective.

1557. "Lost in the Shrouds." 34, No. 4 (Jly 1950), 12-36. Colby.

1558. "Rat Race in Foxtown." 28, No. 3 (May 1946), 72-86. Foxtown is 45 mi. SW of Cleveland; RM's debut in *BM*.

1559. "Richest Man in the Graveyard." 33, No. 2 (Jly 1949), 58-75. Clint Colby.

MARTINS, Colin

1560. "Ho-o-o-o! for Tanago!" 9, No. 4 (Jun 1926), 79-90.

1561. "Stolen Plumes." 9, No. 7 (Sep 1926), 99-109. Set in Florida.

MARVIN, Tom

1562. "Bag o' Bones." 25, No. 9 (Jan 1943), 111-128. 1st-person narrator is 23-year old small town sheriff.

1563. "Blood-Red and Beautiful." 30, No. 3 (Sep 1947), 85-93.

1564. "Harm's Way." 32, No. 2 (Nov 1948), 72-90.

MARZONI, Pettersen

1565. "Fear." 4, No. 3 (Dec 1921), 69-75.

1566. "The Light That Lies." 5, No. 1 (Apr 1922), 35-40.

MATTESON, Herman Howard

1567. "The Proxy Suicide." 7, No. 8 (Oct 1924), 87-98. Ship on high seas bound for Alaska.

1568. "The Wolf Trap." 7, No. 6 (Aug 1924), 31-48. Mystery tale set in salmon cannery in Alaska.

MATTICK, Irvin

1569.   "The Devil's Rocket." 7, No. 6 (Aug 1924), 105-112. Closing act of Koerner's "Greatest Show on Earth."

MEADOWS, Elmer E.

1570.   "Alias Mr. Fate." 21, No. 12 (Mar 1939), 60-65. Jewish boy in NYC's ghetto.

MERRIMAN, Hale

1571.   "Jinx Town." 7, No. 8 (Oct 1924), 110-118. Couple of hoboes.

MEYER, Coleman

1572.   "Gun in His Back." 32, No. 2 (Nov 1948), 67-71. Cop story.

1573.   "You'll Never Grow Old." 29, No. 4 (Mar 1947), 33-41. Bill Cartright, auto racer, tells it.

MICHALEK, Benjamin

1574.   "The Invisible Order of the Living Dead." 8, No. 10 (Dec 1925), 98-117. Advertised as "strange and weird story."

MILLER, Neil C.

1575.   "An Inside Job." 10, No. 4 (Jun 1927), 107-115.

MILNOR, W. R.

1576.   "Identities Changed." 1, No. 4 (Jly 1920), 45-48. Short-short.

MINERS, Harold Freeman

1577.   "Oscar the Terrible." 6, No. 17 (1 Dec 1923), 61-73. Topango John, ancient desert rat; 1st story in series & HFM's debut in *BM*.

1578.   "Topango Catches a Track." 6, No. 19 (1 Jan 1924), 57-66. 2d Topango John yarn.

1579. "Topango Reverses the Decision." 7, No. 6 (Aug 1924), 58-66. 3d Topango John.

1580. "Topango Takes a Long Shot." 7, No. 12 (Feb 1925), 106-117. Last (4th) Topango John story.

1581. "Twisted Trails." 7, No. 1 (1 Apr 1924), 94-102. Western.

MISSIMER, Wilson Clay

1582. "Torn Fingers." 5, No. 12 (15 Feb 1923), 87-97.

1583. "The Uncanny Voice." 2, No. 3 (Dec 1920), 67-75.

MOFFATT, Raymond Jae

1584. "Death in the Dark." 17, No. 5 (Jly 1934), 94-111. Patrolman tries to avenge murdered father.

1585. "Dunnigan of the Morning Call." 17, No. 12 (Feb 1935), 109-121. Cub reporter & cops.

MONTANYE, C[arleton] S[tevens]

1586. "An Adventure in Diamonds." 7, No. 9 (Nov 1924), 78-87. Captain Valentine, that "attractive European scalawag."

1587. "The Creeping Black." 8, No. 3 (May 1925), 55-72. Valentine.

1588. "The Dice of Destiny." 8, No. 5 (Jly 1925), 67-81. Last Captain Valentine caper.

1589. "The Dragon Fly." 5, No. 10 (Jan 1923), 63-69.

1590. "The Final Raid." 1, No. 3 (Jun 1920), 95-102.

1591. "Framed for Hanging." 22, No. 4 (Jly 1939), 108-111.

1592. "The Goat." 5, No. 8 (Nov 1922), 77-82.

1593.   "Jewel Cut Jewel." 3, No. 3 (Jun 1921), 63-70.

1594   "The Jewel of Blood." 5, No. 12 (15 Feb 1923), 33-39.

1595.   "The Lady in Handcuffs." 6, No. 22 (15 Feb 1924), 38-46.
           Captain Valentine.

1596.   "Looking Out for Orchid." 1, No. 2 (May 1920), 104-111.
           Narrated by vaudevillian in dialect; CSM's debut in *BM*.

1597.   "Moron's Holiday." 22, No. 7 (Oct 1939), 65-68. CSM's final
           appearance in *BM*.

1598.   "No Imagination." 20, No. 3 (May 1937), 124-126. Short-
           short; CSM's 1st story in *BM* since Jly 1925.

1599.   "Outwitted." 6, No. 12 (15 Sep 1923), 104-109. Captain
           Valentine.

1600.   "The Perfect Crime." 1, No. 4 (Jly 1920), 93-99. Rider Lott,
           inventor of The Perfect Crime.

1601.   "The Plan That Was Outlined by Monahan." 2, No. 4 (Jan
           1921), 51-57. Young dip, yegg, & wire man.

1602.   "Planned by the Stars." 1, No. 6 (Sep 1920), 37-42.

1603.   "The Pursuing Shadow." 6, No. 20 (15 Jan 1924), 42-48.
           Captain Valentine.

1604.   "The Safe in the Library." 2, No. 1 (Oct 1920), 63-69. Crookdom,
           complete with criminal argot.

1605.   "The Sandalwood Box." 6, No. 21 (1 Feb 1924), 9-27. Valentine.

1606.   "The Second Charge." 3, No. 6 (Sep 1921), 111-117.

1607.   "The Seven Gold Figures." 7, No. 2 (15 Apr 1924), 76-90.
           Valentine, "adventurer and rascal"; see p. 127 for letter
           from CSM.

1608.   "A Shock for the Countess." 5, No. 14 (15 Mar 1923), 59-66. Countess d'Yls steals some pearls; set in France.

1609.   "The Suite on the Seventh Floor." 6, No. 11 (1 Sep 1923), 75-86. Captain Valentine.

1610.   "The Telegram." 3, No. 2 (May 1921), 43-49. 1st of 2 stories in issue by CSM; see also "Told By a Card."

1611.   "Three Candlesticks." 6, No. 8 (15 Jly 1923), 79-87. Captain Valentine.

1612.   "Told By a Card." 3, No. 2 (May 1921), 104-109. 2d of 2 stories by CSM in issue; see also "The Telegram."

1613.   "Told In Glass." 2, No. 2 (Nov 1920), 55-60.

1614.   "What the Moonlight Revealed." 3, No. 1 (Apr 1921), 23-28.

MOONEY, Ralph E.

1615.   "Outside the World." 8, No. 7 (Sep 1925), 44-58. Atempted murder of an editor.

MOORE, Frederick

1616.   "Jerauld of Beranda Island." 7, No. 1 (1 Apr 1924), 33-43. Called "A detective story of the sea."

MOREHEAD, Clyde

1617.   "Death Without Blackstone." 26, No. 6 (May 1944), 59-65, 112, 114. Gabby Blane, attorney.

1618.   "Tears for Little Willie." 26, No. 5 (Mar 1944), 96-97, 113. Short-short.

MORELAND, Dick

1619.   "Blue Dandy." 18, No. 5 (Jly 1935), 54-71. Jim Delf, owner of Blue Dandy Kennels.

MORGAN, Bassett

1620.   "Sinister Orchids." 10, No. 6 (Aug 1927), 37-64. South Seas
             adventure.

MORGAN, Howard E.

1621.   "The Prisoner at Silver City." 9, No. 5 (Jly 1926), 92-99.

1622.   "The Swamp Road." 9, No. 2 (Apr 1926), 117-122. Western;
             Texas-setting.

MORRIS, E. A.

1623.   "Steal Your Own Grave." 33, No. 4 (Nov 1949), 102-123.

MORRIS, E. G.

1624.   "Panic." 19, No. 10 (Dec 1936), 31-39. Petty crook's panic.

MORRISON, David

1625.   "A Small Blister." 1, No. 1 (Apr 1920), 91-96.

1626.   "Thornton Smiled Significantly." 4, No. 3 (Dec 1921), 83-89.

MOSES, Kingsley

1627.   "The 12.32" 5, No. 10 (Jan 1923), 112-118.

MOULTON, Lewis H.

1628.   "The Chess Club Problem." 2, No. 3 (Dec 1920), 57-66.

1629.   "The Voice of the Dead Man." 2, No. 1 (Oct 1920), 70-72.
             Short-short.

MOYNAHAN, James H[enry] S[eymour]

1630.   "Blow-Off." 15, No. 8 (Oct 1932), 105-124. O'Brien, private
             dick.

1631.   "Crime of Passion." 14, No. 11 (Jan 1932), 110-121. Police dick, Tom Flavin.

MULLALLY, Donn

1632.   "The Corpse I Left Behind Me." 29, No. 3 (Jan 1947), 74-90. Martin Fowler in Hollywood.

1633.   "Death Takes a Dive." 31, No. 2 (Mar 1948), 102-125, 130. Charlie Wingate, Hollywood shamus, & Mike O'Reilly, boxer.

MULLINAX, Ira D.

1634.   "Bas Burke Keeps a Date." 8, No. 1 (Mar 1925), 91-100. Western mystery.

MURRAY, Marr

1635.   "Hades and Return." 5, No. 11 ([1] Feb 1923), 24-30. South Seas story.

MYERS, Cleve

1636.   "Strumming Sam Malone." 13, No. 5 (Jly 1930), 65-75. Western; singing fighter.

N

NAPHEYS, Hank

1637.   "Homicide Furlough." 36, No. 1 (May 1951), 40-52. Reprint; not from *BM*.

NATHAN, George Jean

1638.   "Remarks on the Klan." 6, No. 5 (1 Jun 1923); 89. Brief article on KKK in special KKK issue; reprinted from *Smart Set*, Mar 1923.

NEBEL, Frederick L[ewis] [né Louis Frederick N.; see also Grimes HILL]

1639.   "Alley Rat." 12, No. 12 (Feb 1930), 58-80. Captain Steve MacBride, policeman, & sidekick, Kennedy, local reporter.

1640.   "Backwash." 15, No. 3 (May 1932), 66-81. Kennedy & MacBride.

1641.   "Bad News." 17, No. 1 (Mar 1934), 34-49. Kennedy without MacBride who is on leave.

1642.   "Beat the Rap." 14, No. 3 (May 1931), 84-102. MacBride in Richmond City; 2d story (of 2) by FLN in issue; see "The Spot and the Lady" (HILL).

1643.   "Be Your Age." 17, No. 6 (Aug 1934), 66-85. MacBride, Kennedy, & Co.

1644.   "The Breaks of the Game." 9, No. 1 (Mar 1926), 98-103. "Shrimp" Darcy, heist artist; FLN's debut in *BM* (story signed Lewis N.).

1645.   "Champions Also Die." 16, No. 6 (Aug 1933), 73-92. Tough dick Donahue; boxing story.

1646.   "China Silk." 10, No. 1 (Mar 1927), 51-65. "Introducing Buck Jason—booze runner extraordinary"; 1st of 3 BJ stories.

1647.   "Crack Down." 19, No. 2 (Apr 1936), 8-35. MacBride & Kennedy.

1648.   "Death for a Dago." 14, No. 5 (Jly 1931), 58-76. Kennedy & MacBride.

1649.   "Death's Not Enough." 14, No. 8 (Oct 1931), 8-28. Tough dick Donahue.

1650.   "Deep Red." 19, No. 6 (Aug 1936), 8-31. Kennedy & MacBride; their last story (37th) featuring one or the other or both.

& FLN's final appearance in *BM*, excepting reprint; see "The Green Widow."

1651. "Die-Hard." 18, No. 6 (Aug 1935), 34-56. MacBride & Kennedy.

1652. "Dog Eat Dog." 11, No. 8 (Oct 1928), 54-77. MacBride & Kennedy; 2d installment in "The Crimes of Richmond City" series.

1653. "Doors in the Dark." 15, No. 12 (Feb 1933), 8-27. Kennedy & MacBride.

1654. "Dumb Luck." 9, No. 11 (Jan 1927), 1-17. Whitey Fleer, professional crook, in NYC.

1655. "Emeralds of Shade." 10, No. 6 (Aug 1927), 84-99. Buck Jason; 3d & last BJ story.

1656. "Fan Dance." 18, No. 11 (Jan 1936), 38-62. MacBride & Kennedy.

1657. "Farewell to Crime." 16, No. 2 (Apr 1933), 54-72. MacBride & Kennedy

1658. "Get a Load of This." 13, No. 12 (Feb 1931), 34-55. Donahue of Interstate.

1659. "Ghost of a Chance." 18, No. 1 (Mar 1935), 12-45. 15th & last Donahue story.

1660. "Graft." 12, No. 3 (May 1929), 19-41. Kennedy & MacBride; 5th & last installment in "The Crimes of Richmond City" series.

1661. "Grain to Grain." 9, No. 9 (Nov 1926), 86-97. Corson & Gleason, ex-gangster & ex-boxer, turned dicks.

1662. "The Green Widow." 35, No. 3 (Jan 1951), 96-112. Sergeant Brinkhaus; reprint from *Detective Fiction Weekly,* 11 Feb 1933.

1663.   "A Grudge Is a Grudge." 10, No. 7 (Sep 1927), 82-92. Among crooks, that is; police dick.

1664.   "A Gun in the Dark." 11, No. 4 (Jun 1928), 23-35. Steve Callahan & Tony Valenzo, NYPD dicks.

1665.   "Gun Thunder." 13, No. 11 (Jan 1931), 10-32. Donahue.

1666.   "Guns Down." 16, No. 7 (Sep 1933), 65-82. MacBride & Kennedy.

1667.   "Hard to Take." 19, No. 4 (Jun 1936), 36-61. Kennedy & MacBride.

1668.   "He Could Take It." 15, No. 7 (Sep 1932), 23-41. Tough dick Donahue.

1669.   "Hell-Smoke." 12, No. 9 (Nov 1929), 9-30. MacBride with Kennedy.

1670.   "Hell to Pay." 11, No. 6 (Aug 1928), 38-48. Chicago hood; 1st-person narrator.

1671.   "He Was a Swell Guy." 17, No. 11 (Jan 1935), 34-47. MacBride & Kennedy.

1672.   "Hounds of Darkness." 10, No. 2 (Apr 1927), 113-125. Buck Jason on NYC waterfront; 2d BJ story (of 3).

1673.   "It's a Gag." 17, No. 12 (Feb 1935), 12-44. Kennedy & MacBride.

1674.   "It's the Live Ones That Talk." 14, No. 9 (Nov 1931), 8-25. Chet Knox, Eastern States Detective Service.

1675.   "Junk." 14, No. 1 (Mar 1931), 92-110. MacBride, Kennedy, & river pirates; 2d of 2 stories in issue by FLN; see also "The Kill" (HILL).

1676.   "The Law Laughs Last." 11, No. 9 (Nov 1928), 9-30. MacBride & Kennedy; 3d installment in "The Crimes of Richmond City" series.

1677.   "Law Without Law." 12, No. 2 (Apr 1929), 5-24. MacBride & Kennedy; 4th installment in "The Crimes of Richmond City" series.

1678.   "Lay Down the Law." 16, No. 9 (Nov 1933), 43-59. Kennedy & MacBride.

1679.   "A Man with Sand." 10, No. 5 (Jly 1927), 88-100. See p. 128 for data on FLN with small photo.

1680.   "New Guns for Old." 12, No. 7 (Sep 1929), 61-84. MacBride in Richmond City without Kennedy.

1681.   "No Hard Feelings." 18, No. 12 (Feb 1936), 10-36. MacBride & Kennedy in reversed roles.

1682.   "Pearls Are Tears." 14, No. 7 (Sep 1931), 33-49. Tough dick Donahue.

1683.   "The Penalty of the Code." 10, No. 11 (Jan 1928), 88-100. The Code of Silence.

1684.   "The Quick or the Dead." 15, No. 1 (Mar 1932), 77-92. Kennedy & MacBride.

1685.   "Raw Law." 11, No. 7 (Sep 1928), 9-31. MacBride, Jack Cardigan, with Kennedy in minor role; 1st MacB & K story & 1st installment in "The Crimes of Richmond City" series.

1686.   "The Red-Hots." 13, No. 10 (Dec 1930), 62-83. Tough dick Donahue.

1687.   "Red Pavement." 15, No. 10 (Dec 1932), 10-27. Donahue.

1688.   "The Red Web." 15, No. 8 (Oct 1932), 6-27. Donahue, a.k.a. "The Hard-Boiled One."

1689.   "Rough Justice." 13, No. 9 (Nov 1930), 7-29. Introduces Tough dick Donahue of Interstate; 1st of 15 stories; see pp. 114-115 for note on FLN.

1690.   "Rough Reform." 16, No. 1 (Mar 1933), 56-76. Kennedy & MacBride.

1691.   "Save Your Tears." 16, No. 4 (Jun 1933), 6-24. Donahue.

1692.   "Shake-Down." 13, No. 7 (Sep 1930), 79-102. MacBride, *et al.*

1693.   "Shake-Up." 15, No. 6 (Aug 1932), 6-23. Donahue.

1694.   "Some Die Young." 14, No. 10 (Dec 1931), 68-90. MacBride & Kennedy.

1695.   "Song and Dance." 16, No. 5 (Jly 1933), 6-25. Donahue.

1696.   "Spare the Rod." 14, No. 6 (Aug 1931), 55-74. Donahue.

1697.   "Street Wolf." 13, No. 3 (May 1930), 7-45. Napoleon Damiani, gangster.

1698.   "Take It and Like It." 17, No. 4 (Jun 1934), 8-23. MacBride & Kennedy; reprinted, *The Hard-Boiled Detective* (1977).

1699.   "Ten Men from Chicago." 13, No. 6 (Aug 1930), 3-23. Chicago hoods tangle with MacBride & Co.

1700.   "That's Kennedy." 18, No. 3 (May 1935), 8-38. Kennedy & MacBride.

1701.   "Too Young to Die." 16, No. 12 (Feb 1934), 37-55. Kennedy & the group.

1702.   "Tough Treatment." 12, No. 11 (Jan 1930), 7-28. MacBride & Kennedy but not in Richmond City.

1703.   "Winter Kill." 18, No. 9 (Nov 1935), 12-37. MacBride & Kennedy; reprinted, *The Hardboiled Dicks* (1965).

1704.   "Wise Guy." 13, No. 2 (Apr 1930), 9-32. Kennedy & the usual company.

1705.   "With Benefit of Law." 10, No. 9 (Nov 1927), 94-104. Boxing & crooks.

NEEGARD, Genevieve

706.   "The Sandalwood Casket." 8, No. 2 (Apr 1925), 63-75.
            advertised as "a meek man drunk with blood"!

NEVILLE, Marthé

707.   "After Midnight." 1, No. 5 (Aug 1920), 103-121.

NEWELL, William S.

708.   "A Man Reforms." 10, No. 11 (Jan 1928), 111-118. "Louse"
            Eller, a punk criminal.

NORTON, Henry

709.   "Here's Homicide." 27, No. 1 (Jly 1945), 62-73. Barney &
            Brownie, writers of smash-hit radio whodunit show with
            same name.

710.   "High Voltage Homicide." 30, No. 2 (Jly 1947), 58-65. Lee
            Bassler, 'phone company trouble-shooter.

711.   "Murderer's Way." 26, No. 1 (Jly 1943), 111-117, 128.
            Prison setting.

712.   "Slay, Fiddle, Slay." 25, No. 11 (Mar 1943), 45-53, 128-129.
            Steve Wiachek, Polish-American worker.

713.   "Suffer, Little Children." 25, No. 10 (Feb 1943), 66-75.
            Tio Salta, pickpocket.

714.   "Two Pin Man." 25, No. 8 (Dec 1942), 107-110. Sheriff McGill.

O

O'HARA, Scott

715.   "Kiss the Corpse Good-By." 32, No. 4 (Mar 1949), 100-105.

O'HEARN, Marian

1716.   "Diary of a Deadly Dame." 33, No. 1 (May 1949), 30-47.

1717.   "Swansong for an Ugly Duckling." 34, No. 1 (Jan 1950), 104-125.

OLSEN, James P.

1718.   "Gunman's Goal." 14, No. 4 (Jun 1931), 109-118. Western; Tip Wing.

1719.   "Honor of the Show." 13, No. 10 (Dec 1930), 84-91. Deformed sideshow owner, Prince Eco, & murder.

1720.   "Horror Hacienda." 13, No. 9 (Nov 1930), 30-38. Western; Wolf Cazell in New Mexico.

1721.   " 'Shot!' " 13, No. 8 (Oct 1930), 64-71.

1722.   "Six-Gun Glory." 13, No. 12 (Feb 1931), 10-33. Western; with Trent Wirt; story inspires some doggerel from a reader; see 14, No. 2 (Apr 1931), 5.

1723.   "Who Knows?" 14, No. 1 (Mar 1931), 42-45. Western

ONSLOW, John

1724.   "The Damned Rookie." 19, No. 12 (Feb 1937), 103-115. Larry Brogan, rookie cop.

1725.   "The Deal." 15, No. 11 (Jan 1933), 62-74. Gyp Basino, hijacker.

OURSLER, Charles F. and John I. PEARCE

1726.   "The Hand of Judas." 1, No. 3 (Jun 1920), 45-54.

OWENS, Elwin J.

1727.   "Lupsika of the Forest." 6, No. 16 (15 Nov 1923), 37-41. North Woods.

OZAKI, Milton K.

1728.   "The Corpse Didn't Kick." 33, No. 4 (Nov 1949), 50-62, 127.

P

PAGE, Norvell

729.   "Black Harvest." 16, No. 2 (Apr 1933), 111-121. Jules Tremaine in Little Italy, NYC.

730.   "The Confessional." 16, No. 1 (Mar 1933), 30-48. Tremaine in Manhattan & Little Italy.

731.   "Those Catrini." 15, No. 12 (Feb 1933), 79-90. 1st of 3 Tremaine stories; Little Italy; (ed. note) a projected & potentially important series that never developed.

PAIGE, Peter

732.   "...And God Won't Tell." 23, No. 3 (Jly 1940), 49-67. Dan Ryan swaps "his soul for a swastika," i.e., a German American Bund-type group; 1st-person narrator.

733.   "Berlin Papers, Please Copy!" 25, No. 5 (Sep 1942), 112-127. Mr. Q, Allied spy in Europe; PP's last story in *BM*.

734.   "Blackout!" 22, No. 11 (Feb 1940), 6-28. Spy story; set in Paris early in WW II.

735.   "Bomb Heat." 23, No. 9 (Jan 1941), 96-112, 114, 116-126. Gabby Grant & Pepito Valdes in NYC; see also "The Friends of Pepito Valdes."

736.   "Counterfeit Citizen." 22, No. 12 (Mar 1940), 44-65. Espionage; U.S. female entertainer in Berlin.

737.   "Death Is a Souvenir." 25, No. 4 (Aug 1942), 80-107, 129. Captain Hammer (private eye), "one-man war Department."

738.   "The Friends of Pepito Valdes." 23, No. 1 (Apr 1940), 36-55. Gabby Grant; laid in Spain with Civil War background; see also "Bomb Heat."

1739.   "I Guard Nudes." 22, No. 6 (Sep 1939), 108-111. Factual article;
            PP is guard at New York World's Fair; his debut in
            BM.

1740.   "The Night You Shot Hitler." 24, No. 10 (Feb 1942), 104-114.
            116, 118, 120-126, 128-129. Murder of RAF pilot in NYC.

1741.   "Picture Me Dead!" 24, No. 7 (Nov 1941), 62-79. Cold-Trail
            Harris of Missing Persons.

1742.   "Swastika Scourge." 22, No. 9 (Dec 1939), 6-27. Nazi spies
            on the high seas; see p. 111 for letter from PP.

1743.   "Voodoo Frame." 22, No. 10 (Jan 1940), 24-45. Cash Wale,
            1st-person narrator, employee in Moonglow, an
            amusement park.

PANGBORN, Edgar

1744.   "Bullet Song." 21, No. 8 (Nov 1938), 43-63. Tom Paradine,
            music critic.

PATTERSON, Lt. Col. J[ohn] H[enry], D.S.O.

1745.   "The Man-Eaters of Tsavo." 9, No. 8 (Oct 1926), 66-73, Pt. 1;
            9, No. 9 (Nov 1926), 74-84, Pt. 2; 9, No. 10 (Dec 1926), 68-77,
            Pt. 3; 9, No. 11 (Jan 1927), 70-77, Pt. 4; 9, No. 12 (Feb 1927),
            87-96, Pt. 5; 10, No. 1 (Mar 1927), 101-107, Pt. 6; 10, No. 2
            (Apr 1927), 88-91, Pt. 7. Tiger-hunting, etc.; serialization
            of (factual) book (pub. 1927).

PAYNE, Stephen

1746.   "The Fifth Loop." 10, No. 11 (Jan 1928), 40-49. Western.

1747.   "Night-Riding Ruddy." 11, No. 6 (Aug 1928), 96-105. Western;
            with Ruddy Ingersoll.

PEACOCK, H. Randolph

748.   "Bare Facts." 22, No. 2 (May 1939), 60-67. Nudist camp
         setting; epistolary style.

749.   "Dead Alibi." 20, No. 1 (Mar 1937), 86-102. Otto, department
         store dick, 1st-person narrator; 1st of 3; see p. 127 for word
         on HRP.

750.   "Dead Man's Prints." 21, No. 6 (Sep 1938), 66-91. Otto; makes
         $40 week at Klineman's.

751.   "Double Check." 20, No. 4 (Jun 1937), 40-60. Otto.

PEARCE, Dick

752.   "Homicide Hangover." 28, No. 2 (Mar 1946), 8-34, 96-97.
         Major Bill Boyle, just back from WW II.

PEARCE, Jim T.

753.   "Always Leave 'Em Dying..." 34, No. 3 (May 1950), 49-57.

PEARCE, John Irving, Jr. and Joseph FAUS

754.   "The Belled Boomerang." 1, No. 2 (May 1920), 19-24. For JIP,
         see also under OURSLER.

PENTECOST, Hugh [pseud. of Judson Pentecost Philips]

755.   "Murder Lays the Keel." 25, No. 8 (Dec 1942), 44-98. Lassiter
         of Naval Intelligence; set in Portsmouth Navy Yard.

PERKERSON, Angus

756.   "Ether." 3, No. 2 (May 1921), 50-52.

PERRY, Jennings

757.   "The Clear Call." 7, No. 6 (Aug 1924), 67-87. "A Mystery
         of the Sea."

758.   "The Master of the Maisie." 6, No. 21 ([1] Feb 1924), 75-87.

PETERSEN, Herman

1759.   "The Black Gauntlet." 6, No. 10 (15 Aug 1923), 7-35. Advertised
          as "A Long Novelette of South Sea Adventure."

1760.   "Call Out the Klan!" 6, No. 5 (1 Jun 1923), 5-31. KKK yarn
          in special KKK issue.

1761.   "The Gentle Art of Drying Heads." 6, No. 15 (1 Nov 1923), 92.
          Brief article; relates to "One Dried Head" in issue.

1762.   "The Ghost Ship." 5, No. 13 (1 Mar 1923), 3-26. "Complete
          Mystery Novelette of the Cannibal Isles."

1763.   **"A Gold-Digger's Man." 5, No. 5 (Oct 1922), 121-125. 2d of 2**
          stories in issue by HP; see next entry.

1764.   "Half Across the World." 5, No. 7 (Oct 1922), 37-47. 1st of
          2 stories in issue by HP; see previous entry.

1765.   "In Mutiny." 6, No. 4 (15 May 1923), 40-47. "A weird thing."

1766.   "The Knife." 9, No. 5 (Jly 1926), 109-123. HP's last story in *BM*.

1767.   "On Ten Palms Island." 6, No. 24 (15 Mar 1924), 75-88. South
          Seas.

1768.   "One Dried Head." 6, No. 15 (1 Nov 1923), 55-69, Pt. 1; 6, No. 16
          (15 Nov 1923), 70-82, Pt. 2; 6, No. 17 (1 Dec 1923), 103-120,
          Pt. 3. South Seas; see also "The Gentle Art of Drying
          Heads."

1769.   "Painted Skulls." 7, No. 8 (Oct 1924), 41-60. Detective in South
          Seas.

1770.   "Poisoned Gas." 5, No. 6 (Sep 1922), 73-84. 2d of 2 stories
          by HP in issue; see next entry.

1771.   "The Seven Gilded Balls." 5, No. 6 (Sep 1922), 35-42. 1st of
          2 stories by HP in issue (see previous entry) & HP's debut
          in *BM*.

772.	"Shark-Bait." 5, No. 8 (Nov 1922), 19-21. Short-short.

773.	"That Yellow Devil." 6, No. 21 (1 Feb 1924), 101-117, Pt. 1; 6, No. 22 (15 Feb 1924), 83-104, Pt. 2. Madame Pinar, Eurasian.

774.	"Three Lavender Envelopes." 9, No. 2 (Apr 1926), 81-95. Blackmail in NYC.

775.	"The Useless Man." 6, No. 8 (15 Jly 1923), 43-52. Pacific tropical islands.

776.	"When a Wizard Woos." 6, No. 19 (1 Jan 1924), 84-86. Short-short; Wamaba, wizard in New Hebrides.

ETTEE, Florence M[ae]

777.	"The Clue from the Tempest." 3, No. 3 (Jun 1921), 3-38. "A Complete Mystery Novelette."

778.	"The Double-Bottomed Casket." 3, No. 4 (Jly 1921), 55-63.

HILLIPS, Henry Wallace

779.	"A Chance Shot." 12, No. 11 (Jan 1930), 129-132. Western mystery; Red Saunders.

780.	"Chotka Sevier." 10, No. 6 (Aug 1927), 75-83. Western; Chotka is half-breed.

781.	"The Demon in the Canyon." 12, No. 9 (Nov 1929), 129-132. Western.

782.	"For Sale, The Golden Queen." 14, No. 10 (Dec 1931), 61-67. Western; Agamemnon Jones & Hy, 1st-person narrator; Golden Queen is a gold mine.

783.	"Judgment Reversed." 11, No. 5 (Jly 1928), 129-132. Red Saunders relates story about Mike, a Black barber.

784.	"Just a Canter." 12, No. 12 (Feb 1930), 81-87. Red Saunders.

1785.   "The Killing Nerve." 10, No. 7 (Sep 1927), 75-81. Western; 1st Red Saunders story (of 8).

1786.   "The Pets." 12, No. 7 (Sep 1929), 85-89. Saunders.

1787.   "Red Saunders Busts a Lynching." 13, No. 12 (Feb 1931), 116-120.

1788.   "The Spectre of Wickam's Shack." 10, No. 4 (Jun 1927), 38-43. HWP's debut in *BM*.

1789.   "A Touch of Nature." 15, No. 4 (Jun 1932), 106-112. Red Saunders fights "a wild man in kilts"; HWP's final story in *BM* & last (8th) Saunders story.

1790.   "The Wooing of Shah-Layah." 11, No. 7 (Sep 1928), 78-83. Saunders, Jack, & Indian girl, Shah-Layah, who marry.

PHILLIPS, Roland

1791.   "The Sentinel of Green Cove." 28, No. 1 (Feb 1946), 83-92.

PIERCE, Jud

1792.   "Sunrise." 7, No. 7 (Sep 1924), 123-126. Short-short.

POST, William Stanwood

1793.   "Finger Prints." 5, No. 2 (May 1922), 123-124. Short-lived department; not indexed beyond this point.

POWEL, Harford, Jr.

1794.   "The High Jackers." 5, No. 12 (15 Feb 1923), 27-32. HP's debut in *BM*.

1795.   "How Two Men Died." 6, No. 3 (1 May 1923), 116. Brief-brief; 2d of 2 pieces by HP in issue; see next entry.

1796.   "Mystery Ship." 6, No. 3 (1 May 1923), 5-24. 1st of 2 pieces by HP in issue; see previous entry.

1797.	"The Other Immortals." 6, No. 5 (1 Jun 1923), 76-77. Fantasy short-short, featuring Leon F. Czolgosz, John Wilkes Booth, & Judas; in special KKK issue.

1798.	" 'Suffery, You're Dead.' " 6, No. 7 (1 Jly 1923), 115-116. Short-short.

1799.	"What Did She See?" 6, No. 23 (1 Mar 1924), 72-79. Billed as "A Real Black Mask Mystery"; HP's last appearance in *BM*; for HP, see also under Albert LEE.

POWELL, Sam

1800.	"Smoke Out." 16, No. 11 (Jan 1934), 116-125. Gamblers hire Curry as guard; he is framed for murder.

POWELL, Talmage

1801.	"Her Dagger Before Me." 33, No. 2 (Jly 1949), 80-96. Tampa (Florida) p.i., Lloyd.

POYNTER, Beulah

1802.	"The Abandoned House." 1, No. 5 (Aug 1920), 35-44.

PREECE, Harold

1803.	"Boulevard Buzzards." 33, No. 2 (Jly 1949), 76-78. Short-short; Paris in 1880.

PRICE, E. Hoffman

1804.	"I'll Be Slaying You." 27, No. 3 (Nov 1945), 66-86, 92-97. Dave Stanton in military service; Bagdad, California.

PROCTOR, A.A.

1805.	"Unfortunate Gold." 9, No. 2 (Apr 1926), 96-106. Set in France.

PROVOST, Eric

1806.   "Killer's Luck." 25, No. 8 (Dec 1942), 111-127. Jim Sibley,
            NYPD homicide, on vacation in Maine.

R

RAGSDALE, Edith Lyle

1807.   "The Curse of Indra." 6, No. 22 (15 Feb 1924), 105-110.
            Daytime Story.

RAINEY, William B. [pseud. of Wyatt BLASSINGAME]

1808.   "The Garden of Violent Death." 22, No. 10 (Jan 1940),
            112-125. Philip Dumaine, New Orleans private gumshoe,
            & Negro sidekick, Ben Bolt.

RAMMEL, Hal

1809.   "So Spake the Prophet." 9, No. 8 (Oct 1926), 123-126.

RANCK, Edwin Carty

1810.   "The Face That Stared Back at Blaisdell." 1, No. 5 (Aug 1920),
            45-48.

1811.   "Fingers from the Grave." 1, No. 6 (Sep 1920) 43-48.

RANDALL, William R.

1812.   "If the Coat Fits." 2, No. 6 (Mar 1921), 109-118.

RAY, Victor K.

1813.   "Eeney-Meeny-Money—Murder!" 31, No. 4 (Jly 1948), 86-95.
            Bill Baldwin, nightclub bookkeeper, 1st-person narrator.

RAYMOND, Ray

1814.   "The Curse of the Long Tooth." 7, No. 7 (Sep 1924), 30-44.
            South Seas mystery.

RAYNOR, H. C.

1815.   "The Horror of McCandless Bend." 7, No. 3 (May 1924),
            89-97. Billed as "a mystery of three generations."

READE, J. Fortune

1816.   "At the Bottom of It." 6, No. 14 (15 Oct 1923), 52-61. "A Strange
            Detective Problem."

1817.   "The End of the Measure." 6, No. 3 (1 May 1923), 117-122.

1818.   "The Windfall." 7, No. 6 (Aug 1924), 95-104.

REELHEW, Riblew [pseud. of Wilber WHEELER]

1819.   "Eyes of the Night." 10, No. 3 (May 1927), 35-45. Dandy Dan,
            nimble & nimble-witted crook.

1820.   "The Robbing of Ming Tai Low." 10, No. 1 (Mar 1927), 33-40.
            Chinatown character outwits crook.

REEVES, Robert

1821.   "Alcoholics Calamitous." 27, No. 2 (Sep 1945), 62-79. Last
            (7th) Cellini Smith story & RR's final appearance in
            BM.

1822   "Bail Bait." 24, No. 9 (Jan 1942), 11-39. Cellini Smith.

1823.   "Blood, Sweat and Biers." 26, No. 10 (Jan 1945), 10-29.
            Smith & a boxing-fix.

1824.   "The Cat with a Headache." 24, No. 2 (Jun 1941), 56-79. Smith.

1825.   "Dance Macabre." 23, No. 12 (Apr 1941), 8-28. Dime-a-dance
            hostess & Firpo Cole.

1826.   "Dog Eat Dog." 23, No. 5 (Sep 1940), 76-128, Pt. 1; 23, No. 6
            (Oct 1940), 86-128, Pt. 2; 23, No. 7 (Nov 1940), 90-128,
            Pt. 3. Debut of Cellini Smith (Sep 1940) & RR's debut
            in *BM*; serial pub. as *No Love Lost* (1941); see pp. 44-45
            (Oct 1940) for photo & data on RR.

1827.   "The Flying Hearse." 23, No. 11 (Mar 1941), 8-35. Cellini Smith; Hollywood.

1828.   "Murder A.W.O.L." 26, No. 9 (Nov 1944), 10-29. Smith on his induction day, WW II.

1829.   **"Murder in High Gear." 24, No. 4 (Aug 1941), 58-82. Bookie** Barnes, highway detective, posing as truck-driver.

1830.   "A Taste for Murder." 25, No. 7 (Nov 1942), 11-37. Smith.

RENARD, Maurice

1831.   "The Frog." 5, No. 9 (Dec 1922), 64-72. Daytime Story.

RENAUD, Ralph E.

1832.   **"Telling the Cock-Eyed World." 9, No. 4 (Jun 1926), 99-106.**

REYNARD, Lester

1833.   "Don't Call It Air-Tight." 11, No. 9 (Nov 1928), 31-40. Border story with aviation; smuggling Chinese.

1834.   " 'He's Give the Works.' " 12, No. 7 (Sep 1929), 90-100. Ted Bland; airplanes.

1835.   "Ladies Love Diamonds." 13, No. 8 (Oct 1930), 80-89. San Francisco setting.

1836.   "Ritzie Gets Clever." 11, No. 6 (Aug 1928), 87-95. Western; Deputy "Happy" Collins & girl, Ritzie.

1837.   "Saving the Double-Cross." 12, No. 10 (Dec 1929), 118-128.

RICHARDS, Cole

1838.   "No Reprieve." 20, No. 1 (Mar 1937), 124-126. Short-short.

RICHARDS, Phil

1839.   "The Slay's the Thing." 33, No. 3 (Sep 1949), 34-46. James Greer, ex-playwright.

RIGGS, Arthur Stanley

1840.   "Printed, But Not Read." 3, No. 6 (Sep 1921), 35-43.

ROCKEY, Howard P.

1841.   "Alibis and Evidence." 5, No. 3 (Jun 1922), 46-58.

1842.   "False Witness." 5, No. 7 (Oct 1922), 114-120.

1843.   "Madge the Mouse." 5, No. 6 (Sep 1922), 57-67.

1844.   "The Mistaken Sacrifice." 5, No. 5 (Aug 1922), 98-106.

1845.   "When Lightning Strikes." 5, No. 4 (Jly 1922), 107-116.

RODGERS, S.T.

1846.   "How Mr. Bingham Wrote a Little Story for Nothing." 4, No. 6 (Mar 1922), 33-38.

ROHDE, Robert H.

1847.   "Millions of Cops." 36, No. 1 (May 1951), 85-92. Reprint; not from *BM*.

ROLFE, Harry Emmons

1848.   "Tin Cans." 9, No. 5 (Jly 1926), 124-126. Short-short.

ROLLINS, William, Jr.

1849.   "Chicago Confetti." 15, No. 1 (Mar 1932), 104-120. Percy Warren, private eye; 1st PW story; see p. 121 for biographical information on WR.

1850.   "Dead Men of the Marshes." 7, No. 10 (Dec 1924), 55-87. Jack Darrow & double murder; 2d (of 3) JD stories; see also

"Death That Comes After Midnight" & "Treasures That Dead Men Guard."

1851. "Death in the Western Foothills." 8, No. 9 (Nov 1925), 40-73.

1852. "Death That Comes After Midnight." 7, No. 8 (Oct 1924), 9-40. Jack Darrow, 16-year old hero; 1st (of 3) JD stories; see also "Dead Men of the Marshes" & "Treasures That Dead Men Guard."

1853. "Dirty Linen." 15, No. 11 (Jan 1933), 91-105. 4th & last Percy (Buck) Warren story.

1854. "Footsteps of the Dead." 7, No. 3 (May 1924), 55-76. "Complete Mystery Novelette"; sequel to "The Ring on the Hand of the Dead."

1855. "Free Ride." 15, No. 6 (Aug 1932), 102-123. 2d Warren story; framed for murder.

1856. "The House of the Fiend Who Laughs." 6, No. 10 (15 Aug 1923), 52-62. Daytime Story.

1857. "I Am Kidnapped." 17, No. 3 (May 1934), 62-83. Boy in hands of kidnappers; WR's final appearance in *BM*.

1858. "K. O. and the Killers." 16, No. 2 (Apr 1933), 35-53. Kenneth Osborne; 3d (of 4) KO stories.

1859. "K. O. Carries On." 16, No. 1 (Mar 1933), 88-107. Osborne; 2d (of 4) KO stories.

1860. "K. O. Comes Clean." 15, No. 12 (Feb 1933), 61-78. Kenneth Osborne from "No'th Cah'lina," 1st-person narrator; 1st (of 4) KO stories.

1861. "K.O. Makes It O.K." 16, No. 1 (Jun 1933), 105-121. 4th & last KO story.

1862. "The Ring on the Hand of Death." 7, No. 1 (1 Apr 1924), 9-32. See "Footsteps of the Dead" for sequel.

1863.   "Schuydenehome." 6, No. 1 (1 Apr 1923), 45-60. Debut of WR in *BM*.

1864.   "Silent Sentinels." 6, No. 7 (1 Jly 1923), 79-97. KKK tale.

1865.   "A Song of India." 6, No. 9 (1 Aug 1923), 64-77. Billed as an "Oriental adventure in a small town."

1866.   "Stars and Bullets." 16, No. 11 (Jan 1934), 97-115. Durant, investigator, Northeastern Insurance, 1st-person narrator.

1867.   "Treasures That Dead Men Guard." 7, No. 12 (Feb 1925), 81-95, Pt. 1; 8, No. 1 (Mar 1925), 74-90, Pt. 2; 8, No. 2 (Apr 1925), 104-119, Pt. 3. 3d & last Jack Darrow tale; see also "Death That Comes After Midnight" & "Dead Men of the Marshes."

1868.   "Triple-Cross." 15, No. 7 (Sep 1932), 102-121. 3d Percy (Buck) Warren caper.

1869.   "The Wolf of the Du Mont Thiers." 6, No. 18 (15 Dec 1923), 53-63. Advertised as "A Strange Story of Strange People."

ROSE, A.

1870.   "A Substitute for Blood." 5, No. 8 (Nov 1922), 23-28. Story illus. by author who also designed cover of issue.

ROSE, Edward E. and Dorothy S.

1871.   "The Night of November 7th." 1, No. 3 (Jun 1920), 62-67.

ROUGH, William

1872.   "Cops Have Muddy Feet." 25, No. 2 (Jun 1942), 119-130. Ben Slabbe, p.i., who has his own agency; 1st of 5 BS capers.

1873.   "Don't Burn Your Corpses Behind You." 29, No. 1 (Sep 1946), 44-67. Slabbe.

1874.   "Hot Ice." 29, No. 3 (Jan 1947), 42-60. Last Slabbe case.

1875.   "My Gun Hires Legitimate." 28, No. 3 (May 1946), 40-59.
            Slabbe.

1876.   "Shoot If You Must." 28, No. 1 (Feb 1946), 72-82, 93-97. Slabbe.

ROUSE, William Merriam

1877.   "The Cunning of Red Neck." 6, No. 24 (15 Mar 1924), 9-30.
            Mystery novelette set in & around Quebec.

1878.   "The Hour of Vengeance." 3, No. 4 (Jly 1921), 85-93.

ROUSSEL, Hubert de Tavanne

1879.   **"The Eyes in the Alley." 3, No. 3 (Jun 1921), 39-46.**

1880.   "The Hair That Hanged." 3, No. 4 (Jly 1921), 37-44.

1881.   "Marked 'Star-J.' " 2, No. 3 (Dec 1920), 43-53. HR's debut
            in *BM*.

1882.   "The Stained Paper." 3, No. 1 (Apr 1921), 37-39. Short-
            short; 1st of 2 pieces by HR in issue; see also "The
            Yellow Stripe."

1883.   "The Thing Called Luck." 4, No. 1 (Oct 1921), 57-66. Last
            story by HR in *BM*.

1884.   "The Trap." 3, No. 2 (May 1921), 29-31. Short-short.

1885.   "The Yellow Stripe." 3, No. 1 (Apr 1921), 99-102. Set in
            Kalahari Desert (South Africa); 2d of 2 stories by HR in
            issue; see also "The Stained Paper."

ROUSSEL, Royal

1886.   "The Mutt." 6, No. 20 (15 Jan 1924), 94-96. Short-short;
            there may be connection between RR & Hubert ROUSSEL;
            see previous entries.

ROWAN, Victor

1887.   "Inheritance by Proxy." 6, No. 20 (15 Jan 1924), 97-101.
                1st-person narrated crime story.

RUD, Anthony M.

1888.   "The Farson Enigma." 3, No. 2 (May 1921), 3-27.

1889.   "The Silver Screw." 2, No. 1 (Oct 1920), 3-40. "Complete
                Mystery Novelette"; set in Ivory Coast (Africa).

RUSSELL, Robert

1890.   "Greggs Over-Reaches." 6, No. 13 (1 Oct 1923), 74-80. Jewels

1891.   "The Snake." 6, No. 4 (15 May 1923), 106-115.

1892.   "Suspiciously Good Behavior." 5, No. 7 (Oct 1922), 79-90.

S

SACHS, Emanie N.

1893.   " 'Of an Urgency.' " 6, No. 8 (15 Jly 1923), 71-77.

ST. VRAIN, Roy

1894.   "Hands Up!" 1, No. 1 (Apr 1920), 97-102. In the Andes.

SALE, Richard [Bernard]

1895.   "Banshee." 35, No. 3 (Jan 1951), 68-81. Reprint; not from *BM*.

1896.   "The Dancing Rats." 25, No. 2 (Jun 1942),88-118. Nick Adams,
                M.D.; Oahu in WW II; villainous Japanese

1897.   "Nail Down the Lid." 36, No. 2 (Jly 1951), 49-58. Reprint;
                not from *BM*.

SALZ, H. Wolff

1898.   "Handwriting on the Wall." 26, No. 6 (May 1944), 103-106.

SAND, Paul

1899.   "The Advertising Criminal." 5, No. 3 (Jun 1922), 19-28.

1900.   "The Living Mask." 3, No. 4 (Jly 1921), 65-72.

1901.   "The Wire-Puller." 3, No. 3 (Jun 1921), 85-93.

SANDSTONE, Christopher

1902.   "The Knights of the Ku Klux Klan." 6, No. 5 (1 Jun 1923),
             63-70. Article; "the case for"; in special KKK issue.

SANFORD, William

1903.   "The Wife." 5, No. 9 (Dec 1922), 21. Novelty item—a "prose-
             poem."

1904.   "The Wife Stealer." 5, No. 10 (Jan 1923), 59-62. Daytime Story.

SCHERER, Ruth von Bach

1905.   "The Devil's Hoof Prints." 6, No. 7 (1 Jly 1923), 71-78.

SCHLEH, Heydorn

1906.   "The Whitest Man That Ever Lived." 12, No. 5 (Jly 1929), 85-89.

SCHNEIDERMAN, Herb

1907.   "Homicide—According to Hoyle." 34, No. 1 (Jan 1950), 45-51.

SCOTT, Earl and Marion [see also Marion SCOTT]

1908.   "Bitter Business." 13, No. 1 (Mar 1930), 31-48. Phil Craleigh.

1909.   "Brewed at Benetti's." 11, No. 12 (Feb 1929), 25-39. Debut of Phil Craleigh, once brilliant lawyer, now a drunk, given to bouts of reform; 1st of 6 PC stories.

1910.   "Bullets for Murder." 13, No. 7 (Sep 1930), 5-23. Craleigh & million-dollar robbery.

1911.   "Cameo Kirby Takes His Cue." 12, No. 4 (Jun 1929), 64-80. Debut of Cameo Kirby, reformed jewel thief; 1st of 6 CK stories.

1912.   "Cards on the Table." 11, No. 4 (Jun 1928), 105-125. Debut of ES & MS as team in *BM*; however, see Marion SCOTT.

1913.   "Craleigh Comes to Life." 12, No. 10 (Dec 1929), 46-68.

1914.   "Curtains for Porky." 11, No. 10 (Dec 1928), 74-84. Set in a theatre; Pat, actor, 1st-person narrator.

1915.   "Gat Grabs the Shadow." 12, No. 3 (May 1929), 7-18. Gat Wilson, gangster.

1916.   "Hard to Kill." 13, No. 11 (Jan 1931), 77-97. Bob McNary & Pat Ferrell, police dicks & partners.

1917.   "An Hour Before Dawn." 11, No. 7 (Sep 1928), 71-77. Escaped con, Bat Sladen; Flint Williams, detective.

1918.   "Lights Out at Benetti's. 14, No. 4 (Jun 1931), 8-23. Phil Craleigh; Benetti's is nightclub.

1919.   "The Note to Kill." 14, No. 9 (Nov 1931), 43-59. Last (6th) Cameo Kirby story.

1920.   "The Other Cameo." 12, No. 6 (Aug 1929), 53-77. Kirby.

1921.   **"Red Rendezvous." 14, No. 12 (Feb 1932), 102-118. Last (6th)** Craleigh story & final appearance of ES & MS in *BM*.

1922.   "Regards to the Chief." 12, No. 5 (Jly 1929), 29-49. Kirby.

1923.   "The Second Spartan." 12, No. 9 (Nov 1929), 53-70. Kirby.

1924.   "Seven Glass Beads." 12, No. 12 (Feb 1930), 31-49. Kirby &
             Wah Foo Wah, Chinese murderer.

SCOTT, Marion [see also Earl and Marion SCOTT]

1925.   "Folded Evidence." 10, No. 8 (Oct 1927), 32-48. Brent,
             detective from HQ, NYPD; debut of MS in *BM* but see
             under Earl and Marion SCOTT.

1926.   "Fools Rush In." 11, No. 3 (May 1928), 37-47. Steve Burke,
             tenderfoot lumberjack, 1st-person narrator.

1927.   "Poison Enters the Manse." 11, No. 11 (Jan 1929), 9-19. 1st-
             person narrator & kidnapping.

SCOTT, R[eginald] T[homas] M[aitland]

1928.   "Esses Pip Seven." 6, No. 22 (15 Feb 1924), 117-123. Billed as
             "a novelty for veterans."

1929.   "The Trap." 5, No. 1 (Apr 1922), 41-50. Secret Service Smith.

SCOTT, Walker J.

1930.   "Fatal Fridays" 5, No. 12 (15 Feb 1923), 3-26.

SEARLS, Hank

1931.   "Drop Dead Twice." 34, No. 2 (Mar 1950), 44-52.

1932.   "Nice Girls Don't Murder." 34, No. 4 (Jly 1950), 72-89. Pete
             Butler, San Francisco private eye.

SERRANO, Henry

1933.   "The Ghost of the Hesperides." 6, No. 21 (1 Feb 1924), 28-32.

SHAFER, Don Cameron

1934.   "The Hunters." 6, No. 21 (1 Feb 1924), 89-94. Tiger-hunting in
             India.

SHAW, Joseph T[hompson] [see also Mark HARPER]

1935.   "Derelict." 13, No. 12 (Feb 1931), 56-79, Pt. 1; 14, No. 1
             (Mar 1931), 46-71, Pt. 2; 14, No. 2 (Apr 1931), 80-111,
             Pt. 3; 14, No. 3 (May 1931), 60-83, Pt. 4. Murder, romance, &
             disaster on deserted ocean liner; serialization of novel pub.
             (1930).

1936.   "Fugitive." 15, No. 6 (Aug 1932), 24-47, Pt. 1; 15, No. 7 (Sep
             1932), 42-56, Pt. 2; 15, No. 8 (Oct 1932), 66-85, Pt. 3; 15,
             No. 9 (Nov 1932), 38-68, Pt. 4. Jack Henderson; set in
             Far East, e.g., Rangoon.

1937.   "Makings." 9, No. 10 (Dec 1926), 78-100. Western; Alexis
             Gregory, *nom de querre* of Prince Dimitri Gregorejovich
             Alexandrov.

SHAW, Victor

1938.   "Birds of Prey." 12, No. 6 (Aug 1929), 99-120. Getaway from
             road gang.

1939.   "For A Girl Like That." 10, No. 3 (May 1927), 47-62.
             Western detective.

1940.   "Hard Rock." 10, No. 10 (Dec 1927), 40-66. Hard-rock mining
             with Dan Craig; see also "The Tommy-Knocker."

1941.   "Pack Rats." 12, No. 3 (May 1929), 107-124.Mining.

1942.   "The Tommy-Knocker." 10, No. 12`(Feb 1928), 97-110. Dan
             Craig & hard rock mining; see also "Hard Rock."

SHAY, Reuben Jennings

1943.   "Backfire." 13, No. 3 (May 1930), 46-49.

1944.   "Taking His Time." 13, No. 11 (Jan 1931), 98-100. Short-

short; pickpockets in a small town; reprinted, *The Hard-Boiled Omnibus* (1946).

SHEA, Victor

1945.   "Charity." 7, No. 6 (Aug 1924), 125-126. Short-short.

1946.   "Mr. Pentridge Comes Down to Breakfast." 7, No. 4 (Jun 1924), 71-77.

SHEAVELY, Camford

1947.   "Shroud With a Silver Lining." 28, No. 4 (Jly 1946), 8-24, 97. Redondo Beach (Calif.) setting.

SHERMAN, L. R.

1948.   "The Last Cartridge." 9, No. 11 (Jan 1927), 55-60. The Frozen North.

1949.   "The Man Who Would Not Quit. 10, No. 11 (Jan 1928), 107-110. Far North.

1950.   "Reading Sign on the Sagebrush Kid." 12, No. 10 (Dec 1929), 92-102. Western.

SHERWOOD, Robert E[mmet]

1951.   "Film Thrillers." 5, No. 7 (Oct 1922), 126-128. Film-reviews; short-lived department; not indexed beyond this point.

SHIPPEY, Lee

1952.   "Instinct." 9, No. 6 (Aug 1926), 118-128. About a horse.

SIMMONS, Albert

1953.   "Disc-Jockey Dirge." 35, No. 2 (Nov 1950), 60-75, 126.

1954.   "Murder Is the Best Policy." 34, No. 3 (May 1950), 58-73, 128.

SIMON, Harry

1955.   "Beyond Want." 5, No. 10 (Jan 1923), 73-80.

1956.   "The Man Who Passed Judgment." 6, No. 13 (1 Oct 1923), 81-90.

SIMS, Burt

1957.   "To Each His Corpse." 30, No. 3 (Sep 1947), 94-114. Diminutive Clint Morgan, Hollywood eye.

SINCLAIR, Bertrand W[illiam]

1958.   "Ananias and the Sapphires." 14, No. 5 (Jly 1931), 31-47. Western; Andy Nason.

1959.   "Rope's End." 13, No. 10 (Dec 1930), 33-46. Western; Bill Stokes.

1960.   "The Spider in His Web." 15, No. 3 (May 1932), 34-44. Western detective story.

SIODMAK, Curt

1961.   "Donovan's Brain." 25, No. 5 (Sep 1942), 10-36, Pt. 1; 25, No. 6 (Oct 1942), 92-126, 128-129, Pt. 2; 25, No. 7 (Nov 1942), 50-85, Pt. 3. Mystery-sci-fi; pub. as novel (1943).

SMITH, Elizabeth Parker

1962.   "The Burglar." 6, No. 20 (15 Jan 1924), 118-119. Short-short.

SNOW, Walter

1963.   "Boozer Take All." 34, No. 2 (Mar 1950), 53-57.

SOLOMON, David R.

1964.   "Mind-Poison." 6, No. 7 (1 Jly 1923), 5-28. "A Complete **Novelette of Queer Humans.**"

1965.   "The Open Door." 6, No. 11 (1 Sep 1923), 87-94.

SOMERVILLE, Charles

1966.   "The Aeroplane Burglar." 6, No. 22 (15 Feb 1924), 111-116. The Manhunters; see next entry.

1967.   "After Ten Thousand Miles." 5, No. 11 ([1] Feb 1923), 39-51. 1st of 47 articles in The Manhunters series (see pp. 38-39 for data on CS); no effort has been made to sustain the supposed veracity of series; see also under Joseph GOLLOMB, Glenn G. GRAVATT, & Robert Lee HEISER.

1968.   "The Big Surprise." 5, No. 14 (15 Mar 1923), 81-89. The Man**hunters; Captain Fay, German spy, in USA in WW I.**

1969.   "By Wire." 6, No. 1 (1 Apr 1923), 61-70. Manhunters.

1970.   "The Camp Dix Mystery." 6, No. 9 (1 Aug 1923), 85-91. Manhunters.

1971.   "The 'Cat' Detective." 6, No. 21 (1 Feb 1924), 118-125. Manhunters.

1972.   "The 'Cigar Box' Mystery." 6, No. 16 (15 Nov 1923), 103-109. Manhunters.

1973.   "The Clue in the Turf." 6, No. 4 (15 May 1923), 85-96. Manhunters; "Honest John" Brunen, murder victim, & Ellis Parker, detective.

1974.   "The Clue of the Bad Check." 8, No. 1 (Mar 1925), 109-122. Manhunters.

1975.   "The Clue of the Hatband." 6, No. 16 (15 Jun 1923), 93-105. Manhunters.

1976.   "The Clue of the Tattooed Arm." 5, No. 12 (15 Feb 1923), 67-74. Manhunters.

1977.   "The Corpse in the Woods." 7, No. 11 (Jan 1925), 108-122.
         Manhunters.

1978.   "A Crook De Luxe." 6, No. 3 (1 May 1923), 61-70. Manhunters.

1979.   "The Death Ship." 7, No. 12 (Feb 1925), 118-125. Manhunters;
         schooner *Mary Beatrice* & Chinese; see important
         headnote (p. 118) & editorial note (p. 125) relating to series.

1980.   "The Double Stroke." 7, No. 3 (May 1924), 109-116. Man-
         hunters.

1981.   "The False Clue." 6, No. 23 (1 Mar 1924), 115-121. Manhunters.

1982.   "The Great Liverpool Bank Robbery." 7, No. 5 (Jly 1924),
         114-122. Manhunters; "Lord Jim" Manes & $1.5M robbery.

1983.   "The Grey-Green House." 8, No. 2 (Apr 1925), 120-127. Man-
         hunters.

1984.   "The Grim Detective." 6, No. 20 (15 Jan 1924), 73-80. Man-
         hunters.

1985.   "The Gun-Girl." 7, No. 6 (Aug 1924), 113-124. Manhunters;
         Celia Cooney & 42 stickups in 4½ months.

1986.   "The Hackettstown Mystery." 6, No. 12 (16 Sep 1923), 59-66.
         Manhunters; New Jersey.

1987.   "A Hand from the Grave." 7, No. 8 (Oct 1924), 119-128. Man-
         hunters.

1988.   "The Hand of God." 6, No. 15 (1 Nov 1923), 110-119. Man-
         hunters.

1989.   "The Honor of Shan-Tlang." 6, No. 11 (1 Sep 1923), 96-101.
         Manhunters; case told by Chief Police Inspector A.P.
         Wong, Kiangsu province, China.

1990.   "The Insomniac." 6, No. 8 (15 Jly 1923), 101-110. Manhunters.

1991.   "The Ku Klux and Crime." 6, No. 5 (1 Jun 1923), 71-75.
         Article in special KKK issue & "the case against."

1992.   "The Lively Corpse." 7, No. 4 (Jun 1924), 121-126. Manhunters.

1993.   "The Loot Ship." 6, No. 18 (15 Dec 1923), 104-110. Manhunters.

1994.   "The Man in the Little Cage." 6, No. 7 (1 Jly 1923), 106-
         114. Manhunters; the Black Hand in NYC.

1995.   "The 'Masonic Burglar.' " 8, No. 6 (Aug 1925), 120-128.
         Manhunters.

1996.   "The Mole." 6, No. 19 (1 Jan 1924), 100-105. Manhunters.

1997.   "The Murray Hill Mysteries." 8, No. 11 (Jan 1926), 99-109.
         Manhunters.

1998.   "Numbers and Threads." 7, No. 1 (1 Apr 1924), 103-109.
         Manhunters; Detective James McCoy, NYPD.

1999.   "Old Clothes." 5, No. 13 (1 Mar 1923), 88-102. Manhunters;
         "fictitious names are given...changed a bit for necessary
         reasons."

2000.   "A Reporter's Clue." 7, No. 2 (15 Apr 1924), 104-112. Man-
         hunters.

2001.   "The Riddle of Room 14." 6, No. 14 (15 Oct 1923), 79-87.
         Manhunters.

2002.   "The Rough Diamond." 7, No. 7 (Sep 1924), 109-117. Man-
         hunters.

2003.   "The Sleepless Eye." 6, No. 13 (1 Oct 1923), 91-100. Man-
         hunters.

2004.   "The Standard Oil Mystery." 8, No. 5 (Jly 1925), 118-125.
         Manhunters; see also "The Trial of Gerald Chapman" in
         issue.

2005.   "Swift Work." 8, No. 4 (Jun 1925), 118-126. Manhunters.

2006.   "The Tap on the Door." 6, No. 10 (15 Aug 1923), 90-94. Manhunters.

2007.   "The Tracking of a Fiend." 8, No. 3 (May 1925), 117-126 (?). Manhunters.

2008.   "Trapped." 8, No. 10 (Dec 1925), 118-127. Manhunters.

2009.   "The Trial of Gerald Chapman." 8, No. 5 (Jly 1925), 82-86. "Afterthoughts on a famous trial."

2010.   "The Vengeance of the Dead." 6, No. 2 (15 Apr 1923), 89-95. Manhunters.

2011.   "The Vultures' Trail." 6, No. 17 (1 Dec 1923), 81-88. Manhunters.

2012.   "A Weird Detective." 8, No. 8 (Oct 1925), 123-128. Manhunters.

2013.   "Walls Have Ears." 9, No. 3 (May 1926), 119-128. Manhunters; 47th & last piece by CS in series which began in [1] Feb 1923 issue.

2014.   "The Window of Fear." 7, No. 9 (Nov 1924), 119-127. Manhunters.

STAGG, J.J.

2015.   "The Broken Melody." 5, No. 6 (Sep 1922), 109-114. JJS's final appearance in *BM*.

2016.   "The Disappearing Diamond." 3, No. 6 (Sep 1921), 44-49.

2017.   "The Explosive Gentleman." 5, No. 5 (Aug 1922), 75-80.

2018.   "The Finger of Guilt." 5, No. 1 (Apr 1922), 19-26.

2019.   "The Frame-Up." 5, No. 2 (May 1922), 99-104.

2020.   "Getting Away Clean." 4, No. 1 (Oct 1921), 99-106.

2021.   "The Last Message." 4, No. 4 (Jan 1922), 47-53.

2022.   "The Man in Box D." 4, No. 5 (Feb 1922), 65-72.

2023.   "Murdering Uncle." 5, No. 3 (Jun 1922), 87-91.

2024.   "The Mystery of the Stains." 2, No. 5 (Feb 1921), 73-82.
         JJS's debut in *BM*.

2025.   "Post-Mortem Murder." 5, No. 4 (Jly 1922), 38-42(?).

STANTON, John

2026.   "A Fortune at Stake." 9, No. 3 (May 1926), 77-86.

STARR, H. W. [pseud. of Harold WARD; see also Ward STERLING]

2027.   "The Sheriff Takes the Stand." 4, No. 2 (Nov 1921), 76-78.
         3d of 3 stories in issue by HW/WS/HWS; see also "The
         Hand of Destiny" (WARD) & "The Whip of Death"
         (STERLING).

STARRETT, [Charles] Vincent [Emerson]

2028.   "The Case of the Shoeless Man." 3, No. 5 (Aug 1921), 95-104.

2029.   "Footsteps of Fear." 1, No. 1 (Apr 1920), 103-108. Sub-
         titled: "A Fragment Found in a Deserted Mansion."

2030.   "In the Wilds of New York." 3, No. 3 (Jun 1921), 55-61.

2031.   "The Open Window." 2, No. 6 (Mar 1921), 85-94.

STEEN, Sallie Pate

2032.   "The Parrot's Cage." 8, No. 1 (Mar 1925), 63-73.

STERLING, Stewart [pseud. of Prentice WINCHELL]

2033.   "Blow the Man Down." 25, No. 3 (Jly 1942), 11-40. Special
        Squad (Harbor Police), NYPD, & war effort sabotage;
        see p. 8 for letter from SS for background on story.

2034.   "Bullets, Back to Back." 25, No. 8 (Dec 1942), 10-34. Special
        Squad (Pickpocket & Confidence Bureau), NYPD;
        Detective Gaynor; see pp. 8 & 129 for background on story.

2035.   "Coat of Many Killers." 23, No. 8 (Dec 1940), 42-66. Special
        Squad (Safe-and-Loft).

2036.   "Dead as a Duck." 26, No. 1 (Jly 1943), 8-35. Special Squad
        (Air Police); last (of 9) Squad stories & SS's final appear-
        ance in *BM*; see pp. 6 & 129 for letter from SS on story.

2037.   "Don't Bury Me at All." 24, No. 7 (Nov 1941), 11-40. Special
        Squad (Homicide).

2038.   "Kill a Man Dead." 22, No. 4 (Jly 1939), 96-107. Vince
        Mallie; 2d of 3 VM stories; see also "Strictly for Suckers"
        & "Straight Across the Board."

2039.   "Kindly Omit Flowers." 24, No. 11 (Mar 1942), 98-116,
        118-126, 128. Sergeant Helen Dixon, temporarily assigned
        to Special Squad (Homicide).

2040.   "Over My Dead Body." 24, No. 2 (Jun 1941), 10-38. Special
        Squad (Bomb & Forgery); see p. 8 for note by SS on story.

2041.   "The Platinum Pig." 23, No. 11 (Mar 1941), 90-127. Special
        Squad (Emergency).

2042   "Straight Across the Board." 22, No. 9 (Dec 1939), 88-101.
        Vince Mallie at the races; 3d of 3 VM stories; see also
        "Strictly for Suckers" & "Kill a Man Dead."

2043.   "Strictly for Suckers." 22, No. 2 (May 1939), 98-111. 1st of
        3 Vince Mallie stories (see previous entry); SS's debut in
        BM.

2044.   "Ten Carats of Lead." 23, No. 4 (Aug 1940), 26-49. Special

Squad (Pawnshop Detail), NYPD, & Detective Mike
Hansard; 1st (of 9) Squad stories.

STERLING, Ward [pseud. of Harold WARD; see also H. W. STARR]

2045.   "Bram Dwyer's Bonfire." 5, No. 2 (May 1922), 93-98.

2046.   "The Brand of Cain." 5, No. 1 (Apr 1922), 91-96. 2d of 3
stories in issue by WS/HW; see also "The Man Who Was
Two" (WARD) & "Hankenson's Perfect Crime"
(STERLING).

2047.   "The Catspaw." 5, No. 5 (Aug 1922), 114-122. 3d of 3 stories
by WS/HW in issue; see also "The Failure" (WARD) &
"The Police Sometimes Guess Wrong" (WARD).

2048.   "The Concrete Facts About Thomas Hancock." 5, No. 7 (Oct
1922), 31-34. Last story by WS (pseud.) in *BM*.

2049.   "The Devil Takes a Hand." 1, No. 6 (Sep 1920), 77-80. 2d of 3
stories in issue by WS/HW; see also "The Long Arm of
God" (STERLING) & "The Man Who Would Not Die"
(WARD).

2050.   "The Golden Slipper Mystery." 2, No. 6 (Mar 1921), 43-48.
1st of 2 stories in issue by WS/HW; see also "The Man in
the Trunk" (WARD).

2051.   "Hankenson's Perfect Crime." 5, No. 1 (Apr 1922), 120-123.
3d of 3 stories in issue by WS/HW; see also "The Man Who
Was Two" (WARD) & "The Brand of Cain" (STERLING).

2052.   "The Letter in Pedro's Skull." 2, No. 5 (Feb 1921), 51-61.
2d of 2 stories in issue by WS/HW; see also "The Trego
Circus Mystery" (WARD).

2053.   "The Long Arm of God." 1, No. 6 (Sep 1920), 29-38. 1st of
3 stories in issue by WS/HW; see also "The Devil Takes a
Hand" (STERLING) & "The Man Who Would Not Die"
(WARD).

2054.   "The Mystery of the Chessmen." 3, No. 5 (Aug 1921), 35-39.

1st of 2 stories in issue by WS/HW; see also "The Ship on Dunbar's Breast" (WARD).

055.   "The Mystery of Devil's Nest." 1, No. 4 (Jly 1920), 53-63. Debut of WS (pseud.) in *BM*; 2d of 2 stories in issue by WS/HW; see also "The Mysterious 'Captain Who?' " (WARD).

2056.   "The Passing of Bloody Dan." 4, No. 5 (Feb 1922), 119-123. 2d of 2 stories by WS/HW in issue; see also "The Attorney for the Defense" (WARD).

2057.   "The Phantom Bullet." 4, No. 4 (Jan 1922), 61-66. 1st of 2 stories in issue by WS/HW; see also " 'Great Minds Run—' " (WARD).

2058.   "The Riddle of the Tattooed Men." 3, No. 1 (Apr 1921), 55-60. 2d of 2 stories by WS/WH in issue; see also "Under the Crimson Skull" (WARD).

2059.   "The Strange Story of Martin Colby." 1, No. 5 (Aug 1920), 89-94. 3d of 3 stories in issue by WS/HW; see also "Jim Dickinson's Head" (WARD) & "The Valley Where Dead Men Live" (WARD).

2060.   "The Whip of Death." 4, No. 2 (Nov 1921), 57-64. 2d of 3 stories in issue by WS/HW/H. W. STARR; see also "The Hand of Destiny" (WARD) & "The Sheriff Takes the Stand" (STARR).

STEWART, Solon K.

2061.   "The Riddle of the Bonita." 7, No. 8 (Oct 1924), 61-75, Pt. 1; 7, No. 9 (Nov 1924), 88-106, Pt. 2. Mexico in days of Madero & Diaz.

2062.   "The Trail of the Feathered Snake." 7, No. 11 (Jan 1925), 9-41. "A Complete Mystery Novelette."

STINSON, H. H.

2063. "All-American Menace." 21, No. 10 (Jan 1939), 64-88. O'Hara.

2064. "Aw, Lieutenant!" 20, No. 3 (May 1937), 114-123. Sergeant Rockey, cop.

2065. "Calling All Hearses." 24, No. 3 (Jly 1941), 78-97, 130. O'Hara.

2066. "Clamp Down." 23, No. 2 (Jun 1940), 102-128. O'Hara.

2067. "Climb Back In Your Coffin." 24, No. 5 (Sep 1941), 43-61.

2068. "Get Your Own Corpse." 26, No. 11 (Mar 1945), 61-77. O'Hara.

2069. "Give the Man Rope." 16, No. 2 (Apr 1933), 8-34. Ken O'Hara, fighting reporter on Los Angeles *Tribune*; 1st KO'H (of 14) story & debut of HHS in *BM*.

2070. "A Guy Has a Thousand Dollars." 19, No. 9 (Nov 1936), 16-41. Pete Jorn.

2071. "Lay Off, O'Hara." 19, No. 12 (Feb 1937), 44-69. O'Hara.

2072. "Murder Is a Pleasure." 32, No. 1 (Sep 1948), 6-29. Sam Terry, p.i., & partner, Sol Hirshberg; L. A. setting; HHS's final appearance in *BM*.

2073. "Murder's No Libel." 30, No. 2 (Jly 1947), 28-54. Last (14th) O'Hara story; he is now press agent for Hotel Diplomat.

2074. "Murder Sweepstakes." 22, No. 4 (Jly 1939), 8-30. O'Hara; see p. 7 for letter from HHS about O'H.

2075. "My Dough Says Murder." 20, No. 8 (Oct 1937), 90-117. O'Hara.

2076. "No Substitute for Murder." 31, No. 2 (Mar 1948), 8-29. Mac Burnett, L. A. private shamus, & ex-wife Maggie.

2077. "A Noose for Little Nemo." 26, No. 12 (May 1945), 42-61. Sergeant Joe Terry, home on leave.

2078.　　　"North of the Border." 23, No. 8 (Dec 1940), 70-93. O'Hara.

2079.　　　"Nothing Personal." 19, No. 5 (Jly 1936), 30-56. O'Hara.

2080.　　　"Ol' Davil O'Hara." 21, No. 6 (Sep 1938), 8-30. O'Hara.

2081.　　　"Please Kill Me Carefully." 30, No. 4 (Nov 1947), 96-115. 129-130. Ned Healey, L. A. private eye.

2082.　　　"This Murder's On Me." 22, No. 10 (Jan 1940), 58-80. Van Hogan, Worldwide Agency dick, 1st-person narrator.

2083.　　　"Three Apes from the East." 21, No. 1 (Mar 1938), 52-77. Kerry Thorne, detective in L. A.

2084.　　　"Trivial, Like Murder." 17, No. 10 (Dec 1934), 87-111. O'Hara.

2085.　　　"Two Rings for Murder." 26, No. 3 (Nov 1943), 47-72. Sam South, loan company proprietor, & Nazi spies.

2086.　　　"Unholy Matrimony." 28, No. 3 (May 1946), 26-39.

2087.　　　"You Gotta Live Right." 21, No. 12 (Mar 1939), 66-82. Arizona.

2088.　　　"You're the Crime in My Coffin." 28, No. 2 (Mar 1946), 52-68. Gerry Fowler of Fox, Fox, Shapiro & Fox, law firm.

2089.　　　"Your Corpses Are Shwoing." 27, No. 3 (Nov 1945), 10-32. O'Hara.

STIRLING, Stewart [possible pseud. of Stewart STERLING?]

2090.　　　"Boomerang Dice." 14, No. 2 (Apr 1931), 33-41. Johnny Hi Gear, a.k.a. K-5, Undercover Agent; 1st of 8 Hi Gear stories & SS's debut in *BM*.

2091.　　　"Cold Blood." 14, No. 5 (Jly 1931), 48-57. Hi Gear.

2092.　　　"One for the Book." 15, No. 2 (Apr 1932), 64-75. Hi Gear.

2093.　　　"Pushover." 14, No. 7 (Sep 1931), 72-82. Hi Gear & boxing fix.

2094.　　　"600 to 1." 14, No. 10 (Dec 1931), 91-101. Hi Gear & King Collis, Negro policy king; racial slurs.

2095.　　　"Starita Takes a Rumble." 16, No. 3 (May 1933), 71-79. Last (8th) Hi Gear caper & SS's final appearance in *BM*.

2096.　　　"Table Stakes." 14, No. 11 (Jan 1932), 76-86. Hi Gear.

2097.　　　"Two-Timer." 14, No. 4 (Jun 1931), 24-33. Hi Gear.

STOCKARD, Willett

2098.　　　"A Dead Girl in the Moonlight." 5, No. 14 (15 Mar 1923), 37-44. Rural setting; dead girl avenged by badman.

2099.　　　"Hutch Blood." 6, No. 13 (1 Oct 1923), 53-61. Billed as "a real *Black Mask* weirdity."

2100.　　　"The One-Man Mob." 6, No. 10 (15 Aug 1923), 37-43.

2101.　　　"Punctual." 6, No. 17 (1 Dec 1923), 74-80.

2102.　　　"A Shot in the Fog." 6, No. 12 (15 Sep 1923), 67-74. Ad calls this "one of our most unusual stories to date."

STOKES, Horace Winston

2103.　　　"The Devil's Hollow. 5, No. 11 ([1] Feb 1923), 56-61.

STORY, Walter Scott

2104.　　　"Bulling the Bulls." 1, No. 6 (Sep 1920), 121-126.

2105.　　　"Bristow's Sunset." 6, No. 24 (15 Mar 1924), 120-125. Death by snakebite (copperheads).

STOVER, Herbert Elisha

2106.   "Fangs." 6, No. 22 (15 Feb 1924), 64-68.

2107.   "The Guillotine." 6, No. 5 (1 Jun 1923), 84-89. In special
            KKK issue but not Klan piece; see p. 128 for letter from
            HES.

2108.   "The Rattle of Fear." 6, No. 12 (15 Sep 1923), 33-37. Billed as
            "a man, a wife, and an idea."

STRAGNELL, Gregory, M.D.

2109.   "Our Dreams." 5, No. 13 (1 Mar 1923), 117-120. Short-lived
            Department devoted to "one of the newest sciences—
            psychoanalysis"; not Indexed beyond this point.

STRATTON, Ted

2110.   "Accounts Deceivable." 28, No. 1 (Feb 1946), 57-59.

2111.   "Call the Undertaker." 26, No. 5 (Mar 1944), 98-105. Trigg.

STREET, MacAllister

2112.   "$1000 a Day." 19, No. 12 (Feb 1937), 116-122. Hade, private
            'tec.

STUEBER, William H.

2113.   "Bill Comes Home." 10, No. 10 (Dec 1927), 116-120. Man
            just out of the Big House.

SURREY, George

2114.   "The King of Pearls." 9, No. 5 (Jly 1926), 100-108.

SUTER, J. Paul

2115.   "The Absent-Minded Cannibal." 10, No. 6 (Aug 1927), 5-25. The
            Reverend McGregor Daunt; see p. 128 for info, with

photo, on JPS.

2116.　"Beyond Justice." 6, No. 14 (15 Oct 1923), 45-51. Daytime Story.

2117.　"By His Own Hand." 6, No. 12 (15 (Sep 1923), 38-43. Advertised as "a real ghost story"; JPS's debut in *BM*.

2118.　"The Cat Mocker." 8, No. 1 (Mar 1925), 33-48. Reverend Daunt.

2119.　" 'Caught.' " 7, No. 5 (Jly 1924), 104-113.

2120.　"The Ether Demon." 8, No. 6 (Aug 1925), 97-119. Hospital mystery; Daunt.

2121.　"The Foot-Washing Baptist." 9, No. 6 (Aug 1926), 94-117. Daunt.

2122.　"The German Field Glass." 8, No. 10 (Dec 1925), 64-84. Daunt.

2123.　"The Grandover Diamond." 9, No., 7 (Sep 1926), 76-98. Daunt.

2124.　"The King of the Earth." 8, No. 5 (Jly 1925), 47-66. Daunt.

2125.　"The Little Blond Nightmare." 7, No. 11 (Jan 1925), 64-86. Reverend Daunt again.

2126.　"The Loud Voice of Time." 7, No. 12 (Feb 1925), 35-54. Daunt & one of his problems.

2127.　"The Man in the Bus." 10, No. 8 (Oct 1927), 70-90. Daunt.

2128.　"The Problem of the Man Who Sowed the Wind." 7, No. 9 (Nov 1924), 107-118. Debut of The Reverend McGregor Daunt, "clergyman by profession and detective by choice"; 1st of (15) McGD stories; see p. 118 for a "letter" from McGD himself!

2129.　"The Tail of the Serpent." 9, No. 12 (Feb 1927), 108-128. Daunt; robbery & murder in archeological museum.

2130.　"Ten Dead Policemen." 12, No. 1 (Mar 1929), 47-66. Last

(15th) Daunt story & last story by JPS in *BM*.

2131.   "The Terror by Night." 9, No. 2 (Apr 1926), 56-68, Pt. 1; 9, No. 3 (May 1926), 102-118, Pt. 2. Daunt.

2132.   "The Uncomfortable Buddha." 8, No. 3 (May 1925), 32-54. Daunt.

SUTHERLAND, Harry M.

2133.   "The Shot in the Blizzard." 5, No. 2 (May 1922), 113-122.

2134.   "The Weeping Killer." 4, No. 3 (Dec 1921), 30-32. Short-short.

SUTTON, Michael

2135.   "Concerto for Guns." 30, No. 2 (Jly 1947), 66-99. Johnny Dillon, L. A. private 'tec, 1st-person narrator.

2136.   "Jail Will Be Lonely." 27, No. 1 (Jly 1945), 53-61. Steve Duncan, hotel bouncer.

SWAIN, John D.

2137.   "Mahogany Brogues." 3, No. 1 (Apr 1921), 93-97. Cocaine addict kills bully on NYC subway.

2138.   "The Man Who Knew Too Much." 4, No. 3 (Dec 1921), 107-112.

SWETT, Oliver

2139.   "Crossed Lead." 12, No. 5 (Jly 1929), 61-84. Western.

T

TAHNEY, C.G. [pseud of Charles Green; do not confuse with Charles M. GREEN]

2140.   "And a Little Child Shall Bleed Them." 24, No. 10 (Feb 1942), 76-103. Nickie & Uncle Pat; see "Satan in Short Pants" for data on this series.

2141.   "A Brain for Sale." 26, No. 4 (Jan 1944), 8-48. Nickie.

2142.   "Murder in Ten Easy Lessons." 24, No. 3 (Jly 1941), 32-59.
          Nickie, a.k.a. Sherlock in short pants.

2143.   "Satan in Short Pants." 24, No. 1 (May 1941), 82-103.
          Debut of Nickie & slow-witted Uncle Pat, private dick,
          formerly K. O. Sherwin, middleweight champ.

2144.   "There's Dough in Murder." 27, No. 4 (Jan 1946), 10-36.
          Last Nickie story.

TANQUERY, William

2145.   "At Stillson's." 21, No. 5 (Aug 1938), 116-122. Newspaper
          reporter; Stillson's—a bar.

2146.   "Getting Maizie." 22, No. 11 (Feb 1940), 75-85. Mac MacGrath
          & Jennie Komorawski, rival reporters.

TAYLOR, Eric

2147.   "Boulevard Louis." 11, No. 9 (Nov 1928), 68-77. "Boulevard
          Louis" Meyer, international jewel thief, in NYC.

2148.   "The Calloused Hand." 19, No. 5 (Jly 1936), 10-29. Hastings
          ("Hasty") Sparks, a dick with World Detective Agency.

2149.   "Jungle Justice." 11, No. 4 (Jun 1928), 98-104. Hobo jungle
          setting; ET's debut in *BM*.

2150.   "The Murder Rap." 11, No. 5 (Jly 1928), 120-128. "Tip"
          Banning, sneak thief in 'Frisco.

2151.   "Murder to Music." 19, No. 3 (May 1936), 73-97. Jess Arno,
          private eye.

2152.   "A Pinch of Snuff." 12, No. 4 (Jun 1929), 53-63. Irene, lady-
          crook in Montreal (Canada).

2153.   "Red Death." 18, No. 10 (Dec 1935), 36-59. Gene Terry,
          detective, Metropolitan Agency.

TAYLOR, Joe

2154. "Alias 'Claire.' " 6, No. 3 (1 May 1923), 94-101. My Underworld series.

2155. "At Eleven." 6, No. 7 (1 Jly 1923), 98-105. My Underworld; portrait-drawing of JT, p. 98.

2156. "The Doublecross." 6, No. 14 (15 Oct 1923), 62-72. My Underworld.

2157. "The Fixer." 5, No. 11 ([1] Feb 1923), 77-91. My Underworld; billed as fiction.

2158. "The Life of a Hold-Up Man." 5, No. 8 (Nov 1922), 41-48. 1st (of 12) tales in My Underworld series; JT is advertised as 'Ex-Automobile Bandit" with 15 years' experience in crime; early-on, listed as fact; later, as fiction; see p. 40 for photo-portait of JT.

2159. "The Meanest Thief." 6, No. 2 (15 Apr 1923), 52. Brief-brief.

2160. "Monty's Last Job." 7, No. 4 (Jun 1924), 109-120. 12th & last piece in My Underworld series; JT's final appearance in *BM*.

2161. "My Underworld." 5, No. 9 (Dec 1922), 73-81. 2d in series by Ex-Auto Bandit; see next entry.

2162. "My Underworld." 5, No. 10 (Jan 1923), 89-94. 3d in series; not a serial, however; see previous entry.

2163. "Playing Both Ends." 5, No. 14 (15 Mar 1923), 67-73. My Underworld; fiction.

2164. "Ragged Seams." 6, No. 4 (15 May 1923), 97-105. My Underworld.

2165. "Stumbling Feet." 5, No. 12 (15 Feb 1923), 98-102. My Underworld.

2166. "Tell It to Toots." 7, No. 3 (May 1924), 117-126. My Underworld; "fictionized experiences of a bandit—by an ex-bandit."

TAYLOR, Joe and G[eorge] W. SUTTON, Jr.

2167.   "Burnt Hands." 6, No. 1 (1 Apr 1923), 96-104, Pt. 1; 6, No. 2 (15 Apr 1923), 79-88, Pt. 2 (subtitled, "A Splinter of Steel"). GWS was then editor of *BM*.

TAYLOR, Merlin Moore

2168.   "Chains That Bind." 6, No. 22 (15 Feb 1924), 47-63. Billed as "A gripping detective novelette."

2169.   "Ivywild." 6, No. 24 (15 Mar 1924), 41-66, Pt. 1; 7, No. 1 (1 Apr 1924), 67-93, Pt. 2. Family secret in ancient English castle.

2170.   "One of Five." 6, No. 9 (1 Aug 1923), 48-63, Pt. 1; 6, No. 10 (15 Aug 1923), 95-108, Pt. 2; 6, No. 11 (1 Sep 1923), 102-115, Pt. 3.

2171.   "Ripe Peach Odor." 11, No. 4 (Jun 1928), 72-81. MMT's last story in *BM*.

2172.   "The Wheel Within the Wheel." 1, No. 2 (May 1920), 112-117. MMT's debut in *BM*.

2173.   "The Young Squirt." 6, No. 14 (15 Oct 1923), 7-28. Advertised as "A Complete Mystery Novelette."

TEPPERMAN, Emile C.

2174.   "Death for Sale." 22, No. 2 (May 1939), 68-88. Vacuum cleaner salesman.

2175.   "Death—to the Highest Bidder." 22, No. 1 (Apr 1939), 58-81. Broadway auction house; see p. 57 for note by ECT on story.

2176.   "Stormy Nocturne." 20, No. 6 (Aug 1937), 67-73. 1st-person narrator.

THIBAULT, David

2177.	"The Contract." 10, No. 12 (Feb 1928), 117-128. Louisiana lumber swamps in Mississippi Delta; Irish dialect.

2178.	"Muddy Waters." 11, No. 2 (Apr 1928), 66-73. Fighting crooks against Mississippi-flood background.

THOMAS, Merle

2179.	"The Lettered Telegraph." 10, No. 8 (Oct 1927), 107-112. RR holdup & telegraph operator's daring.

THOMAS, Peter G.

2180.	"The Bell in the Fog." 13, No. 1 (Mar 1930), 116-128. River pirates in NYC.

THOMEY, Tedd

2181.	"Come Hell or Hot Water!" 34, No. 1 (Jan 1950), 67-75.

2182.	"Homicide Honeymoon." 34, No. 3 (May 1950), 39-48. Mario Giovani, rookie cop.

THORNE, J. Frederic

2183.	"The Death Warrant." 4, No. 1 (Oct 1921), 67-97, Pt. 1; 4, No. 2 (Nov 1921), 89-105, Pt. 2. "A Mystery Novel"; 2d of 2 stories (Nov 1921) by JFT in issue; see also "The Man Who Died Twice.

2184.	"In the Jury Room." 3, No. 6 (Sep 1921), 95-105.

2185.	"The Man Who Died Twice." 4, No. 2 (Nov 1921), 41-50. Narrated by defendant to jury; murder of twins in Seattle & Hong Kong; 1st of 2 stories by JFT in issue; see also "The Death Warrant," Pt. 2.

2186.	"The Man Who Was Seven." 1, No. 5 (Aug 1920), 3-25. "Complete Novelette."

2187.	"The Multiple Murder Mystery." 4, No. 4 (Jan 1922), 83-98,

Pt. 1; 4, No. 5 (Feb 1922), 73-93, Pt. 2; 4, No. 6 (Mar 1922), 89-104, Pt. 3. JFT's final appearance in *BM*.

2188. "The Prisoner Speaks." 4, No. 3 (Dec 1921), 3-19. "A Complete Mystery Novelette."

2189. "Who and Why?" 1, No. 1 (Apr 1920), 3-37. Billed as a complete short novel; *"Black Mask* presents...to its readers...by all odds the best mystery novel of the last three years"; story has the honor of being the lead story in 1, No. 1.

THORNE, Pearce

2190. "A Jury of His Peers." 6, No. 19 (1 Jan 1924), 24. Brief-brief.

TICHENOR, L. King

2191. "False Impressions." 10, No. 5 (Jly 1927), 57-69. Told in prison near execution time.

2192. " 'A Just Price.' " 8, No. 7 (Sep 1925), 71-84. The Senator.

2193. "The Law Steps In." 8, No. 4 (Jun 1925), 105-117. A confidence yarn.

2194. "A Thousand Dollar Bill." 8, No. 3 (May 1925), 73-82.

2195. "Twisted Evidence." 8, No. 5 (Jly 1925), 93-108. "A detective story."

TINGLEY, Richard Hoadley

2196. "The Sultan's Diamond." 6, No. 23 (1 Mar 1924), 122-125.

TINSLEY, Theodore A.

2197. "Ball and Chain." 15, No. 12 (Feb 1933), 28-39. Jerry Tracy, wisecracking columnist on the daily *Planet*.

198. "Behind the Column." 18, No. 6 (Aug 1935), 76-99. Tracy; column used for numbers racket.

199. "Beyond All Light." 15, No. 11 (Jan 1933), 51-61. Tracy.

200. "Body Snatcher." 18, No. 12 (Feb 1936), 37-57. Tracy.

201. "Death By Arrangement." 18, No. 1 (Mar 1935), 46-71. Max Ward, "the famous little Broadway ticket broker"; erroneously titled "Death By Appointment" on TofC p.

202. "Five Spot." 18, No. 9 (Nov 1935), 65-86. Tracy.

203. "Guide to Murder." 22, No. 3 (Jun 1939), 6-28. Tracy; murder at New York World's Fair.

204. "He Asked for It." 16, No. 3 (May 1933), 59-70. Tracy.

205. "Help Wanted." 16, No. 1 (Mar 1933), 108-119. Tracy.

206. "Keep On Asking." 18, No. 3 (May 1935), 78-95. Tracy.

207. "Little Guy." 19, No. 11 (Jan 1937), 46-71. Tracy.

208. "Make It Murder." 21, No. 6 (Sep 1938), 40-65. Tracy.

209. "Manhattan Whirligig." 20, No. 2 (Apr 1937), 10-37. Tracy.

210. "Murder Is News." 20, No. 6 (Aug 1937), 6-37. Tracy.

211. "Murder Maze." 19, No. 7 (Sep 1936), 103-125. Tracy meets a Coney Island "Hindu."

212. "Murderer's Guest." 18, No. 5 (Jly 1935), 6-30. Tracy.

213. "My Candle Burns." 23, No. 1 (Apr 1940), 4-29. Last (of 25) Jerry Tracy stories & TT's final appearance in *BM*.

214. "No More Limericks." 21, No. 2 (Apr 1938), 44-68. Tracy.

2215.   "Park Avenue Item." 15, No. 10 (Dec 1932), 28-37. Tracy.

2216.   "Party from Detroit." 15, No. 8 (Oct 1932), 54-65. 1st (of 25) **Jerry Tracy capers; columnist on (NYC)** *Planet;* **"mixer with poor and rich, the crooked and the straight, trailer of trouble and happiness"; TAT's debut in** *BM.*

2217.   "Smoke." 17, No. 4 (Jun 1934), 60-82. Tracy.

2218.   "Somebody Stole My Pal." 16, No. 5 (Jly 1933), 49-60. Tracy.

2219.   "South Wind." 15, No. 9 (Nov 1932), 27-37. Tracy in North Carolina; see *BM,* Mar 1933, p. 124 for note on story; reprinted, *The Hard-Boiled Omnibus* (1946).

2220.   "Station K—I—L—L." 21, No. 8 (Nov 1938), 18-42. Tracy.

2221.   "Storm Signal." 19, No. 4 (Jun 1936), 83-103. Tracy.

2222.   "Ticketed for Death." 18, No. 7 (Sep 1935), 51-75. Tracy.

TIPTON, Everett H.

2223.   "El Tigre *Was* Bad." 11, No. 6 (Aug 1928), 106-115. Bobby Warren, reporter, in Juárez (Chihuahua).

2224.   "Hunted." 11, No. 3 (May 1928), 94-101. Western.

2225.   "Killers Should Run." 11, No. 1 (Mar 1928), 74-81. Western.

2226.   "Leather Mask and Cowhide Vest." 10, No. 12 (Feb 1928), 60-68. Western.

2227.   "Noose Law." 11, No. 2 (Apr 1928), 74-81. Western.

2228.   "One Bad Man." 10, No. 9 (Nov 1927), 78-85. Western; EHT's debut in *BM.*

2229.   "A Song in the Night." 11, No. 8 (Oct 1928), 47-53. Border tale; Juárez; EHT's final appearance in *BM.*

TOOMBS, Robert P.

2230.   "A Kill for the Bride." 34, No. 3 (May 1950), 74-98, 129.
             Billed as a "Suspense-Packed Crime-Adventure
             Novelette."

2231.   "Not Necessarily Dead." 33, No. 3 (Sep 1949), 84-103.

2232.   "These Dead Hands Reaching." 33, No. 2 (Jly 1949), 110-130.

TOPHAM, Thomas

2233.   "The Confession of Brick McTigue." 9, No. 1 (Mar 1926),
             48-61. Brick has a gift of gab.

TORREY, Roger

2234.   "Always a Lady." 20, No. 1 (Mar 1937), 57-65. Lieutenant
             Delehanty, a cop.

2235.   "Beginner's Luck." 17, No..11 (Jan 1935), 98-110. 1st of 4
             stories starring 1st-person narrator Mike O'Dell, ex-
             wrestler, now bodyguard.

2236.   "Black and White." 22, No. 12 (Mar 1940), 27-43. Allen, in-
             vestigator for United Indemnity, 1st-person narrator;
             murdered police dog, a Filipino, jewel thieves, et al.

2237.   "Blackmail Is an Ugly Word." 16, No. 8 (Oct 1933), 83-104.
             Dal Prentice; see "Police Business" for data on series.

2238.   "Border Blockade." 19, No. 6 (Aug 1936), 56-71. George
             Killeen; California, i.e., Mexican border.

2239.   "The Breaks." 17, No. 7 (Sep 1934), 108-124. Prentice.

2240.   "The Case-Hardened Samaritan." 16, No. 2 (Apr 1933), 95-110.
             Prentice—"hard when it comes to handling killers."

2241.   "Clean Sweep." 16, No. 12 (Feb 1934), 71-86. Prentice; re-
             printed, *The Hard-Boiled Omnibus* (1946).

2242.   "Concealed Weapon." 21, No. 9 (Dec 1938), 80-95. Marge
         Chalmers & Pat McCarthy; see "Jail Bait" for info
         on series.

2243.   "Dangerous Crossing." 18, No. 6 (Aug 1935), 100-111. Killeen
         plays at "framing the framer."

2244.   "Dead Men Can Talk." 18, No. 4 (Jun 1935), 35-47. Last
         (11th) Prentice caper.

2245.   "Death Calls the Hand." 22, No. 10 (Jan 1940), 82-99. Marge
         & McCarthy; see p. 81 for letter from RT on story.

2246.   "Death Plays Tag." 21, No. 5 (Aug 1938), 72-89. McCarthy.

2247.   "Gardenia Kill." 21, No. 7 (Oct 1938), 100-120. McCarthy.

2248.   "Hay Ride." 20, No. 7 (Sep 1937), 35-56. McCarthy & Co.

2249.   "Hay Time." 22, No. 5 (Aug 1939), 84-102. Marge & McCarthy.

2250.   "Hell and High Water." 24, No. 12 (Apr 1942), 66-84. Bryant;
         4th & last CCC novelette; see pp. 8 & 129 for letter
         from RT about CCC; RT's final appearance in *BM*.

2251.   "Hillbilly Stuff." 20, No. 4 (Jun 1937), 72-93. Shean Connell,
         private peep; 1st of 4 SC stories.

2252.   "Hospital Case." 16, No. 6 (Aug 1933), 54-72. Prentice.

2253.   "The Irish Have It." 19, No. 10 (Dec 1936), 86-106. McCarthy.

2254.   "Jail Bait." 19, No. 8 (Oct 1936), 38-59. 1st (of 14) in McCarthy
         series, with Marge Chalmers often his "sidekick"; he is
         ex-NYC cop, ex-agency man (Chicago & St. Louis) who
         dislikes cops.

2255.   "Just a Nice Girl." 20, No. 6 (Aug 1937), 74-92. Connell.

2256.   "Kill That Witness." 22, No. 7 (Oct 1939), 48-64. McCarthy.

2257.   "Law and Disorder." 17, No. 9 (Nov 1934), 62-85. Prentice;
         see next entry for same title.

2258. "Law and Disorder." 23, No. 12 (Apr 1941), 73-89. Johnny Riordan in Miller's Landing; see previous entry for same title.

2259. "Mail Racket." 19, No. 9 (Nov 1936), 113-126. Last (5th) George Killeen tale.

2260. "Murder—For No Reason." 23, No. 4 (Aug 1940), 6-25. Debut of Bryant (4 stories), a regular U.S. Army man, who works in a CCC camp; 1st-person narrator.

2261. "Murder for Your Money." 22, No. 11 (Feb 1940), 56-74. 14th & last in McCarthy-Marge series.

2262. "Murder Frame." 19, No. 11 (Jan 1937), 116-124. Cassidy, cop, is framed.

2263. "Murder in Jail." 16, No. 7 (Sep 1933), 29-45. Prentice.

2264. "Murder's Never Funny." 19, No. 12 (Feb 1937), 70-91. Marge & Pat McCarthy.

2265. "Murder Link." 21, No. 3 (May 1938), 78-97. Marge & Pat.

2266. "A Night in Menlo." 16, No. 1 (Mar 1933), 49-55. Western; Deputy Marshal Henry Corbin in town of Menlo.

2267. "No Gashes Were Deep." 23, No. 10 (Feb 1941), 60-79. Bryant —at another CCC camp.

2268. "Nose Trouble." 18, No. 5 (Jly 1935), 91-102. Mike O'Dell.

2269. "Off-Stage." 17, No. 1 (Mar 1934), 85-97. Killeen.

2270. "One Good Turn." 20, No. 9 (Nov 1937), 94-111. Connell.

2271. "Party Murder." 17, No. 2 (Apr 1934), 84-99. Prentice.

2272. "Police Business." 15, No. 11 (Jan 1933), 75-90. Debut of Magna City police dick, Dal Prentice, one tough guy; 1st (of 11) DP stories & RT's debut in *BM*.

2273.   "Private War." 16, No. 11 (Jan 1934), 28-41. Debut (of 5) of George Killeen, private 'tec in L.A., & 1st-person narrator; with Lieutenant McFee, Homicide.

2274.   "Rat Runaround." 20, No. 3 (May 1937), 96-113. Marge & McCarthy.

2275.   "Relative Trouble." 20, No. 11 (Jan 1938), 90-112. Last (of 4) Shean Connell yarns.

2276.   "Robbery—With Violence." 16, No. 4 (Jun 1933), 43-59. Prentice.

2277.   "Sanitarium for Sale." 20, No. 12 (Feb 1938), 74-93. McCarthy & Marge.

2278.   "Snakes in the Grass." 24, No. 2 (Jun 1941), 80-97. Bryant; in a Southern CCC camp.

2279.   "Thirty Grand Reward." 22, No. 8 (Nov 1939), 97-104. Cop-hating Joe Evans, newsboy.

2280.   "Too Many Angles." 23, No. 2 (Jun 1940), 40-70. Donovan, the "hard-luck shamus."

2281.   "Too Much Action." 19, No. 5 (Jly 1936), 82-100. 4th & last Mike O'Dell.

2282.   "The Vanishing Miss Vance." 23, No. 1 (Apr 1940), 98-112. Joe Mahoney, private eye, 1st-person.

2283.   "Win—Place—and Show." 18, No. 3 (May 1935), 39-53. O'Dell.

TREAT, Lawrence

2284.   "A Night's Work." 21, No. 4 (Jun 1938), 100-123.

2285.   "Once Upon a Crime." 24, No. 12 (Apr 1942), 108-128. Bim Marlow, State Trooper; LT's final piece in *BM*.

2286.   "Sing a Song of Murder." 22, No. 3 (Jun 1939), 102-111.
         G-Man.

2287.   "Swampers' Gold." 22, No. 5 (Aug 1939), 103-112. Pirate
         treasure.

2288.   "Three Magic Bullets." 20, No. 7 (Sep 1937), 117-124. Barry
         Denton, ex-prosecuting attorney & racket-buster; LT's
         debut in *BM*.

TRUSLOW, Fergus

2289.   "The Corpse with the Green Hair." 31, No. 2 (Mar 1948),
         30-39. Forbes, studio trouble-shooter in Hollywood,
         1st-person narrator.

2290.   "Death on Ice." 27, No. 1 (Jly 1945), 79-86. Hendricks,
         rookie cop in L.A.; FT's debut in *BM*.

2291.   "Hardboot Homicide." 27, No. 3 (Nov 1945), 45-51, 89-90.
         Ex-jockey Nick Apelman.

2292.   "The Killing Was Mutuel." 28, No. 2 (Mar 1946), 76-88, 90-
         92. Private snoop Galahan around Del Mar (California).

2293.   "Murder Makes the Cock Crow." 30, No. 3 (Sep 1947), 6-27.
         Malott & McCool, L.A. gamblers.

2294.   "Pardon My Poison Platters." 33, No. 1 (May 1949), 8-29.
         The record business; FT's last *BM* story.

TUCKERMAN, Arthur

2295.   "Cross-Channel." 2, No. 5 (Feb 1921), 23-31.

TURNER, Robert

2296.   "For the Rest of Your Death." 35, No. 3 (Jan 1951), 82-86.

2297.   "Hell Is What You Make It." 35, No. 2 (Nov 1950), 39-49, 128.

2298.　"Man's Best Friend." 33, No. 3 (Sep 1949), 8-33. A dog named Satan.

2299.　"Nine Kills to Paradise." 34, No. 4 (Jly 1950), 106-127.

V

VAN, Juliette

2300.　"At the Dragon's Dip." 6, No. 2 (15 Apr 1923), 5-42. Billed as "A Complete Double-Length Detective Mystery Novelette."

VAN DER RHOER, Edward

2301.　"Crime Waits for No Man." 33, No. 4 (Nov 1949), 97-101.

2302.　"The High Cost of Dying." 32, No. 4 (Mar 1949), 74-76, 130.

W

WADE, Lashire

2303.　"The Fall Guy." 9, No. 2 (Apr 1926), 123-127. Police in The Windy City.

2304.　"The Wisdom of Bink." 9, No. 1 (Mar 1926), 91-97. Bink Stevens, epistoler.

WALLACE, Carl S.

2305.　"Scott's Shoes." 4, No. 4 (Jan 1922), 99-103.

WALSH, Thomas

2306.　"Best Man." 17, No. 8 (Oct 1934), 109-123. Carver, plainclothesman, Homicide; reprinted, *The Hard-Boiled Omnibus* (1946).

2307.　"Break-Up." 17, No. 1 (Mar 1934), 111-123.

2308.   "Death Can Come Hard." 18, No. 5 (Jly 1935), 31-53. Dr.
          Ed French, interne, 1st-person narrator.

2309.   "Diamonds Mean Death." 19, No. 1 (Mar 1936), 107-118. Joe
          Keenan, private copper; TW's last appearance in *BM*.

2310.   "Double Check." 16, No. 5 (Jly 1933), 110-123. Flaherty
          & Mike Martin, a couple of cops; TW's debut in *BM*.

2311.   "Tip on the Gallant." 16, No. 9 (Nov 1933), 108-121. Chicago
          Drake, "bane of the bookmakers."

WALTON, Bryce

2312.   "Skid-Row Slaughter." 34, No. 2 (Mar 1950), 85-95.

WANDREI, Donald

2313.   "Come Clean." 21, No. 9 (Dec 1938), 52-57. DW's final
          piece in *BM*.

2314.   "Corpse on the Campus." 21, No. 6 (Sep 1938), 31-39. Murder
          at Midville State University.

2315.   "Game of Legs." 21, No. 3 (May 1938), 36-45. Wrestler.

2316.   "Make Me a Death Mask." 21, No. 5 (Aug 1938), 90-104. Young
          artist.

2317.   "The Rod and the Staff." 19, No. 12 (Feb 1937), 124-126.
          Short-short; DW's debut in *BM*.

2318.   "Tick, Tock." 21, No. 8 (Nov 1938), 9-16. Time bomb.

WARD, Harold [see also Ward STERLING and H.W. STARR]

2319.   "The Attorney for the Defense." 4, No. 5 (Feb 1922), 63-64.
          Short-short; 1st of 2 stories in issue by HW/WS; see also
          "The Passing of Bloody Dan" (STERLING.)

2320.   "Dollars and Scents." 5, No. 6 (Sep 1922), 3-31. "Complete
          Mystery Novelette."

2321. "The Failure." 5, No. 5 (Aug 1922), 72-74. Short-short; 1st of 3 stories in issue by HW/WS; see also "The Police Sometimes Guess Wrong" (WARD) & "The Catspaw" (STERLING).

2322. " 'Great Minds Run—.' " 4, No. 4 (Jan 1922), 104-106. Short-short; 2d of 2 stories in issue by HW/WS; see also "The Phantom Bullet" (STERLING).

2323. "The Green Eyes of O'Dowd." 4, No. 6 (Mar 1922), 57-60.

2324. "The Hand of Destiny." 4, No. 2 (Nov 1921), 33-39. Secret Service op, 1st-person narrator; 1st of 3 stories in issue by HW/WS/HWS; see also "The Whip of Death" (STERLING) & "The Sheriff Takes the Stand" (STARR).

2325. "Jim Dickinson's Head." 1, No. 5 (Aug 1920), 65-70. 1st of 3 stories in issue by HW/WS; see also "The Valley Where Dead Men Live" (WARD) & "The Strange Story of Martin Colby" (STERLING).

2326. "The Man in the Black Mask." 2, No. 2 (Nov 1920), 3-25.

2327. "The Man in the Trunk." 2, No. 6 (Mar 1921), 75-83. 2d of 2 stories in issue by HW/WS; see also "The Golden Slipper Mystery" (STERLING).

2328. "The Man Who Returned." 2, No. 1 (Oct 1920), 118-121.

2329. "The Man Who Was Two." 5, No. 1 (Apr 1922), 57-60. 1st of 3 stories in issue by HW/WS; see also "The Brand of Cain" (STERLING) & "Hankenson's Perfect Crime" (STERLING).

2330. "The Man Who Would Not Die." 1, No. 6 (Sep 1920), 93-110. 3d of 3 stories in issue by HW/WS; see also "The Long Arm of God" (STERLING) & "The Devil Takes a Hand" (STERLING).

2331. "The Menace of the Air." 3, No. 6 (Sep 1921), 3-26.

2332. "The Mysterious 'Captain Who?' " 1, No. 4 (Jly 1920), 3-23.
1st of 2 stories in issue by HW/WS; see also "The Mystery of Devil's Nest" (STERLING).

2333. "The Mystery of Doctor Steele." 5, No. 10 (Jan 1923), 119-122.

2334. "The Mystery of the Haunted House." 2, No. 3 (Dec 1920), 54-56. Short-short.

2335. "The Mystery of the Mary Ann." 5, No. 4 (Jly 1922), 103-106.

2336. "Out of the Jaws of Death." 3, No. 2 (May 1921), 62-64. Short-short.

2337. "The Police Sometimes Guess Wrong." 5, No. 5 (Aug 1922), 107-113. 2d of 3 stories by HW/WS in issue; see also "The Failure" (WARD) & "The Catspaw" (STERLING).

2338. "The Ship on Dunbar's Breast." 3, No. 5 (Aug 1921), 85-94. 2d of 2 stories in issue by HW/WS; see also "The Mystery of the Chessmen" (STERLING).

2339. "The Stolen Soul." 1, No. 1 (Apr 1920), 39-42. HW & *BM* share debuts.

2340. "The Story-Book Clue." 3, No. 3 (Jun 1921), 47-54.

2341. "The 'Tail' of a Cat." 1, No. 2 (May 1920), 25-30.

2342. "The Trego Circus Mystery." 2, No. 5 (Feb 1921), 3-21. 1st of 2 stories by HW/WS in issue; see also "The Letter in **Pedro's Skull**" (STERLING).

2343. "The Turning of the Worm." 6, No. 2 (15 Apr 1923), 115-118. HW's final bit in *BM*.

2344. "Under the Crimson Skull." 3, No. 1 (Apr 1921), 29-36. Two detectives & Cora Morgan, "Government operative"; 1st of

2 stories by HW/WS in issue; see also "The Riddle of the Tattooed Men" (STERLING).

2345.   "The Valley Where Dead Men Live." 1, No. 5 (Aug 1920), 81-88. Spiritualism & WW I; 2d of 3 stories in issue by HW/WS; see also "Jim Dickinson's Head" (WARD) & "The Strange Story of Martin Colby" (STERLING).

2346.   "While the Blizzard Raged." 2, No. 4 (Jan 1921), 3-26. People marooned with murderer; 1st-person narrator.

2347.   "The Woman Who Cursed a Man." 4, No. 3 (Dec 1921), 77-82.

WARD, J. R.

2348.   "The Bamboozler." 4, No. 2 (Nov 1921), 65-75. 1st of 2 stories by JRW in issue; see next entry.

2349.   "The Emperor of Blunderland." 4, No. 2 (Nov 1921), 107-115. 2d of 2 stories in issue by JRW; see previous entry.

2350.   "The Reward." 3, No. 6 (Sep 1921), 118-123. *N.B.* It is possible that JRW is also a pseudonym of Harold WARD.

WARE, Edward Parrish

2351.   "The Border Buckoes." 11, No. 11 (Jan 1929), 93-108. Western; Kid Shelley, 1st-person narrator.

2352.   " 'Gangway!' " 6, No. 19 (1 Jan 1924), 67-75. 1st-person narrator; set in Arkansas, complete with dialect; mule skinner.

2353.   "The Hay-Bag." 6, No. 23 (1 Mar 1924), 103-114. Headnote: "Another mule skinner story, written in breezy slang."

2354.   "The Jungle Buzzard." 7, No. 6 (Aug 1924), 49-57. Mule skinner tale.

2355.   "The Kid's Hole Card." 6, No. 21 (1 Feb 1924), 95-100. Western.

2356.   "The Rebellious Egg." 10, No. 8 (Oct 1927), 98-106. Crookedness
         & RR-building.

2357.   "The Six-Gun Showdown." 12, No. 2 (Apr 1929), 36-53.
         Western novelette; EPW's last appearance in *BM*.

2358.   "Slim Baker Horns In." 11, No. 10 (Dec 1928), 65-73. Western;
         Baker horns in on a necktie party.

2359.   "The Snitch." 6, No. 14 (15 Oct 1923), 104-108. EPW's
         debut in *BM*.

WATSON, Henry S. and Asa STEELE

2360.   "The Trap Thief." 4, No. 3 (Dec 1921), 37-48.

2361.   "The Yellow Door." 3, No. 6 (Sep 1921), 79-88.

WEAVER, Sarah Harbine

2362.   "The House Across the Way." 1, No. 1 (Apr 1920), 43-52.

2363.   "A Knight's Night Out." 9, No. 8 (Oct 1926), 103-112.

WEBSTER, K.

2364.   "One Fall for Murder." 28, No. 2 (Mar 1946), 69-75. Steve
         Ransom, reporter; wrestling story.

2365.   "Prison Break." 22, No. 2 (May 1939), 89-97.

2366.   "Underwater Kill." 21, No. 11 (Feb 1939), 102-111. Cop
         goes under sea-surface to nab his man.

WELLS, Stewart

2367.   "The Puzzle of the Hand." 1, No. 1 (Apr 1920), 59-64.

WELSH, Emmet

2368.   "The Slippery Eel." 6, No. 17 (1 Dec 1923), 7-31. Billed as "A Complete Fast-Moving Novelette"; NYC police; oddly, in 15 Nov 1923 issue (p. 42) author is listed as Robert E. WELCH.

WHEELER, Wilber [see also Riblew REELHEW]

2369.   "The Perfect Plot." 10, No. 4 (Jun 1927), 88-99. Dandy Dan.

2370.   "The Trail of Sudden Death." 11, No. 1 (Mar 1928), 30-37. Western.

WHIPPLE, Kenneth Duane

2371.   "Pursuit." 4, No. 4 (Jan 1922), 107-117.

2372.   "Tainted." 7, No. 12 (Feb 1925), 96-105.

WHIPPLE, Willard

2373.   "The Gun." 2, No. 4 (Jan 1921), 114-120. Honor among crooks via revenge.

WHITE, Leslie T.

2374.   "The City of Hell!" 18, No. 8 (Oct 1935), 84-106. Four honest cops "put the Indian sign on a city of graft."

WHITEHEAD, Henry S.

2375.   "Gahd Laff!" 9, No. 4 (Jun 1926), 107-115.

2376.   "The Gladstone Bag." 8, No. 7 (Sep 1925), 37-43.

WHITFIELD, Raoul F[auconnier] [See also Ramon DECOLTA]

2377.   "About Kid Deth." 13, No. 12 (Feb 1931), 92-115. Gangland novelette; Joey (Kid) Deth; 2d of 2 stories in issue by RFW; see also "Diamonds of Dread" (DECOLTA).

2378.   "Black Air." 9, No. 5 (Jly 1926), 74-91.

2379.   "Black Murder." 11, No. 3 (May 1928), 72-80. Verner,
                Federal man, & greyhound racing; Black Murder = dog.

2380.   "Blue Murder." 11, No. 5 (Jly 1928), 38-51. Mac, Ben Breed,
                & The Wop; 2d segment (of 6) in Border Brand series;
                see next entry for same title.

2381.   "Blue Murder." 15, No. 7 (Sep 1932), 6-22. Don Free, private
                dick; 3d & last DF story; see also "Man Killer" &
                "Walking Dynamite"; see previous entry for same title.

2382.   "Bottled Death." 10, No. 4 (Jun 1927), 116-128. 5th (of 7)
                Chuck Reddington story; aviation & border-running.

2383.   "The Carnival Kill." 12, No. 5 (Jly 1929), 50-60. 6th (of 9)
                segment in Laughing Death series, featuring Gary Greer.

2384.   "Dark Death." 16, No. 6 (Aug 1933), 6-30. Ben Jardinn,
                Hollywood private cop, & earthquake; 2d & last BJ story;
                see also "Murder By Request"; BJ also in "Death in a
                Bowl."

2385.   "Dead Men Tell Tales." 15, No. 9 (Nov 1932), 8-26. Jay
                Cameron, hard-boiled city editor; 1st of 2 stories in issue
                by RFW; see also "The Magician Murder" (DECOLTA).

2386.   "Death in a Bowl." 13, No. 7 (Sep 1930), 35-71, Pt. 1; 13, No. 8
                (Oct 1930), 90-119, Pt. 2; 13, No. 9 (Nov 1930), 76-113, Pt. 3.
                Ben Jardinn, Hollywood eye, & murder in Hollywood
                Bowl; serial (originally titled "The Maestro Murder") pub.
                as novel (1931); see also "Dark Death" & "Murder By
                Request" for BJ.

2387.   "Death on Fifth Avenue." 16, No. 12 (Feb 1934), 56-70. Ben
                Carey, private peeper, 1st-person narrator; RFW's final
                appearance in *BM*.

2388.   "Delivered Goods." 9, No. 9 (Nov 1926), 68-73. Aviator hero;
         see headnote for data on RFW.

2389.   "Face Powder." 14, No. 2 (Apr 1931), 6-32. Pittsburgh
         rub-out; Ben Annison, police dick.

2390.   "First Blood." 11, No. 4 (Jun 1928), 5-22. Mac, 1st-person
         narrator (aviator), Ben Breed, & The Wop (villain);
         1st segment (of 6) in Border Brand series.

2391.   "Flying Gold." 9, No. 7 (Sep 1926), 110-120. "Hen" Darrow,
         joy-hopping pilot.

2392.   "For Sale—Murder." 14, No. 4 (Jun 1931), 78-107. Gil
         Baggart, a square dick; sequel to "Soft City."

2393.   "Ghost Guns." 11, No. 8 (Oct 1928), 78-88. 5th (of 6)
         segment in Border Brand series.

2394.   "Green Ice." 12, No. 12 (Feb 1930), 88-108. Mal Ourney;
         Pt. 3 (of 5) of "The Crime Breeders"; see "Outside" for
         data.

2395.   "High Death." 11, No. 6 (Aug 1928), 49-61. 3d (of 6) segment in
         Border Brand series.

2396.   "High Murder." 16, No. 11 (Jan 1934), 52-69. Murder on
         airliner; Ash Evans & Chink Chaddon, L.A. County cops.

2397.   "High Odds." 12, No. 3 (May 1929), 79-89. Gary Greer; 4th
         (of 9) segment in Laughing Death series.

2398.   "Inside Job." 14, No. 12 (Feb 1932), 8-31. Tim Slade, de-
         tective, & Hugh Fresney, editor; reprinted, *The Hard-
         Boiled Omnibus* (1946).

2399.   "Jenny Meets the Boys." 9, No. 4 (Jun 1926,) 91-98. Border
         air-story.

2400.   "Killers' Show." 13, No. 2 (Apr 1930), 107-128. Mal Ourney; Pt. 5 (last) of "The Crime Breeders."

2401.   "Little Guns." 11, No. 2 (Apr 1928), 30-39. Police & gangsters in Center City.

2402.   **"Live Men's Gold." 10, No. 6 (Aug 1927), 26-36. 6th (of 7)** Chuck Reddington story.

2403.   "Man Killer." 15, No. 2 (Apr 1932), 6-28. Don Free, private eye; 1st of 3 DF stories; see also "Walking Dynamite" & "Blue Murder"; 1st of 2 stories by RFW in issue; see also "The Siamese Cat" (DECOLTA).

2404.   "Money Talk." 16, No. 8 (Oct 1933), 54-73. Shamus Dion Davies; 2d & last DD caper; see also "A Woman Can Kill."

2405.   "Murder Again." 16, No. 10 (Dec 1933), 60-80. L. A. County dicks; Hollywood story.

2406.   **"Murder By Mistake." 13, No. 6 (Aug 1930), 36-56. Don** Burney, private cop; see pp. 120-121 for data on RFW.

2407.   "Murder By Request." 15, No. 11 (Jan 1933), 8-30. Ben Jardinn, shamus; 1st of 2 BJ stories; see also "Dark Death" plus "Death in a Bowl."

2408.   "Murder in the Ring." 13, No. 10 (Dec 1930), 7-32. Boxing, gamblers, racketeers, with Primo Carnera-like boxer; reprinted, 36, No. 1 (May 1951), 2-32; 1st of 2 stories in issue **by RFW; see also "The Caleso Murders"** (DECOLTA).

2409.   "Not Tomorrow." 16, No. 9 (Nov 1933), 60-76. O'Rory, hard-fisted lawyer, & Rollo, his assistant, in NYC.

2410.   "On the Spot." 11, No. 12 (Feb 1929), 11-24. Gary Greer; 1st (of 9) segment in Laughing Death series; presented as separate stories rather than conventional serial; pub. as *Five* (1931) under pseudonym of Temple FIELD.

2411.   "Out of the Sky." 12, No. 1 (Mar 1929), 35-46. Gary Greer; 2d (of 9) segment in Laughing Death series.

2412.   "Outside." 12, No. 10 (Dec 1929), 27-45. Mal Ourney; Pt. 1 (of 5), "The Crime Breeders"; presented as separate stories rather than conventional serial; pub. as *Green Ice* (1930).

2413.   "Oval Face." 13, No. 1 (Mar 1930), 96-114. Ourney; Pt. 4 (of 5), "The Crime Breeders."

2414.   "The Pay-Off." 12, No. 2 (Apr 1929), 54-65. Greer; 3d (of 9) segment in Laughing Death series.

2415.   "Red Pearls." 10, No. 9 (Nov 1927), 86-93. Police dick, Lou Kyle.

2416.   "Red Smoke." 12, No. 11 (Jan 1930), 88-106. Ourney; Pt. 2 (of 5), "The Crime Breeders."

2417.   "Red Terrace." 14, No. 7 (Sep 1931), 50-71. Alan Van Cleve; 2d (of 6) segment in The Skyline Murders series.

2418.   "Red Wings." 11, No. 7 (Sep 1928), 32-42. Mac, Ben Breed, *et al.*; 4th (of 6) segment in Border Brand series.

2419.   "River Street Death." 12, No. 6 (Aug 1929), 78-87. Greer; 7th (of 9) segment in Laughing Death series.

2420.   "Roaring Death." 9, No. 6 (Aug 1926), 67-93. Lee Brooks, reporter, in Steel City, plus airplanes.

2421.   "Sal the Dude." 12, No. 8 (Oct 1929), 117-134. Greer; last (9th) segment in Laughing Death series.

2422.   "Scotty Scouts Around." 9, No. 2 (Apr 1926), 107-116. Bill Scott; aviation & smuggling on the Border; see next entry.

2423.   "Scotty Troubles Trouble." 9, No. 1 (Mar 1926), 82-90. Bill Scott & Bing Russell apprehend kidnappers; see previous entry; RFW's debut in *BM*.

2424. "Sixty Minutes." 10, No. 8 (Oct 1927), 9-23. Buck, who flies a Jenny, 1st-person narrator, & Sam Ellis.

2425. "The Sky Club Affair." 14, No. 6 (Aug 1931), 6-27. Alan Van Cleve, wealthy sportsman, man-about-town; 1st (of 6) segment in The Skyline Murders series; presented as separate stories rather than conventional serial; pub. as *Killer's Carnival* (1932) under pseudonym of Temple FIELD; 1st of 2 stories in issue by RFW; see also "Diamonds of Death" (DECOLTA).

2426. "Sky-High Odds." 10, No. 1 (Mar 1927), 41-50. 3d (of 7) Chuck Reddington story; airplanes & machineguns.

2427. "The Sky's the Limit." 10, No. 11 (Jan 1928), 119-128. 7th & last Reddington story.

2428. "Skyline Death." 14, No 11 (Jan 1932), 12-34. 6th & last segment in The Skyline Murders series; Van Cleve.

2429. "The Sky Trap." 11, No. 9 (Nov 1928), 109-120. Mac, Ben Breed; finale (6th) of Border Brand series.

2430. "Soft City." 14, No. 3 (May 1931), 6-34. Center City yarn; see "For Sale—Murder" for sequel; 1st of 2 stories by RFW in issue; see "Red Dawn" (DECOLTA).

2431. "Soft Goods." 10, No. 12 (Feb 1928), 26-34. Little Bennie, a hood, & Charlie Harmer, detective, in Center City.

2432. "South of Savannah." 10, No. 3 (May 1927), 120-128. 4th (of 7) Reddington story.

2433. **"The Squeeze." 12, No. 7 (Sep 1929), 101-111. Gary Greer;** 8th (of 9) segment in Laughing Death series.

2434. "Steel Arena." 14, No. 8 (Oct 1931), 29-47. Van Cleve; 3d (of 6) segment in The Skyline Murders series; 1st of 2 stories in issue by RFW; see also "Shooting Gallery" (DECOLTA).

2435. "Ten Hours." 9, No. 10 (Dec 1926), 51-66. Chuck Reddington & Jake Bailey; aviation, etc.; 1st of 7 CR stories.

2436. "Uneasy Money." 9, No. 11 (Jan 1927), 108-117. Aviation on the Border; Buck, 1st-person narrator.

2437. "Unfair Exchange." 14, No. 10 (Dec 1931), 102-121. Van Cleve; 5th (of 6) segment in The Skyline Murders series; 2d of 2 stories in issue by RFW; see also "The Javanese Mask" (DECOLTA).

2438. "Van Cleve Calling." 14, No. 9 (Nov 1931), 60-82. 4th (of 6) segment in The Skyline Murders series.

2439. "Walking Dynamite." 15, No. 3 (May 1932), 6-26. Don Free, private snoop; 2d of 3 DF stories; see also "Man Killer" & "Blue Murder."

2440. "White Murder." 9, No. 12 (Feb 1927), 98-107. Reddington, 2d of 7 CR stories.

2441. "Within the Circle." 12, No. 4 (Jun 1929), 98-107. Greer; 5th (of 9) segment in Laughing Death Series.

2442. "A Woman Can Kill." 16, No. 7 (Sep 1933), 6-28. Dion Davies, partner in a private 'tec agency; 1st of 2 DD capers; see also "Money Talk."

WICKHAM, Harvey

2443. "Something in Writing." 1, No. 4 (Jly 1920), 25-33.

WIGGINS, Donegan

2444. "The Double-Cross." 29, No. 3 (Jan 1947), 73. Brief-brief.

WILCOX, Samuel

2445. "The Witness." 2, No. 1 (Oct 1920), 73-74. Short-short.

WILKIE, Valleau

2446.   "The Strange Case of Ivan Milukov." 8, No. 6 (Aug 1925),
              42-52. Burke, reporter.

2447.   "The White Elephant." 8, No. 7 (Sep 1925), 59-70. Billed
              as "A Last Minute Mystery."

WILLIAMS, Edward S.

2448.   "Bloody Answer." 22, No. 5 (Aug 1939), 40-65. Corporal John
              Harmon, State Trooper, narrator.

2449.   "Body of a Well Dressed Man." 20, No. 5 (Jly 1937), 45-65.
              Tim Walsh, private eye.

2450.   "Deadly Secret." 21, No. 11 (Feb 1939), 44-61. Rex Flynn,
              private dick.

2451.   "Death Has Green Eyes." 19, No. 1 (Mar 1936), 88-106. Mike
              Dunneen, private 'tec; ESW's debut in *BM*.

2452.   **"For Valor." 35, No. 4 (Mar 1951), 26-35. Reprint; not**
              from *BM*.

2453.   "Leave the Door Open." 20, No. 9 (Nov 1937), 12-37. Peter
              Nelson, young M.D., in the slums.

2454.   "Murder for Her Birthday." 22, No. 8 (Nov 1939), 74-96.

2455.   "Someday I'll Kill You." 23, No. 3 (Jly 1940), 68-91.
              Clee Dunn, shamus; ESW's final appearance in *BM* except
              for reprint.

WILLIAMS, Valentine

2456.   "The Mystery of the Brown Leather Suit-Case." 1, No. 3
              (Jun 1920), 69-80.

2457.   "The Mystery of the Missing Finger." 1, No. 2 (May 1920), 45-55. Desmond Okewood, British Secret Service.

WILSON, Elsy

2458.   " 'For Sale.' " 5, No. 9 (Dec 1922), 50-56.

WILSON, Mitchell

2459.   "Fatal Friday." 25, No. 12 (May 1943), 107-116. Twist & Saratoga, private peepers.

WILSON, N.H.

2460.   "The Head of Clampini." 5, No. 11 ([1] Feb 1923), 31-37. Daytime Story.

WINNETT, Ralph

2461.   "Poison Gloves." 22, No. 3 (Jun 1939), 29-35. Boxing.

WINSLOW, Thyra Samter

2462.   "Blueberry Pie." 5, No. 5 (Aug 1922), 3-18. "Complete Mystery Novelette."

WIPPLE, Willard

2463.   "The Gun." 2, No. 4 (Jan 1921), 114-120. Cop story; NYC.

WITT, Arthur Seymour

2464.   "The Crawling Crime." 2, No. 1 (Oct 1920), 51-61.

2465.   "The Recoil." 2, No. 6 (Mar 1921), 67-74. "Duffy, The Soup," old-time yegg.

WOLFE, Charles S.

2466.   "The Finishing Touch." 4, No. 3 (Dec 1921), 33-36.

2467.   "Speaking Steel." 4, No. 4 (Jan 1922), 54-58.

2468.   "Unlucky Friday." 4, No. 5 (Feb 1922), 59-62.

WOOD, Edwin Goodenow

2469.   "Crimson Gold." 8, No. 5 (Jly 1925), 3-31. Billed as "A
               Mystery-Adventure Novelette."

2470.   "Devil's Bowl." 6, No. 22 (15 Feb 1924) 9-33. Advertised
               as "A Novelette of Strangeness and Swiftness."

WOOD, J. Ainsworth

2471.   "Beyond." 5, No. 7 (Oct 1922), 48. Brief-brief.

WOOD, Joe

2472.   "The Devil's Tale." 9, No. 1 (Mar 1926), 9-37. Flinty
               McElvy of the Mounties.

WOODBURY, Herbert A.

2473.   "Nothing to Worry About." 20, No. 8 (Oct 1937), 118-122.

WOODFORD, Jack

2474.   "Blank Fingers." 8, No. 7 (Sep 1925), 107-115. Article;
               fingerprints; cf. under John Nicholas BEFFEL.

WOODS, Clee

2475.   "Hoofprints of Law." 11, No. 3 (May 1928), 48-71. Western;
               subtitled, "A Neck in a Noose."

WOOLFORD, Cynthia

2476.   "The Pink Nails of Marylin Hart." 2, No. 6 (Mar 1921),
               119-123.

WOOLRICH, Cornell [pseud. of Cornell George Hopley-Woolrich]

2477.   "After-Dinner Story." 20, No. 11 (Jan 1938), 35-50.

2478.   "Borrowed Crime." 22, No. 4 (Jly 1939), 46-69.

2479.   "Cab, Mister?" 20, No. 9 (Nov 1937), 38-51.

2480.   "C-Jag." 23, No. 6 (Oct 1940), 6-32. Cocaine jag makes murderer forget what he's done with body.

2481.   "Collared." 22, No. 7 (Oct 1939), 32-47. See p. 31 for letter from CW on this story.

2482.   "Cool, Calm and Detected." 23, No. 12 (Apr 1941), 107-128.

2483.   "Crime by the Forelock." 22, No. 6 (Sep 1939), 73-85.

2484.   "Dime a Dance." 20, No. 12 (Feb 1938), 59-73. Ginger, dime-a-dance gal, 1st-person narrator; see p. 59 for glossary of slang in story.

2485.   "Dormant Account." 25, No. 1 (May 1942), 70-93.

2486.   "Dusk to Dawn." 20, No. 10 (Dec 1937), 42-60. Lew Stahl.

2487.   "Face Work." 20, No. 8 (Oct 1937), 31-46. Jerry Wheeler; reprinted as "Angel Face," *The Great American Detective* (1978).

2488.   "He Looked Like Murder." 35, No. 3 (Jan 1951), 40-67. Reprint; not from *BM*; orig. pub., *Detective Fiction Weekly*, 8 Feb 1941.

2489.   "If the Dead Could Talk." 25, No. 10 (Feb 1943), 36-45, 128. Trapeze-artist, 1st-person narrator.

2490.   "I'll Never Play Detective Again." 20, No. 3 (May 1937), 10-25. 1st-person narrator imagines best friend a murderer.

2491.   "Men Must Die." 22, No. 5 (Aug 1939), 66-83.

2492.   "Mimic Murder." 20, No. 4 (Jun 1937), 112-126.

493. "Murder on the Night Boat." 19, No. 12 (Feb 1937), 92-102. Police dick on honeymoon; Sergeant James Q. Bradford.

494. "Nelli from Zelli's." 20, No. 7 (Sep 1937), 58-75. 1st-person narrator is an American in Paris.

495. "Of Time and Murder." 35, No. 2 (Nov 1950), 96-122. Reprint; not from *BM*; orig. pub., *Detective Fiction Weekly,* 15 Mar 1941.

496. "Picture Frame." 26, No. 7 (Jly 1944), 8-28. Hollywood; excepting reprints, CW's final appearance in *BM*.

497. "Post-Mortem." 23, No. 1 (Apr 1940), 56-73.

498. "Shooting Going On." 19, No. 11 (Jan 1937), 107-115. Hollywood murder; CW's debut in *BM*.

499. "3 Kills for 1." 25, No. 3 (Jly 1942), 106-129.

500. "Through a Dead Man's Eye." 22, No. 9 (Dec 1939), 28-46. Boy vs. murderer.

WRIGHT, Alan

501. "Jaw Bone." 7, No. 5 (Jly 1924), 123-126. Story of U.S. Army life.

WRIGHT, Geroge A.

502. "The Mountain Comes to Mohammed." 7, No. 7 (Sep 1924), 118-122.

WRIGHT, Sally Dixon

503. "The House on the Dunes." 5, No. 8 (Nov 1922), 99-111.

WRIGHT, Sewell Peaslee

504. "The Nod." 13, No. 6 (Aug 1930), 76-80. Gangster tale.

2505.   "The Road That Led Nowhere." 11, No. 10 (Dec 1928), 29-37.

Y

YOUNG, J.A.

2506.   "The Meanest Thief." 6, No. 3 (15 Apr 1923), 52. Brief-brief.

Z

ZASTROW, Erika

2507.   **"The Crook Who Wanted To Be Straight."** 10, No. 7 (Sep 1927), 31-37.

2508.   "Joe's Woman." 10, No. 1 (Mar 1927), 88-91. In street-dialect.

2509.   "A Moll and Her Man." 11, No. 7 (Sep 1928), 84-90. Billed as **"A Drama of the Underworld."**

CPSIA information can be obtained
at www.ICGtesting.com
Printed in the USA
BVHW070308090223
657979BV00010B/46